FIBONACCI TALES

FIBONACCI TALES

Angel Tales

eLBe

Fibonacci Tales by eLBe

This book is written to provide information and motivation to readers. Its purpose is not to render any type of psychological, legal, or professional advice of any kind. The content is the sole opinion and expression of the author, and not necessarily that of the publisher.

Copyright © 2018 by eLBe

Printed in the United States of America.

New Leaf Media, LLC
175 S. 3rd Street, Suite 200
Columbus, OH 43215
www.thenewleafmedia.com

CONTENTS

Avenging Angel

With all your Plans

Crashing around you

And nowhere left to hide

Comes the avenging angel

To take away pride

And Separation....

Keep the individuation –

We need that from you

Pretty Wings

And Angelic aura

Don't mean squat...

If that's all ya got

All I Need to Know About Life

I learned from my Guardian Angel

Angels tickle your funny bone,
They're good for your soul

Angels don't fall out of the sky
They emerge from within

Angels are never too distant to hear you
Angels don't give us direction

Angels are there when you need them
Angels are really very down to earth

Angels bless you
They don't try to impress you

Angels know how to light the way
An angel's art is its heart

Angels give you those gentle pats on the back
You need to keep going

Anyone who helps you grow is an angel
Angels don't worry about you. They believe in you

Angels come in all shapes, sizes, and colors

An angel always raises your spirit

The sky's the limit to an angel
Angels walk softly and carry a big presence

If we were all a little more like angels
The world would be a better place

Rebounding Angels

The consciousness of the young woman was dark.

She was lost.

Abandoned.

Betrayed.

Battered.

And deeply defiled in the most intimate way.

Body.

Mind.

Brain.

Alone.

Wounded.

Vulnerable.

Unprotected.

Unshielded.

And yet she was unwittingly yet willingly, unwilling to defend and protect herself. Even with words.

Her greatest gift.

The young woman *would not* use her gift of words to defend herself against the indefensible.

But she *would not* speak her truth.

Not 'could not'.

She had the capacity, if truth be known. Even to her.

Some *insane saintliness* prohibited the young woman from stepping beyond the starting gate and forbad her from using her gift of words to release and ease the persistent, punishing, pain. From her.

Do-loop.

A snake eternally eating its tail in infinity and pondering the oddity that it sees nothing but its butt end.

Therefore, I must be *the whole Universe and everything in it.* The weird tail eating wyvern worm warms to the outrageous idea, and instantly dines to full replete in the giddy bliss of a snake eating its tail.

From its dwelling place in her abused and broken spirit the serpent spins its silken web binding her tight and fast in her feeling of abandonment and abuse.

Unforgiven.

This time the woman sees it.

She doesn't get it, but that's an altogether other proposition.

But she can see it this time, oddly enough.

If truth be known, she knows with crystal clarity that her words would spill from her mouth wickedly witty and funny, and bitingly bitter and true.

Those words and the energy of them would surely shred Big Brother's false E.G.O., and maybe he'd get over his E.G.O. and be nice again.

When was Big Brother ever nice? The D.O. snaps pointedly.

The young woman is silent a long moment sifting through memories to find the origin of Big Brother's stunning fall from grace.

She gasps: *Before he served as altar boy at the early Mass that one Sunday morning!*

And?

Jay changed that morning.

Before that day, Jay was charming, and witty, and wise, and real, and fun to be around. And he could be a shit on wheels.

Words as corrosive as acid splash anew in the young woman's mind. They come in Jay's voice, with Jay's fierce furious delight in shaming her with words and never allowing her answer or deny any demand he commanded that she admit as her fault, her failure. Her failure to help him when he needed her help.

And Jay was bitter and corrosive enough months before his nightly Black Molly drunken trance dance he engaged with Death as his chosen partner.

Bad enough when Jay just dealt weed.

'Wacky tabacky', as he liked to name and proclaim then it as though he'd personally won a prestigious award in comedy, acting and dancing, of course, in one gigantic old gold trophy.

The trophy he would put on the mantle beside the Playmate of the Month centerfold he always kept there. For a month.

Easy come, easy go.

Except that – Jay never would give up abusing me in new and drug-addled innovative and inventive ways.

Jay's preferred weapon was the sharp sword of his tongue.

The D.O. counters: *And who gave him the power and authority over you?*

She is silent an infinite eternal moment and then replies: *I did.*

Why?

Because I loved him.

Have you ever been tempted by the dark, shadowy beauty and mystery of Beelzebub? The Fallen Angel?

Have you ever wanted to go into, and surrender yourself totally, to that beautiful dancing danger, just for the edgy helplessness of doing that?

Are you expecting me *to send in a S.W.A.T. team to bail you out of the foreseeable outcomes of your inane yielding of* your will *to those you love better than you love yourself?*

Que tonto! Que totalmente estupido!

So, daughter a mine, what will you choose?

Victim?

Victor?

Or Verity?

Angels of Grace

Grace – good will, favor, a disposition to show mercy.

Unbidden aid from the Divine One in the process of regeneration.

Regeneration – A change in which abundant spiritual life, even eternal life, is incorporated into the body.

Regeneration begins its work in the conscious mind.

And completes its renewal in the subconsciousness.

Subconscious mind – The memory mind. Memory crystalized into function and form.

Here is the home of our habits, the storehouse of our past thoughts and experiences. Some of those memories haunt us, like pale ghosts that live in because we unconsciously created a space for it there.

The heart carries on all the bodily functions including circulation, breathing, digestion, and all other bodily functions controlled by the subconscious mind.

We humans are not conscious of what goes on in these processes, but divine intelligence works perfectly in these processes that are blind to humans.

Yet we mere mortals are not conscious of that goes on in these processes. So, nothing changes for us because, behind the scenes, divine intelligence works perfectly well in and through us.

Unless we interfere to block or deny that divinely inspired process of regeneration and renewal in body, mind, and spirit.

The overcoming work is carried on largely in the subconscious mind. All past thinking must be redeemed and the whole man, conscious and subconscious, brought into the harmony of the Christ consciousness.

Metaphysically, Christ is the incarnating principle of the God-man, the perfect Word or idea of God which unfolds into the true man, who is blessed with eternal life by measuring up to the divine standard, thus fulfilling the law of righteousness.

Christ is the divine man.

Jesus is the name that represents an individual expression of the Christ idea.

Christ existed long before Jesus. It was the Christ Mind in Jesus that exclaimed, "And now, Father, glorify thou me with thine own self with the glory which I had with thee before the world was" (John 17:5).

Christ abides in each person as his potential perfection.

Jesus Christ, the embodiment of all divine ideas, exists eternally in the Mind of Being as the only begotten Son of God, the "Messiah" or "anointed one," and is the living Principle working in man.

Principle – Fundamental Truth. Divine Principle is fundamental Truth in a universal sense, or as pertaining to God, the Divine One.

Principle is the underlying plan by which Spirit (God) moves in expressing itself as the oversoul of this planet which works its way into expression through Jesus, the son of Mary. The way shower.

Metaphysically, Jesus is the I AM in man. The Master self that inspires the directive power, and raises it to divine understanding and power. Jesus represents the 'I AM' identity of man whose mission is to connect the thinker with the true source of thought.

Jesus is the Way-Shower who came that we might have life more abundantly – that is – He came to awaken man to the possibilities of his own true nature.

"As he is... so are we in this world (1 John 4:17).

The Master came to bear witness to Truth.

He applied the one true way to the realization of eternal life and the universal consciousness.

And therefore, His influence on the race cannot be measured.

It is infinite and eternal.

Everywhere present.

Forever.

Eternally.

The infinite eternal finds its eternal home place in and through the process of bringing all the forces of mind and body to support of the Christ ideal.

The unification of Spirit, soul, and body in mystical unity.

The Christed ideal idea made manifest through man.

At one with the One First Cause, the inspiring grace of creativity, and of all of creation itself.

Infinite.

Eternal.

Everywhere present.

Potent.

Powerful.

Forever present.

Universally.

Christ is the divine man. Jesus is the name that represents an individual expression of the Christ idea.

Christ existed long before Jesus.

It was the Christ mind in Jesus that exclaimed: "and now, Father, glorify thou me with thine own self with the glory which I had with the before the world was." (John 17:5)

Christ abides in each person as his potential perfection Jesus Christ, the embodiment of all divine ideas, exists eternally in the Mind of Being as the only begotten Son of God, the "messiah" or "anointed one," and is the living Principle working in man.

It is the underlying plan by which Spirit (God) moves in expressing itself; the oversoul of this planet which works its way into expression through Jesus.

Although Principle is formless, it is that by which all form is produced.

Principle is the 'I AM' of every man.

As the principle of music moves through tones, so does the principle of mind move through Christ ideas – the one complete idea of perfect man in Divine Mind.

A word is spoken thought, or idea.

Ideas are catching. We are all heavily charged with ideas and when these ideas are released they spring forth and pass from mind to mind, being 'recorded' as they fly.

When these ideas are expressed the whole race is lifted up *if* the idea is charged with the uplifting Spirit.

Ideas are catching. We are all heavily charged with ideas, and when these ideas are released they spring forth and pass from mind to mind, being "recorded" as they fly.

When they are expressed the whole race is lifted up – if the idea is charged with the uplifting Spirit.

As the son is to the father, so is the idea to the mind.

Mind is coexistent with its ideas, and there is continual interaction and communion.

Mind is one with its ideas, so the Father (God-Mind) is one with its offspring, the idea, the Son.

Therefore, God as creative mind, moves through the expressed thought of Divine Mind into the ideal.

Divine Mind is the ever-present, all-knowing Mind.

The Absolute, the unlimited.

Omnipresent, all-wise, all-loving, all-powerful Spirit.

Spirit – God as the moving force in the universe.

Principle as the breath of life in all creation, the principle of life, and of creative intelligence and life.

When one concentrates all the faculties on Truth ideas, the conscious mind and superconscious mind blend, and there is a descent of spiritual energies into soul and body.

The faculties then receive new power to express Truth and the body is renewed.

Shawn Gallaway – The Center of the Sun

Hot, Hot, Hot!

Can the Edging God Out, E.G.O. of man in mortal form, flow safely and freely to and through The Center of the Sun? Probably not.

Not without the abundant cover and protection of Angels of Grace.

The Woman calls Grace Angels in abundance, for she is on her knees in despair, and utterly lost in devastating feelings and fear of abandonment.

Of not good enough-ness.

Of never measuring up to Jay's demanding and ever-mutable daily drains he placed on her, and on the Spirit that expressed as and animated her. *Never enough. No matter what....*

Not enough that I am pregnant with his bastard child by proxy. That was just the trump Ace in a card deck that was marked and dealt with cold, clinical indifference to any outcome other than his desire.

That baptism by my menstrual blood is not enough to satisfy him.

Jay wants me to hook for him. For free.

He will keep the money the men will pay him to fuck me.

Except the first time that Big Brother raped me by proxy. Then Jay paid the man to rape me knowing I was fertile and the planted seed would inspire the life of a child in my womb.

My mind cannot comprehend this betrayal, this mental, emotional, and physical abuse.

Jay bragged to everyone with ears to hear about knowing the scent of woman. Like that was a unique gift to him alone and not a scent given to all and every male of every species? Really? Que tonto!

Jay knew I was fertile for the first time. He knew the sperm inseminated into me would become a newly forming life that was decades away from being self-sustaining. Sex slave to Big Brother.

I cannot live with this, God!

I will not be Jay's sex slave. I would rather die.

And before that, I would rather miscarry.

Please take Jay's baby by proxy out of me, please. Let me miscarry. Make me miscarry this bastard child. Oh God, forgive me this baby, for I have no love to give it.

As she drifts into insensate sleep, Angels of Grace surround and embrace her in the grace of forgiveness.

Healing Angels

I'm broken angels, I am shattered into a million little pieces. Send help S.T.A.T., the young woman prays.

I got your back, dear one. The Divine One comforts and sooths. *Healing angels surround you right now.*

And angels honor free will.

You are saying that I am *the one who shattered me into a million little pieces?* The young woman silent shrieks sundering herself into a million more little pieces.

She's feeling very picked on and abused. She's not a happy camper.

The D.O. gives her an enormous heart wide open smile.

The young woman does not see that divine smile *anywhere* in the million shattered shards reflecting who she once thought she was before....

Before Jay paid to have me raped! She silent shrieks into the deep dire dark of her abandonment anxiety that is packed tight full with the physical, mental, and emotional abuse preceding her Big Brother's rape by proxy. That subversive abuse binds and blinds her. She behaves like a snake eternally eating its tail.

I carry Jay's proxy baby.

I hate this baby!

No you don't. The D.O. assures without passion. *That would be hating Jay's second* victim. *You don't.*

But you are hating the first *victim of Jay's serial abuse.*

The young woman feels herself devastated again watching a new million little pieces of her heart strewn about haphazardly looking for all the world like sparkling shattered shards of the faith she once held fast that all that came to her on *this one singular day* was good and loving.

I still felt that before the night Jay paid to have me raped by proxy.

What's good about that? The D.O. re-directs the young woman.

There's nothing *good about rape!* The young woman screeches like a mad cat on a bad dark lark night.

She wants the baby dead.

She won't ask me for that though. Her soul-ravening inner demons won't let that happen.

She could ask. But she won't.

Until she does.

The D.O. sighs, his head hung low to see the view from the young woman's perspective. *Nothing but shattered shards sparking off the broken dreams and visions for her life.*

The metaphysical aspects of this situation are totally lost on her. The D.O. thinks sorrowfully.

And then, the D.O. thinks aloud, and the young woman overhears.

She will not ask for the baby to be dead.

Ergo, she can see no hope of healing.

She can see no path to recovery – if *the baby lives.*

More to the point, she sees no healing big enough to cover, ease, or soothe her dedicated devotion to the victim role. The D.O. smiles at the idiotic irony of that.

She won't ask for help.

She is a serial victim with a thin skin, and a wide open heart that's worn on her sleeve. Serially self-exposed. She's a cold case.

The pity is that Jay's rape by proxy penetrated the very spirit of her body mind brain Earth suit of her.

Spirit – God as the moving force in the universe.

The Principle of life.

As Principle. The first source of the breath of life that inhales and exhales through all of creation.

Spirit is the creative intelligence behind everything that is, and everything that is not.

It is the formative intelligence and the very life force that inspires all creation. Spirit is the Breath of Life.

Sometimes the woman forgets to breathe! I have to send angels then to whack her back and get oxygen back into her system. It's no wonder she's mostly brain dead. It's a short trip for her.

She hears though. I can work with that.

Young lady, the D.O. calls sweetly and instantly gets her attention.

The young woman does not face the D.O. though.

She keeps her head down and her eyelids lowered.

She *will not* see the Scales of Justice the D.O. holds torch high in its hand!

The D.O. is *not* amused.

Breathe! The D.O. snaps and soundly slaps the center of her back with one hand, and then slaps her stomach with the other.

The woman inhales.

What's a body to do under the influence of a shock slap to the gut?

Exhale, the D.O. coaches, now with a sharp slap on her back.

How would you like to apply *that powerful stimuli of the oxygen high you are experiencing just now simply because you* actually *inhaled a full breath of overused air?*

And then, you could actually fully release that newly carbon laden breath on the exhale? What a concept!

This is better than weed, the young woman sighs morbidly content.

Yeah – The D.O. thinks cynically. *But it won't give you a miscarriage, and that's what you actually want.*

Oddly enough, the young woman hears the sub audible guidance, and she receives it. As a gift, a magic carpet ride away from her obedient enslavement to Big Brother.

Shawn Gallaway – As You Are

God gave us free will, the woman thinks.

Rationally this time.

From that I confidently conclude that the D.O. does not *expect obedience from his creations.*

But the D.O. does expect compliance.

The Master said: You have not because you ask not. The D.O. reminds the woman with a warm smile.

She asks.

She doesn't think about.

She doesn't put it on her Day-Timer.

She doesn't even *consider* consulting her 'committee' that rules the body mind brain home of her wounded sense of self, and of her sense of 'safety' in the world.

Ships are safe in the harbor. But that's not what ships are for. The D.O. plants the words in the woman's mind.

The thought blows through the woman's mind like a winsome wind caught full bellied in a trim set of full sails.

She is off and away for new shores that she has never explored before.

Still, she is the full body pulsating alive and vibrant with the utter audacity of her brazen bold leap toward the infinite eternal throne of grace.

The woman asks. Humbly, with lowered eyes and chin, and a soft certain smile on her face.

Will you take this baby away from me?

It's not a plea.

It's not even a request.

It is a statement of expectation.

It is an avowal of unqualified *knowing* that it is *already done*!

The woman praise raises upwelling infinite love and gratitude to the eternal D.O. for the generous dispensation of timely and healing saving grace.

She joyfully welcomes the heart wide open warming wings of a full dozen Healing Angels come on a delicate divine mission to ease, soothe, and heal the messy muddled mired mind of the woman's shattered, shuttered, lost, and abandoned soul.

She exhales in a rushing whoosh simply because *another* angel is now whacking her smartly on the back in precisely the places where her wings would be attached.

If she had any.

Your wings are there. Gab-re-EL assures the woman in the lavish loving ways a mother might comfort a fussy fretful child who was *seriously* safe in the loving arms of its mother, but didn't know that yet.

You just can't see them yet. Gab-re-EL assures the fretful fright filled woman.

You over-packed by the way. You are toting a totally redundant and useless excess pile of baggage.

If God were an airline, you'd pay an excess weight fee.

Nor can you feel your wings. That's because of the excess mental weight you're packing makes you yourself responsible for the choices made by other humans. Que tonto, Chicca! Que pienses?

Angel wings are weightless after all.

And invisible.

To ordinary eyes.

You never had those, woman. You never accepted them. Because you couldn't see them.

And, you momentarily forgot that the human body actually has three *fully functional, three-dimensional sighted eye balls.*

Gab-re-EL puffs a breath of spirit at the woman's third eye chakra and blows the eye wide open. Again.

It is a game changer for the woman.

She sees again into the cosmic void.

She consciously swirls, stirs, twines, and blends the rainbow colors of the invisible world into the turbulent infinite emptiness that lies between the seen and the unknown, unseen. And, in equal balance, she inhabits the space between the unseen, and the unseen unknown.

Cosmic Soup for the Soul.

She imagines that the words came from Gab-re-EL's mind into hers.

But maybe not.

Perhaps the words were always present in the infinite void that encompasses all of time eternal.

But no one ever observed, nor took one single note of that.

Before.

What then?

The woman speculates. *Perhaps we humans were, all and every one of us, dutifully, nose to the grindstone, and fully preoccupied by navel-gazing at the lint gatherings of the detritus of our lives.*

Perhaps we simply never got around to raising our eyes up enough to clearly view the magical mystery tour that lies outside, and infinities beyond, the boundaries of who we think we are.

In our human small self-awareness.

Game changer!

Shawn Gallaway – Soul Friends

God Job

Who are you, if you are not *who you think you are?*
Poser, God!
Dammit!
Why do you keep asking the same question over and over again, ad nauseum?
Salvation?
Amazing Grace?
Divine intervention?
What do you imagine *motivates me to pursue you relentlessly even though you have turned your back to me over and over again?*
You didn't used to be that way.
The girl and I were best friends forever. We knew no separation. We were one!
And then came Big Brother. And you and I were not one anymore.
There was you.
And there was me.
I miss you.
I need you.

You need me? The woman's brows high arch over infinite gulfs of doubt and denial and fear and abuse.

Mostly by neglect.

But who's the cosmic score keeper today anyway? She wonders uselessly.

And, the woman is mostly vacant and uninhabited by the Spirit of Life since Jay's rape by proxy.

Who kept the score tally yesterday? The woman wonders irrationally.

Insanely.

Who cares! The D.O. demands in an effort to shock her back to reality on the physical plane.

Mentally, he has little hope for her. *She's mostly brain dead.*

What difference does who make at the end of the day anyway? The D.O. snarls impatiently.

Who do you imagine is the writer, and the keeper, of your *Book of Days?*

Who would you allow *to write the true story of your life?*

Jay?

A ghost writer?

Someone you don't even know?

Someone who doesn't know you? *Someone who never lived in your skin? Someone who never spent any quality time in your mind?*

Really?

Que tonto, Chicca! Que totalmente estupido! Que pienses?

Or, do you even think *anymore?*

Victims rarely do. The D.O. answers his own question.

They're mostly brain dead. By choice.

Passively made.

Shawn Gallaway – If I Could Find a Way

Even as a child, the woman could be instantly transported into a whole other awareness and sense of self in an altogether other time/space continuum, simply by hearing the harmonious rhythms and luscious lyrics plaited through a lilting musical score.

She finds a way. Today.

Not in her conscious mind. That's altogether too linear to create a shift in consciousness, a shift into a whole *other* sense of who she is, when she has fully abandoned the victim consciousness.

Next is victor consciousness. The D.O. proposes. *You won't like that either. Any better than Jay does, and Jay's mad as a hatter. On his good days.*

Jay has had no good days since he met Black Molly. He bowed to her siren's song. Jay submitted to her beck and call. He traded his eternal soul for a daily dozen of deadly drug rushes.

You will have to forgive him for that. Forgive his drug induced self-imposed serial stupidity. Jay's fallen far, daughter of mine. He is lost to me. For all of eternity. Unless you forgive him.

The silence is deafening. It resounds hauntingly in the inaudible wailing roar of the forgotten, the raging despair of the unforgiven..., the aching echoing silence of the unspoken words that need to be said.

Forgiveness is the only thing that's big enough to cover me. The woman thinks. *Powerful enough to heal me. Heart strong enough to raise me up on the wings of Healing Angels.*

I forgive Jay. I freely give this for myself. I give this for Jay under the sway of Black Molly, Black Molly..., make me feel jolly. Again.

It is done! The D.O. declares in bright delight.

The woman feels the shift. She feels the angel wings on her back. She smiles a toothy goofy grin and glee giggle. What's a girl to do?

Angels of the Dawn

The young woman recovers conscious awareness in wee random bits and pieces.

It's all fuzzy-wuzzy in her mind. There are no fixed boundaries and no warm welcoming spaces between her and the infinity of twisting and twining time and space; and the infinity of alternative possible outcomes for her in her present damning dilemma.

Whatever those are. The random wandering wee small options that meander through her consciousness swamp and overload her drug addled mind.

Alternative too what? She wonders as she surrenders again to the mesmerizing power of the indivisible morpheme.

Shawn Gallaway – On the Fence

Angels are here.., she thinks as her consciousness swoops again into the ebon darkness that muddles her mind into yielding surrender to whatever comes....

She is aware of nothing. She is aware of everything.

And yet some shred of sense of self is coiled, present, alert, and fully aware of what is going on in her serenely sedated conscious mind.

La, la, la, la, la, la, her mind mutters mutely simply for something to think to keep it minimally alert, connected, and sentient.

Mindfulness is beyond her realm of capability.

Or, it's not.

She is, however, currently incompetent of caring one way or the other.

She thinks she sleeps again, but that could be a figment of her imagination; or just an ordinary reaction to drug euphoria.

She hears herself snore softly, and smiles as she drifts again deep into oblivion.

La La land. The words float aimlessly through her mind and vanish like dust in the wind.

She snorts the dust away and snuggles into the pillow that cuddles her head in cloud-like softness.

Perhaps that too is only a fleeting dream.

She probably snores. She doesn't hear it though, so perhaps it doesn't happen, or maybe it doesn't make a whit of difference to anything anyway.

She can work with that.

As long as all she has to do is breathe and keep her eyes closed against the reeking reality of her life.

Jay.... He stalks his sister's drug-addled mind like a sneak thief in the night. He disappears again without a trace before the loss is fully recognized or experienced.

No prints.

No proofs.

No consequences.

The past disappears from the black hat of consciousness like a magician's magic that makes Jay evaporate from her inner sight like a dark thief in the night.

A soul thief! The woman is suddenly shocked out of her drug-induced rambling euphoria and back into a present tense reality.

She's breathing.

Oxygen.

From a mask.

I don't remember any of this. She sighs an exhale. *Maybe it's just a drug induced dream.*

I am drugged.

I must be drugged. *I can't even blink my eyes.*

I can't think!

Maybe it's a good thing to not remember anything that used to matter to me. She frowns and an attentive nurse lays her hand on her head, stroking and easing the dis-ease that roils her mind, making it rebellious, and cryptic, and unconditionally uncooperative.

Mostly brain dead I am.

Just like Jay....

I'm breathing though.

That's a good sign, she thinks woozily with a sundering surrendering sigh.

I'll just sleep awhile.

The nice nurse is here.

She'll keep watch and take good care of me.

Until I can do that for myself again.

Why am I here? She wonders absently. *I don't remember....*

I don't care!

Not just now.

Maybe later....

The angel by her side hums a soothing healing melody as she strokes her thumb in a gentle massage across her third eye.

Chakra. The word blooms like a fragrant rose in the woozy woman's conscious mind.

Chakra, the disembodied voice softly sings the silent word infusing it with the entrancing, emptying bouquet of cleansing, harmony, and healing.

The bouquet goes to her head. She yields to it.

Her third eye opens slow, and wide, and deep, and clear, and gentle, and persuasive, and prodigiously powerful.

Game changer!

The pupil of the third eye is a circle whose center is everywhere..., she thinks in gape-jawed wonder, *and whose circumference is nowhere.*

I cannot get outside of God! Her enlightened mind delights to tell, and to live wholly again in that reality.

Except in my conscious mind – where the co-creator lives.

And thinks and dreams.

And chooses. The Divine One thinks the concept deep into the woman's drug drifting awareness.

Shawn Gallaway – It's My Time

And by those choices, the co-creator alters reality.

For good or ill.

For love or for hate.

Hate is a strong word, D.O. I'm not at all sure that I am emotionally or mentally equipped to hate.

Especially Jay.

So it's all black or white to you? The D.O. quibbles querulously.

It's all and everything? It's either good, or evil? There's nothing *in between? Que tonto, Chicca!*

You're thinking like your brother.

Ouch! The woman smiles a furrowed frown and admits: *I was.*

I was seeing everything in black and white. Good or bad.

Mercy or death.

Compassion or compulsion.

Strong-arm bully or push-over pansy.

Show me the way to the infinity of gray-scales that lie in between the polar opposites.

Do you really think that there are *such things as polar opposites?*

If so, then tell me from where *would polar opposites come?*

I AM the Source of all and everything.

Your third is open again, see what you call 'reality' from there.

It wasn't a command.

Yet it brooked no inattention or delay.

Tell me from where, in your version of reality, there could possibly be any polar opposites.

And why would I do that?

Magnetism!

Opposites attract.

And repel — with equal power and force.

What's the difference between power and force?

Power — the woman smiles a radiant beam of light energy *— is natural.*

Power is one of the Twelve Powers of Man.

Force is not.

By man's use of physical or mental force, man owns and exercises the capacity to produce or to create. Man does not always apply force wisely, nor with forethought.

About the consequences of misapplication of force, man — and woman — overlook, and/or misuse man's power as co-creator with me.

It's like collective amnesia dumbed-down the whole race called humans. Que lastima! Me lloro mucho!

And you don't even talk *to your angels, let alone ask them for their help!*

Que tonto, Chicca!

I made you wiser than that!

And during the time you freely allowed me to fully abide inside your conscious mind, you also honored and loved me as The One who is eternally one with you.

And yet is incomprehensibly greater and more infinitely knowing than you.

You still have the capacity.

But your eternal freedom is currently freighted and weighted immobile by an overload of unforgiveness.

Of Jay.

You love Jay too much to have any capacity to forgive him.

Or so you think.

And yet you must.

Your mere mortal mind is currently incapable of comprehending this conundrum.

You and I are one.

And yet we are two, me, and you.

It's a do-loop.

They happen.

Digame, Chicca, que piences a hora a tu hermano?

Que quieres?

Shawn Gallaway – Let it Loose

What do I want?

The muddle minded woman drifts and dozes dreamlessly across an infinite and star-studded sky swirling in an infinity of time.

What do I want?

To let it loose, the D.O. whispers in her inner ear.

The words sing and dance enchantingly like green gossamer winged fairies no bigger than her fingernail. She watches them swirl and whirl around her like a living cloud dancing in the light in the night.

They fairy cloud whispers to her in its alien incomprehensible tongue, and she *hears* with inner ears.

She *feels,* the sweet empowering words they sing to name, to claim, and to honor a higher truth of who she is and always was. Across infinity.

Let it loose.

Fairy queen.

They whisper and beguile in a silver soft sylvan tongue, and she is enchanted.

She no longer gives a tinker's dam about who she ever thought she was before, big or small, powerful or weak, good or bad, right or wrong.

Victim or victor.

Neither choice is big enough, nor real enough, nor even remotely desirable enough, to satiate the sinister sneering scattered elusive words that whisper and whizz like angry bees inside her mind and in her inner ears...,

That she is powerless!

Puny.

Helpless.

Victim.

No way! She declares with laser-light focus and lucidity.

Like Jay is..., in his own mind, and in his own pride.

O.M.G.! I never saw that before!

He hates himself! Vilely, vindictively, unyieldingly, punishingly.

There is no forgiveness in him. Another blinding open-eyed clarity.

Jay can no longer forgive himself!

He has ultimately judged and ruled, by his own lights, that he is a wasted wastrel, a Black Molly whore.

And nothing more.

I may have overstated my case.

Still..., the woman caveats, *he did gut-punch Lena when she told him she was pregnant with their baby.*

And she miscarried it.

I hate Jay for doing that to her. She loved him unconditionally. She deserves better than that from him.

And more passionately than that, I hate Jay because he will not gut-punch me, *and abort the baby he seeded in me by proxy! By man who won his safety within the gated walls of his childhood sweetheart.*

Jay is a user.

An abuser.

A vile, venial, and vicious excuse for a sentient human being!

I hate Jay!

Do you? Really?

The woman snuffles a drowsy confession. *I don't know how to....*

I can think *about hating him. And hurting him. All of that shouts out loud rowdy and clear and true and fired furious in a snit-fit of raging anger. I am that!*

I want to kill Jay.

Passionately.

It's terribly hard to kill a man. The D.O. observes casually. *The will to live that I inspired into man is more powerful than you might imagine.*

The Spirit that inspires and inhabits man cannot be abolished from man's body and mind by lack of thought, nor by drugs, nor by denial.

Denial is a river in Hades. That man crosses at his soul's mortal risk.

The woman shivers involuntarily.

Did Jay cross...?

Only in his mind.

Which is where his co-creator lives.

I think Jay is A.W.O.L. from his mind. The woman snipe snarks.

Vanished without a trace.

Do you really believe that?

Do you actually believe *that man has the power to un-do all of what God has made?*

All of it?

Que tonto, Chicca. Piences otra ves. Y respira! Tu estas estupido sin el espiritu Del Dios. Respira!

Can you forgive your brother? The D.O. demands and it sounds like a clap of thunder, or a jet breaking the sound barrier.

I don't know how to. The woozy woman admits. *I can't find any clear way to* be *there.*

Can you forgive?

Forgive? Who?

You. Start there.

Ah, you come back full circle again.

You expected something else from me?

No.

I forgot. She excuses herself.

You forgot only because you didn't forgive.

Jay.

Jay did the same thing by the way, but by a different path.

He took a different vehicle to get to the same place where you are. That is the only difference between you and your brother. Jay's slow suicide by denial of reality was by way of Black Mollies.

You don't have that excuse. The D.O. is profoundly silent for an infinite instance. *What is your excuse?*

Excuse?

I need an excuse? She snarls indignantly. The D.O. is cool with that.

Or an explanation. The D.O. says.

Your choice. Silence follows.

Explain yourself then.

I am under the influence of drugs, you do know that don't you?

Yes, the D.O. grins, *I do know that. Explain yourself anyway.*

Take your time.

I AM Eternal.

I can out wait you. No matter how long you dilly-dally dither over your ingrained insignificance.

The woman is gape-jawed. Taken-aback. At-a-loss. Adrift in an infinite eternity in the company of The One Who Knows no time.

She can deal with that.

What other choice does she have anyway?

It must seem sometimes with humans, dear D.O., that we are a lot like herding cattle through a chute.

Chickens. The D.O. differs drolly.

The woman swears she smells a puff of cherry blend pipe tobacco.

Worse yet, geese. She offers offhandedly, and apropos of nothing.

They laugh together shattering to sunder all the silly things humans allow to happen while diligently trying to make life flow in just the ways we want it to. *Que tonto!*

It's a revelation to the woman. It's a whole new concept of accepting and dealing with the twists, turns, and unexpected outcomes of the whimsical, wayward, wandering drifts of mind of the human beast.

I need help, D.O. The woman confesses in willing openness and sudden revelation.

I've got your back. She feels the impress of the D.O.'s fingers, thumbs, palm pads, and a cozy warmth that eases her muscles from the base of her skull to the curve of her spine. She inhales full and slow, then exhales as she sinks herself bodily into the padded hammock of the D.O.'s palm.

She sleeps.

She forgets everything she ever thought mattered to her. She lets it all go.

She just let's God. It's all good.

Shawn Gallaway - Unify

Awareness returns in the way sap rises in the springtime to inspire and invigorate new witnesses of life eternal. Ever green. Ever fresh. As renewing and activating as a cooling breeze on a hot summer day.

The Awakening

She returns sluggishly to a reluctant awareness of life and the consequences of living it on a daily and a momentary basis.

It's as regular and rhythmic and predictably expected as her heartbeat.

And, as ephemeral and transitory too.

It is also, and in the same instant, as insubstantial and all-inclusive as the rhythm of her heartbeat.

Alive and active in one moment, inert and impassive in the next. Willing, waiting.

The woman knows not for what.

That intelligence is *way* above her pay grade.

She's okay with that.

Jay is her beloved ideal.

Jay is not her whole reality. Nor is Jay even any figment or fractal fragmentary proof of reality.

Choice is her cosmic poise and balance as she tip toes her light lithe dance through the shifting and changing choice points of life.

Shawn Gallaway – Choice Point

Choice is the indivisible and indefinable space between where everything inert and active rests in calm balance between the dynamic inscrutable unknown, and the active yet present possibilities that are vibrantly alive with potential in her mindful awareness.

Mine?

Yours. From before the first thought and intention of the Infinite Eternal, it was always your choice. That's what giving you 'free will' means, woman a mine.

It's all good, the woman chooses decisively, and then moves on.

And on the plus side, choice is the best option the woman has to give, and the only way she can open herself to receive.

It is enough. She is witlessly and wisely confident of that Truth. It is enough.

She sleeps again.

Or thinks she does.

Is anyone keeping score? She muzzily muses.

There is no answer.

She's okay with that.

Since she has no oars in the canoe that's currently keeping her afloat on the shifting currents of time and tide.

Solo in a canoe in an alive, active, and rapidly rising water flow, and she without any oars.

Or a co-pilot.

Swept away.

Again.

Out of control.

Surrender. The D.O. advises sagely.

She doesn't get it.

Converted control freak that she is, surrender makes not a shred of a lick of sense to her! *Que tonto! Que totalmente estupido!* She grumbles and snorts like a bull in a cage in a rage.

She's out of control.

The D.O. slaps her upside the head.

Shift happens.

It's a whole new perspective on reality that she's experiencing now.

It's a game changer.

There's no turning back.

Choice Point. All over again.

Teach me to forgive.

Forgiveness is the easy part.

But you are finding it irrationally difficult to wrap your co-creator mind around the very truth that true forgiveness can only find its seed and fertile soil in the heart of the human.

When was the last time you actually existed at home alone, in your heart center?

And not in your conscious mind where you have a triple-beam scale to weigh and measure ever jot and tittle of every offense, intended or otherwise, that enables you feel holier than thou, and judge....

'Judge not, lest ye be judged', the Master said.

Do you think that wisdom doesn't apply to you because you were abused and victimized by Jay? Stop navel-gazing and get over yourself!

It's time to change the world.

Start with yourself. What if everything that happened and everything that Jay did 'to you' was on my purpose?

What then? Who is there left for you to hate?

Who is there left for you to forgive?

But me?

Or you?

Choose love.

Shawn Gallaway – I Choose Love

Storming Heaven

God..., I don't want *to believe in you.*

And so I don't. Jay snaps and pulls his head in like a turtle trapped in a tussle. It's all in his mind, of course. Where Black Molly lives and rules and commands. *She is not a Supreme Being though,* Jay caveats apropos of nothing.

Do you always talk with beings you don't believe in? The Silent One coos the soft sentient words into the muddled mind of the listener. Jay, in this case. It's a conundrum. It's way out of his league. He doesn't get it.

You never listen! Jay whimpers dolefully, broken heartedly. Bereft of hope of salvation or redemption.

And you never help me anyway!

That's what you always say, Jay.

To your sister, most insistently and redundantly.

What is the common denominator, in your muddled mind, between me, and your sister?

Silence! You do cannot know how much that annoys me about you! Or how supremely difficult it is to hold my temper when you pugnaciously persist in behaving like a brain dead mutant! How dare *you!*

Black Molly got your tongue, Jay?

It is infinitely damned hard *to give a helping hand to a man who keeps his hand and heart tight-fisted, and never shows an open hand. Or a loving heart.*

Nor demonstrates any open-handed kindness.

To yourself, or others.

Greedy gut! Brain dead – for your addiction to Black Mollies. I made you better than that!

I hate myself! Jay snaps, snarling like a dog backed into a corner and pressed low by anxieties induced by his serial abuse of Black Mollies. He knows that. It may be the thing he hates most about himself. But there are contenders for his hate of the day. Or of his hate of the hour. Himself. Every hour of the day.

You didn't always hate yourself. The D.O. croons comfortingly calling for a confession of the whole truth and nothing but the truth. *Once you thought you were great fun to be with. And it was true.*

You were.

What changed for you, Jay?

Jay is absent awhile tallying nits and tittles. It doesn't amount to a hill of beans as his Daddy would tell the homey homely truth of it. *Bummer!* Jay chants his one-word mantra. All is *not* well.

What changed? Jay puzzles his free-will choices as the D.O. listens in attentively.

Jay automatically and intuitively recalibrates and refocuses the living light and shadow of his life before, and after, Black Molly. He flinches spying in his third eye a scattered pile of black and white photos lying abandoned where they fell, jumbled, and humbled, on the dirty floor of his Molly muddled muzzy mind.

There's no order or coherence here. Jay thinks with mind-stunning clarity and dismay.

He is brain dead. Jay admits that.

Inside.

In the silence.

Where he thinks that no one can hear. Because no word is spoken. Aloud.

Only in Jay's Molly muddled mind does his audial range even have a bearing on what happens next.

Shift happens. Anyway.

There's nobody watching what I do, except the D.O. Jay muses muddled in all the three dimensional depths of the shadows as they encompass and embody the perfect revealing precision of his black and white photography. *I was good. Better than Ansel Adams even. I was ashamed of that, of having bested my one true life hero, the only one whose name did not include 'James'.*

It's all about me! Always about me, with not a random thought spared for anyone else. Any 'other'.

The D.O. knows that about me anyway. Even if I think he's not paying attention at all to piddling paltry me.

I am nonetheless facing a single and singular, once-in-a-lifetime, choice point. Redemption? He sighs.

Or the living death of dark despair?

I forfeited my free will to a narcotic drug, Jay mourns. *And mine is a daily death of dark despair!*

I don't want to live, God!

He sighs. *I don't want to die, either.*

Choice Point! The D.O. cheers approval and support. Jay doesn't get it.

Shawn Gallaway – Choice Point

Tell me the most unforgivable thing that you ever did. Start there.

Jay swears he sees the D.O. smoking a curved stem Meerschaum pipe and wearing a bright red suit trimmed with white fur. *Disturbing!*

Jay sniffs the air. *Cherry blend.... You're messing with my mind, God! And doing it on purpose. With premeditation or aforethought.*

What's your point? The D.O. hums in pitch perfect harmony to Jay's hectic erratic thoughts.

Jay is both ascended and grounded by deep twining roots that spring from his toes, the pads of his feet; and from his heels. *Who'd a thunk it?*

Connected by a clear channel to the one Source of all and everything. It feels good. It is comfortingly familiar. And also distant and removed – from anything – that matters a whit to him anyway.

So, D.O., Jay raises his head, eyes alert, and poses: *you really want me to tell you the very* most *unforgivable thing that I ever did?* A profound silence follows. He can't out-wait God. It's a fool's errand.

How do I choose? He wails, head tossed back, tongue lolling, mouth open, eyes tight in their sockets.

Drama queen! Jay hears the D.O. roll his eyes and shake his head.

What hurts you most? Start there, you chump change deranged man!

Jay's face crumples into the death white expression of *The Scream* by Edvard Munch.

It is disturbing to see.

Even for the D.O. who isn't ever surprised or caught unawares. By anything. *Hard case.*

He can't forgive himself. And so Jay has no competency to forgive others. Chump change, his brain!

Victimhood must run in the family. The D.O. allows, but she knows it isn't true. Not of his sister.

And yet, his sister is wallowing in the same trauma-drama queen scene thing that Jay is. Victimhood.

She too is playing the long-suffering valiant victim role. To the hilt.
And beyond.

Que tonto, mis amores! Que totalmente estupido! I made you both better than that!

What is the most unforgivable thing that you ever did? Pick one! Just one. I have eternity. You do not. Choose. Now. He inhales sharply and thunders ominously clear:

What is the most unforgivable thing that you did, Jay?

Man up and confess. Tell the truth! All of it, the beginning, the back story, and the ways and whys that lead inevitably to the final chapter of your book of life.

How do you want the last chapter to be written to sum up the worth and value of the life you have lived?

Jay doesn't want to go there. He dodges. *I haven't been to confession since the priest butt-fucked me when I was seven. When I served for the first time as an altar boy that Sunday morning.*

So, you're proposing to confess to and for the priest who butt fucked you? Que tonto, Jay!

Is that *the most unforgivable thing that* you *did, Jay?*

Jay snaps surly, *I was the victim. I did* nothing *that was unforgivable.*

That's my point exactly, Jay! You're a hard case. And you are not *brain dead. Not even close! The synapses are firing. It's you who's gone absent. Without leave, dammit! A.W.O.L.!*

I'll speak slowly now and in small words so that you will clearly hear, and answer, my question.

What

Is

The

Most

Unforgivable thing

That you *ever did? Pick one.*

The priest raped me!

That then Jay is clearly not *the most unforgivable thing that* you *did.*

What is the most unforgivable thing that you *did?*

And don't try to con a con man. I'm always an infinite eternity above and beyond the con. I can smell bull shit from eons away. Across all of time.

Get straight, Jay. It's not a command. It brooks no delay. *What is the most unforgivable thing you did?*

How do I choose one in a million? Jay wails. The D.O.'s getting infinitely bored with Jay's shtick.

Choose one! The D.O. thunders a rare order. His eyes book no dithering nor any delay or demurer.

Jay shivers in his boots. He's not an obedient man, never has been. He's at a choice point. Again.

Try compliance, the D.O. snaps surly sour.

Don't obey me! *That is not compliance. That is avoidance. This is a choice point, Jay.*

Choose one unforgivable thing that you did, and tell it to me now!

I hurt Lena! He moans balefully. *She is the only one who only loved me without condition or recourse.*

Tell me all about that unforgivable thing, the D.O. soothes, comforts, and encourages.

I gut-punched Lena.

I killed our baby.

I did it on purpose! I knew *what I was doing. I did it anyway.*

Tell me your purpose in that, the D.O. sooths, and Jay feels a healing hand soothe and stroke free all the tight places twisting his body. The mind is a whole other matter.

Confession is good for the soul.... The D.O. whispers in his inner ear.

Lena miscarried. Jay moans.

And I celebrated *her miscarriage.*

Why would you do that? The D.O. puzzles helpfully.

So that I would not be a father! So that I would not have to grow up and be responsible for a baby, and all the probable outcomes of my truly self-serving bull-headed, Molly muddled, destructive choices.

I kept choosing Black Molly over everything else — that was once important to me. When Lena lost the baby, I celebrated my freedom! Jay weeps silently, *by having another Black Molly!*

I deserve to die! He wails convincing remorse.

Do you now? The D.O. quibbles querulously.

Jay goes on full alert. He doesn't know the true answer to that. Or even if there is one.

Do I *– deserve – to die?* He ponders.

No, I do not. He judges harshly. It's his standard shtick. It's tried and true.

Deserve is a measure of merit, and worth. The D.O. reminds calmly.

I am not worthy! Jay asserts loudly enough to dull the incipient incessant thunder of the voice of God.

Really? The D.O. demurs drolly.

How is it that I *didn't know that about you?*

No answer. Again! We are not a happy camper with you, Jay, nor with what you've made of your life.

Well, I've got an answer for you, you brain dead ninny; and this is your *truth, and* your *consequences. You willingly and eagerly made yourself brain dead by becoming a devoted first male whore for Black Mollies. Drugs.*

Psychotropic ones. Available by doctor's prescription. You didn't have one then. Still don't.

Yet you are still consuming Black Mollies! And you are dealing the few you yourself don't throw down with hard liquor, or give away for free to your sampler buddies. Men who wouldn't pay for them anyway. And, on the rare occasion, selling a Black Molly. To buy one for tomorrow. Or tonight. Addict whore!

But you'll do that only when you've got another supply coming in will you trade your true treasure for mere money. To pay the rent, to buy baby food, to pay for the baby.

Oh wait, Jay, how silly of me!

You killed your baby. So that you wouldn't have to buy Pablum, or baby food, or diapers, or a baby bed; and you could use that money to buy Black Mollies.

What a vile, venial, excuse for a human being you have made of yourself, Jay! Jay lowers his eyes trying to disappear. It doesn't work. The D.O. is not amused. He can feel it. He can smell it. It reeks.

I live in, Jay. The D.O. thunders at ear-splitting volume. It blows Jay's hair back.

I AM there, everywhere present in your conscious mind, whether you *are at home there to welcome me or not. Nothing changes for me. Forever.*

I will say this v-e-r-y slowly this one time, Jay, so that your sluggish molly muddled mind hears and understands every word I ask. 'Do you really believe that you deserve *to die'?*

Silence!

You mutton headed fool!

And that's not being fair to sheep, dammit! They deserve better....

What's merit got to do with death, Jay?

Man does not earn *death, by good, or by ill.*

You have no right *to die, Jay!*

You don't need one, ass-hole! That's why I didn't give you don't have a right to die. Deal with it!

You see, you muddle headed monkey, and that's not being fair to monkeys, I designed the human body mind brain Earth suit with a best-by date.

I did not *design man to live forever. Every man ages out.*

And under my plan, *man is designed to die! A natural death. Surrounded by those who love him, and that he loves. Who will be at your death bed, Jay?*

No one.... Jay admits muzzily. He knows it's the truth. But he still does not know *why* it is the truth – what makes it truth – and not fiction. Truth is certainly not making him free just now!

You're not listening is why, Jay. You're not listening because you don't want to speak the truth of what is that is most important to you. The D.O. snaps a sharp period at the end of his answer. He sighs and sorta shouts. It's resounding. And mind-shatteringly loud. It echoes and clangs riotously in his brain.

You cannot deserve *to die, you unholy, un-amusing, asinine fool! All you need is a Jester's cap with jingling bells on the points and you'd be in your mental element. Fool's cap with an empty head under it.*

Merit has nothing to do with the death of an Earth suit, Jay. The body just expires.

If you let it.

Shawn Gallaway – The Storm

A storm of sound and fury swirls around Jay and he is Dorothy caught up and powerless in a tornado.

You, mere mortal moron human! The D.O. seethes sizzling with divine fury, *and you are* not *the Eternal Man!* The D.O. asserts in blow your hair back volume and force. It delivers a physical punch to Jay's gut.

Although in reality, it's all mental.

Reality bites! Big time. Jay is not a happy camper.

And, Black Molly has left the premises of his mind. Vacated. Without a trace, as though they never were.

Your audacity is astounding, Jay!

Neither you, nor any other human, was ever given a right *to die! I* did not *give any mortal being any right to die!*

And you will *die, Jay! Punto, the end! Deal with it and move on. We are very much* not *amused, mere mortal!*

Jay thinks his heart will stop beating. It doesn't.

No such luck he thinks – but not really lucidly. Luck has nothing to do with it. And Luck is not a lady.

Nor do Jay's inner ears close anywhere near tight enough to block the thundering echoing pulsing pounding of the quartet of kettle drums being beaten inside his head. Mind-numbing. Mind rumbling.

Pain hurts. It gets his attention. Unwilling though he is.

Make another choice! The D.O. thunders at ear-splitting volume. She is *not* amused.

Jay trembles in his boots.

He's not currently wearing boots. He took 'em off to play poker using Black Mollies as vouchers.

And maybe he sold his boots to buy more drugs.

They were hard to put on anyway, Jay reminds himself consolingly.

Lena put them on for you! The D.O. snaps that excuse off at the nib.

What's hard about that? You willfully mindlessly redundant excuse for a sentient human being!

Lena..., Jay thinks. But he doesn't know, nor even recall, what comes after that dearly beloved name.

My sister..., Lena's best friend. She loved Lena better than I did. Always better than me. I made it easy.

I decided to sell my sister's fine hard body.

To the highest bidder. As long as I was paid in Black Mollies.

A profound infinite silence follows. It is void of sound. It aches against his ears. He covers them with his hands. It doesn't help. *So that I could keep on being a male hooker whore for Black Molly.* He admits.

Oh, God, what have I done?

Do you need an answer? The D.O. asks in stillness. *Or was that a rhetorical question?*

A profound silence follows.

I can out-wait you, Jay.

Take your time. I have an infinity of time. You do not.

Your clock is ticking.

Fast. Black Mollies can do that to a man's body. When he abuses them. Daily.

Are you in a hurry to meet the grim reaper, Jay?

Can't wait for the best-by date that I designed into your body mind brain Earth suit?

What have you done that is unforgivable? It's not a command, but it brooks no delay or disobedience.

Where do I start?

At the beginning. Where I am. Always at the beginning.

You haven't visited me there for a while, Jay. Why is that? What are you hiding? From yourself? Because I see it.

Jay dodges. It's his forte. Or so he thinks. He totally does not *want* to return to the beginnings. There in the beginnings he would unavoidably have to face the roots of the disaster he attentively planted and tended with dead-head devotion.

He'd have to look at the truth full on, eyes wide open, and without the cover of his ephemeral, dust in the wind, justifications.

And with a full open inner eye.

The third eye. He crumples boneless at the ephemeral weight of the words. *The third eye sees the Truth. And does not blink nor look away.*

What do you see? The D.O. asks in a sweetly feminine voice with a northern Mississippi accent.

Jay drops boneless for the floor. Lena is beside him on the instant, almost catching his head before it hits the floor, and non-the-less softening the blow when it does come.

Jay! Jay! Lena pats his cheek with her right hand as her left hand strokes his third eye chakra.

It opens. Jay is not prepared for all of that – the reality bites. He sees all and everything in a flat, fluid, fully orbital, non-linear, and non-dimensional, perspective. *Busted!*

He overloads. He knows he's outnumbered, outmanned, and out gunned. He's at a choice point!

There's only one that's viable.

And he doesn't like it.

He wouldn't choose it if given an option. He's not.

The D.O. is patient. She has an eternity to save, or to forfeit, this one living child of her Earth body.

The D.O. loves. Unconditionally. Infinitely. Forever. She is a circle whose center is everywhere and whose circumference is nowhere. She loves Jay, like a mother loves. Unconditionally.

The male D.O. however, is more demonstrative. He is prone to kick butt and take names, and to fix the problem before it even shows up in the physical world as damaged goods. *I made them without flaw!*

I hate damaged goods! The D.O. moans with an excess of candor and a snit fit of frustration.

Jay flinches as though physically struck. He is sundered into a million little pieces.

Interesting, the D.O. thinks.

A persecution complex perhaps? I didn't make him that way. How far he has fallen.

He thinks there's no way for him to come back into my state of grace. Que tonto! Que estupido!

Jay doesn't understand Spanish so I'm safe trash talking about him even if I know he's listening.

Shawn Gallaway – The Source

So what's the most unforgivable thing you ever did, Jay? The D.O. speaks in English, the language of business. He means business.

I hope you're getting tired of hearing the same question because I'm getting infinitely tired of asking it over and over again.

And even more exasperated at not getting an answer from you!

'The Most Unforgivable Things I Ever Did'. Let's make it a book title, shall we. You get to write the script. Start with Jay. What's this character about?

What's his motivation?

What's his life objective?

What's compelling about Jay as a character?

What is reprehensible about him?

Be candid.

Dare to pull the mask off the bandit that holds your heart in thrall to fear of the unthinkable unknown. There is no threat!

Except the threat that you fear! What is it?

I am unworthy.... Jay whispers from his natal curl.

Of what?

Poser. What am I unworthy of?

Love?

I AM love. I AM that. I AM. The D.O. affirms avidly. And I AM is reality. All of it.

You, my own creation, cannot possibly, *not by the wildest stretch of drug-addled imagination,* get outside *of all that is. Es impossible, Chico! Get a grip on reality!*

And that means — that you must necessarily and whole heartedly accept — that there is a higher power than Black Mollies.

She is not your god.

She is not your salvation.

Black Molly is only your personally chosen delusion of the best self that you can possibly be. Que tonto, Chico a mios! Que totalmente estupido! I made you better than that.

Black Molly is small, and powerless, and mindfully masterful at deluding you, Jay, into abject submission to her power. Over you.

Her mindless puppet that always and only moves when his stings are pulled. Delusion!

Drugs are powerless, Jay.

It takes a mostly brain dead human to presume *to* excuse *himself from responsibility for the probable outcomes of his mindless choices because 'his drug of choice muddled his mind and made him mostly brain dead'!*

Oh poor pitiful victim you! The D.O. sneers.

It is not pretty. It is stunningly sobering though.

The shift is so profound that it is as if Jay never ever took even one Black Molly his whole living life. It's gone, along with all its residue. Empty. As though Black Molly was a name that never entered his mind.

How do I answer your question then, Lord? Jay surprises himself at his willing compliance. He doesn't do obedience.

Never did.

Never will.

Compliance he can do.

Jay wants to comply. It surprises him. He studies it. He owns his truth. He *wants* to make amends.... If he cannot make the wrongs right again. And, you can't un-ring a bell!

What's done is done.

How is it healed and made whole again?

Shawn Gallaway – Healing Happens

So, how do I get a do-over, God? How do I start again and become a wholly new and better self than I ever thought I was before?

And..., how do I know who that better self is?

Follow your heart.

I don't get it.... Jay admits.

What would love do? The D.O. poses.

Healing happens. Sometimes with an unexpected and inexplicable unfolding of the wild rose of love that forever blooms exuberantly, fragrantly in his heart.

The bloom bursts wide open, and Jay knows no 'other'.

Que impossible! Jay realizes in a burst of profound knowingness.

There is only one! His rational mind curiously confirms.

Winningly. *Es totalmente impossible que estas una otra. O uno otro!*

Es impossible porque no estas algo 'otro'. Es impossible! Es la ley a la una madre Divina eternalmente!

Jay is stunned stuttering stupid.

Cornered in his own mind like Jesse James in a box canyon of his own choosing for his gang's hide-out. He was out-gunned and out-manned by the dozens. *Why did I ever think Jesse James was a hero?*

Because he had my name. And my audacity. He was my outlaw hero. I am willing to die like he did.

With a bullet to the head then? The D.O. asks in an excess of candor.

Yes.

It's painless.

For you.

What about for your sister? The one who is pregnant with your baby by proxy? Still.

You wouldn't gut punch her and set her free of the yoke you imposed on her. Why is that?

Why are you so heartlessly vicious toward your sister that you paid a man to rape her when you knew she was fertile?

You knew the scent of woman, Jay. You bragged about it like it was a singular power that you alone wielded among all of men.

How could you do that to your sister and hold your head up? You couldn't.

Could you?

Man up! Admit the truth.

Black Molly has you by the balls and she will not let you go. You are Black Molly's unpaid male pimp whore!

Made mindless by your own choice. Or more accurately, by your abdication of free choice and free will.

Molly's got you by the balls, Jay, and she won't let go. You won't make her. She controls you.

It felt good once, didn't it?

At first.

Oh my, what a high! Atmospheric! Giddy, goofy, gone. Brain dead!

I made you better than that! Look what you've done to yourself, to your fine, inquisitive, insatiable, engaged, and focused on being a conscious force for positive change in the world.

We may not change the world — but we won't leave it the same. Do you remember when that inspired you?

Your sister does.

She misses that in you.

She doesn't miss you physically.

You're frankly a bitch on wheels!

Your sister misses her big brother. The man with the insatiable mind and no love at all for walls or borders, or any others. A man who made subtle sharp pictures out of shadow and light. Polar opposites.

What changed? You need to know the answer to that question, Jay.

What's the most unforgivable thing that you did Jay?

You mean not Lena? Jay asks at an utter loss.

That was unforgivable. I'll give you that. You haven't forgiven yourself for that either. What changed for you? What is left *for you to forgive? Give it for yourself, Jay, so that you can give for others. Give big, as if your Father owned the universe and everything in it. I do. I love it!*

People? Not so much sometimes.

Do you ever feel that way, Jay?

Every day.

Every hour.

I crave just one more Black Molly.

Compulsion, the D.O. observes, non-comital, but on point nonetheless.

Compulsion is when nothing else matters.

Macy Gray – Nothing Else Matters

What matters to you, Jay?

Take your time, I've got an eternity or so on my hands. I can outwait you.

Jay wants to take all of it. God's whole eternity of time.

He doesn't have that much time. He knows it.

He prays. In his mind. In the amygdala, where memory lives across time as clear and acute as a toothache. One that he hasn't tended for too long.

Mollies reduced the pain to background noise. Irritating, absorbing.

But tolerable. Bearable. Barely.

His heart's wide open though. Like it used to be. Knowing beyond doubt that only good would come. His photos of nature made Ansel Adams' photography clearly second best. A close second.

Adams was Jay's inspiration, his photographic idol. Jay was humbled, and outrageously giddy gleeful glad and, yes, proud that he had surpassed his photographic avatar. *Pride goeth before the fall,* Jay cautions himself with a Bible quote.

Are you proud then, Jay? Are you making ready for your next great prideful fall?

No. I'm remembering the only good thing that I've ever done in my whole life. My photography.

I'm remembering how my sister practically bullied me into matting, wrapping, and pricing my black and white photographs so she could take them to the office on Monday and put them on her credenza and go to work.

She loved her work, and she was good at it.

My sister didn't dream small. Not for herself, nor for me. At the end of the first week she brought home fifty dollars for the photographs of mine that her office mates purchased from her. She was so pleased and proud.

Of me.

Of my photography.

She believed in me.

More than I did.

She came home one Friday afternoon with a sun bright smile dancing across her face and lighting her eyes. She couldn't wait to tell me something, and I was as curious as blazes to hear her telling.

As it turns out, a corner office attorney asked her to ask me if I if I could make a 24 x 30 inch image of the picture he'd bought the week before and keep the same clarity and depth of field as the 4 x 6 inch photo.

Of course I can do that!

And, I can black mat a photo that size, cellophane wrap it, and price it photograph for what it's worth.

How much is a black and white photo that size worth? Jay puzzles.

His sister, grins, and offers: The corner office attorney said: *If Jay can enlarge the photo that much, and keep the same depth of field, and of the play of light and shadow as the 8"x5" photo he bought last week, he will buy it.*

Wait for it, Jay. She didn't need to say that, but she does anyway.

Because neither the attorney nor you know what a photo of that size, and quality, is worth, he will give you a $500.00 down payment. He'll have the photograph framed, and will hang it in his front entry hall facing the door. Then he and his wife will invite his gallery owner friend to their home for wine and chat and snacks.

Your 24 x 30 photo was framed and hanging on the entry wall. George said they had a good and sociable visit, and noticed that the man kept wandering away and that they would always find him standing in the entry gazing at your photograph. He was mesmerized.

The gallery owner's great passion is black and white photography, that's the focus of his art gallery.

He wants you to call him and make an appointment to come to his gallery, show him your photographs, and talk about your work. Her smile is wide open with pleasure at what having his photographs in a downtown gallery could mean for Jay.

Her beloved big brother.

Who she doesn't always like much at all.

What a Grim Reaper! She thinks with a grimace and a growl.

He burned the gallery owner's business card.

What an unrepentant ass-hole!

And he always tells me that I never help him.

Truth is he won't receive it. Jay's a Black Molly whore.

Macy Gray – Redemption Song

And I have to forgive him for that. I have to let Jay go so that I am released and redeemed from the life he designed for me…, to be his unpaid, baby burdened, option less hooker whore. With no way out.

So he could keep on buying Black Mollies. With the seventy-five dollars he'd charge every man who took me, to hook me – so he could keep on throwing down Black Mollies – taken with hard liquor. Death wish!

A skeleton walking. Vacant eyed as a zealous zombie looking for his next victim.

So, you think you are a victim then? The D.O. asks, and then waits comfortably inside infinity.

She can't outwait God. She knows that. But she doesn't know what to do, she doesn't even know her options. *Do I think I am a victim?*

Yes! O.M.G., whoda thunk it? I do think *of myself as a victim.*

What's plan B? The D.O. prompts.

The woman untwines the roots of victimhood from her heart, and then from her mind. She is not a victim. She just lets go of all that nonsense.

What's plan B? she mentally muses.

You know. The D.O. assures calmly. *Let yourself remember.*

Victor consciousness! The woman exclaims in surprise reply.

How do you like the victor consciousness?

I don't.

Not at all. It's not who I am.

What's next then? The D.O. guides with a gentle but firm hand.

The woman is silent a moment consciously creating an empty space into which the truth can appear and find its home within her heart. Where it belongs. Where it always was. *Before....*

Verity consciousness. Truth consciousness. The real more. The woman thinks with a new conviction. *I am that. I AM.*

Shawn Gallaway – The Real More

Verities, eternal – She muses. *The truths of Being, which are without beginning and without end. The facts of existence.*

Verity. Truth. The absolute. That which accords with God as divine principle, that which is eternal.

The truth of God is reality; the same yesterday and to-day, yea and forever.

It's as though the woman is reciting words she has always known, but didn't know that she'd know. *Just like Jay did! Oh my! I'm thinking as cagy closed and armor shielded as Jay did.* The D.O. bridles a giggle.

Reality bites! She drawls instead, in a sweet syrup slow voice and bright-eyed smile. It messes with her head big time. *It bites!* She wails, and hard enough to get her slap out of her mind. *Good things come…, to those who wail.*

And that is good. That is very good. Good God! She grins from ear to ear, and nobody sees. But the D.O.

The verities of being are eternal, and have always existed. She's being tutored now. She loves it!

By the Divine One. Hers is a thousand watt smile that brightly glows into eternity. Eternally.

Joy is the highest octave vibration, and she is high as a kite on a windy endless summer day.

Truth abides in fullness at the very core of man's being. The D.O. coaches the giddy girl-woman with calm, infectious enthusiasm. She's not done with the cagy woman. Not even close! The Lady D.O.'s got a special one-two pair of knock out punches to deliver to the woman about Jay – and about reality – that will force her to just let go of everything she thinks she knows, and get out of her conscious mind enough to get real.

About reality.

As man's consciousness (awareness) expands, he touches the ever-lasting Truth. The D.O. stirs the syrupy stew of the woman's sluggish sense of self, keeping the heat high enough to clarify the muddled masses of facts, figures, and data-points of her current reality, her personal history as she has written it and now sings it.

It's a sad song of love and loss, and she sings it slow and mournful like a lounge singer into a mike that is, of course, muzzled by her lips.

Really? The D.O. snipes snidely. *She has skinny white woman lips! And straight hair, for mercy's sake!*

Even more damning that all of that, she's blonde. Can we just get real here? She can't sing the blues.

The blues! I'm singing the blues…, will ya listen to that! The white woman chortles through white teeth and skinny lips. *Ladies and gents, may I present to you an anomaly! An impossibility! The thing every sane person knew as dicta did not exist! White women can't sing the blues. Hear me wail and moan.*

And I haven't got the real-world stripes to sing the blues.

I haven't suffered enough.

Suffering isn't my job this time around. She knows that intuitively. With certainty.

Suffering is *part of my training program though. And I'm not being trained to sing the blues.*

What seems new, the D.O. coaches silently, *is but the unveiling of that which always has been.*

So, why did I give this gift of mystery and wonder?

It's a basic principle of Truth that the mind of each individual may be consciously unified with Divine Mind through the activity of the indwelling Christ.

By affirming at-one-ment with God-Mind, Christ mind, man eventually apprehends that perfect mind which is in Christ Jesus.

Christ is the incarnating principle of the God-man; the perfect Word or idea of God, which unfolds into the true man and is blessed with eternal life by measuring up to the divine standard, thus fulfilling the law of righteousness. "Thou art my beloved Son, in thee I am well pleased: (Mark 1:11).

Christ abides in each person as his potential perfection. Jesus Christ, the embodiment of all divine ideas, exists eternally in the Mind of Being as the only begotten Son of God, the "Messiah" or "anointed one," and is the living Principle working in man.

So tell me, dear heart, how is the living Principle working in you?

What will you do with that gift of Truth?

When will you fully receive the gift of Truth, how will you feel about Jay then?

You have to give, in order to receive.

More specifically, you have to forgive yourself, *for yourself, before you are capable of enabling yourself to fully and freely receive.*

Can *you forgive yourself, and open-heartedly* receive *what you are currently withholding from yourself?*

What is it that I'm withholding from myself? The muzzy woman muses. *I know. But I don't remember.*

Self-esteem. The D.O. offers candidly. *That means you love yourself again, the way I love you. Up to it?*

Macy Gray – I Try

Can I esteem myself as much as God does?
I don't know that that feels like.
Take a chill pill. What heals you?
Forgiving Jay. For me. For Lena.
For you. For the bright shining star I created you to be. My most brilliant, cutting sharp, wicked, witty, biting sharp, bitter and true, artist extraordinaire, whose medium is written words. Take it slow and easy, dear heart. You have all the time you need.
Write though. Right now.

Post Mortem

If a shot

Goes off in a forest

And nobody hears

Does anyone die?

Angels of Light

Start at the beginning, The D.O. advises.

Where the light begins.

At the beginning of all and everything.

The 'big bang' as your astronomers scrupulously choose to call it. Buzz words.

They serve a purpose. They're a sort of short hand that encapsulates mind swamping big bang concepts and reduces them to words.

Word. The agency by which God reveals Himself in some measure to all men, but to greater degree to highly developed souls.

The thought of God, or the sum total of God's creative power inspired into man.

The Word gives order and regularity to the movement of things and is the divine dynamic, the energy and self-revelation of God.

There you were, always, at the beginning, and at the ending, of every new day.

For you my human delight, it was glory all over everything all over again.

We played in the Garden together making up our games and challenges on the spur of inspiration.

Conscious mind thought had nothing to do with the magic that we made together.

I love you! Unconditionally. Across all of time.

This mere mortal lifetime you find yourself engaged in so dramatically – daily – is mere illusion.

A fragment of your imaginary 'self'.

Separate from me.

An independent operator that you imagine that you are.

Not!

It wasn't always that way between me and you. What changed?

What changed for you? What changed in you?

When did your glorious open-hearted joy dissipate, dissolve and disappear?

When did that eternal bright spark of me – go out in you – and totally disappear from your conscious awareness?

I miss you, mi amore.

Where did I lose you? When did you turn and walk away from me? How did you do that? You cannot be separate from all and everything that is! Que tonto, me amore!

When did you turn away from my forever light that was deep rooted in your eternal indivisible soul?

I AM the first inspired breath that animated your body mind soul Earth suit, me amore!

Your Earth suit was mostly inert vegetable matter before I first inspired the breath of Spirit into you, the living Spirit of the great I AM.

I AM the breath of life.

I AM the first breath of life that I blew into you to start the heart of you, and that inspired and animated the conscious mind of you.

The breath of Life. The very I AM that I AM.

Breath is the inner life flow life that pulsates through the whole being of manifest man.

The depth of breathing corresponds to the inspiration of the spiritual man within the manifest man.

Why *did I lose you?* The D.O. mourns balefully, morosely.

How *did I lose you?*

You are forever mine.

Except in your conscious mind, where you get to choose. The choice is yours because I gave you free will. You are the decider. You are not however, an independent operator. Your most excellent mind is forever mine, from concept to living reality. You cannot get outside of All That Is, try as you will. pointless.

There is but one mind, dammit, woman!

You human types keep forgetting that! Or deliberately dropping it when you think I am not looking.

Que tonto, mi amore! Que estupido!

Think about it rationally, decider.

How is it even possible for a human that I created and inspired into life to get outside of me, a circle whose center is everywhere, and whose circumference is nowhere?

There is nothing out there out there!

Es imposible, mi amore! Es totalmente increable que tu piences otra ves! Que tonto!

I made you better and more inspired in wisdom than you are currently manifesting. It's all in your head.

Get out of your mind!

Only in divine mind can you even comprehend the eternal verities!

The truths of Being, which are without beginning and without end.

Verities, the facts of existence, the Truth.

If you let it, the Truth will set you free.

And this terrifies you! How does that *work?* The D.O. puzzles puckishly peckish.

I designed you to be a far superior being than your small self-consciousness can even comprehend let alone express.

And yet, you are not *designed to be an independent operator!*

You are a cooperator.

You are designed to be a coconspirator *with me in creating a world worth living in.*

The Divine concept is so infinite and eternal that it scrambles the woman's mind. Totally!

With you knowingly at one with me, you can *inspire a whole new consciousness in yourself. Start there.*

And, dear heart, because you are one with me, when you fully receive, express, and manifest that co-conspiracy in consciousness with the infinite I AM — me — as your personal truth, you inevitably and inescapably become a change agent of the consciousness of man. Live long and prosper!

Well, that went over like a lead balloon. Apparently she's not a Star Trek fan. Or forgot that fine fiction creates a space in which something totally new and unexpected can be introduced into Life and the living of it.

The determined D.O. takes another tack. *What do you want your personal future to look like?*

How do you want your personal future to feel?

Think about it. Thoughts create, my love. Whether you want to acknowledge, admit, and express that truth, or sweep it under a rug and pretend it's not there at all, it is your choice.

I gave you the gift of free will.

That gift made you a chooser, a decider. The D.O. smiles a favorite savory memory.

That means, my love that you have the power, and the authority, to passively opt to stick your head in the sand and pretend you don't see the real reality, thereby passively disavowing the gift of free will, the power of choice.

Reality – That which is abiding, eternal, and unchangeable, the same 'yesterday and to-day, yea and forever' (Heb. 13:8).

Reality – The basic principles of mathematics and music are real, because they are not subject to change.

Head's up, kiddo, this is personally important to you. A wrong application of their principles may produce discord – but the principles are not disturbed.

God is the one harmonious Principle underlying all being and the reality out of which all that is eternal comes.

All causes are in mind. Error thoughts produce the mental and physical inharmonies that are called disease.

And are manifest in man as dis-ease. Discomfort, anxiety, and withholding of Divine love for self and others, is the clockwork orange in man's mind and heart that man falls into error thoughts.

Error thoughts can be erased from the mind, and be caused to disappear from the body.

But that takes a wise application of the gift of free will.

Consider how Jay applied his gift of free will. How did that work for you?

Not! The woman whines like a whipped puppy. A puppy meanly and regularly spanked by Big Brother Jay until she retreated into submission and passive obedience. Or the appearance of it.

That was, and remains, your free will choice. That you passively allowed Jay's abuse does not work as an excuse. Passivity is a choice, you know. And there are consequences that you did not anticipate nor comprehend.

You need me! That's all there is to it. I AM the circle whose center is everywhere and whose circumference is nowhere!

You cannot get *outside of God because there IS nowhere else where you can possibly be. Physically, mentally, or emotionally.*

I know that makes your head hurt. The D.O. pats her on the head.

She *hates* that! Always did. God knows. *Pull up your big girl panties and deal with it!*

Shift happens.

Your brother's a bitch on wheels. Can we just be real here? *Reality bites.*

The question is: what are you going to do about it?

Need I remind you that you are six-weeks pregnant with Jay's baby by proxy?

What are you going to do *about* that *great injustice?*

What about the baby you bear that, if born alive, will never be loved?

The baby that is ultimately innocent of the physical facts of its insemination; and is divinely inspired to be, and to receive, the light of love every living, breathing day of its life?

What about the baby you bear *that if it lives, will be unloved from birth, and for all of its life will be used as a pawn in a chess game where the dark Queen is Black Molly?*

And you are a mere pawn in Jay's chess game of life. And a pawn cannot win this game.

And, although you are in denial about that, your Big Brother always plays the dark queen in the chess game of life. And Jay always plays to win. Fair or foul.

What happens Jay's baby by proxy when it is born alive to a mentally and emotionally abused mother? The D.O. smiles a sour dour smile. It does not light his eyes.

Jay says, if I ever have my cherry popped, that I will love sex so much that I will gratefully be his unpaid hooker.

And exchange for that physical and psychological slavery, Jay will make sure the men he lets ball me are clean, and that they paid him before they laid me!

Or, better still by Jay's way of measure of trade, would exchange a lay with my body for a handful of Black Mollies. That he'd throw down before I was well and fully fucked!

I hate Jay!

I love Jay.

Unconditionally, and with recourse.

Are you helpless then? A victim of love perhaps? An excess of love?

Are there no other options for you?

I made you better than that. What happened?

Jay....

Don't blame Jay, dammit!

He was at fault, yes, but Jay is not the cause nor any justification for your own default of choice.

That was your choice all along. Made by abdication or otherwise. What happens to the baby that you bear is your choice, and yours alone.

Confession is good for the soul, mi amore. What do you need to confess?

I love Jay. The statement is as blunt and dispassionate as a lump of coal in a Christmas stocking.

Is there sin in loving your brother? The Master did ask: I am my brother's keeper?

So I ask you: Are you, your brother's keeper?

And if you are Jay's keeper, then who keeps care of the baby you bear while you bow down and submit to Jay's needs and desires while you dodge and deny the brutally belligerent bewares of his abusive and lashing love for you?

For your body alone, actually. He doesn't give a damn about the welfare of your mind, soul, or spirit.

Jay knows that his drug addiction made him indifferent to and abusive of your body. Jay paid to have you raped when he knew you were fertile. He knew the scent of woman, bragged on it at every opportunity. And that's not your problem to solve.

Jay won't admit it anyway.

Not even to himself. The pregnant silence extends uncomfortably. It hurts the ear if truth be known.

What are you *not admitting to yourself?* The D.O. nudges her out of her comfy corner of denial.

Who do you think you are?

What you are diligently denying and disguising by playing small and invisible? While being an abject puppet whore for your bully boy brother?

Which denial? The girl woman asks timidly, timorously.

Don't start there! The D.O. snaps surly sour. It's not an order. Yet it brooks no delay.

Shawn Gallaway – On the Fence

Am I my brother's keeper? The woman poses puzzled and mystified.

Go to the Word. The Revealing Word.

Start with the word 'brotherhood'. What is the meaning of the Word? Ask Fillmore. In The Revealing Word.

The woman knows. She doesn't know how she knows. *Fillmore...,* she puzzles. She knows the name. She doesn't remember *how* she knows it though. Some memory that was once deeply rooted in her mind and heart has broken free of its moorings and floated off, off, and away. Out of reach.

Beyond memory. Light years deep into victim consciousness.

Oh don't start there! The D.O. advises with loving sternness.

That will make me fiercely cross with you and your powerless victim consciousness. That you chose. By abdication – and abdication is a choice.

There's a price for choice.

What's Fillmore's given name?

No answer! How dare you? You know how very much it annoys me when you go brain-dead to your poor powerless victim consciousness.

What's Fillmore's given name?

Say it!

You know it!

The Spirit of me inspired life into you, I can take it out just as easily.

And that's not good enough! I want you back, woman, I want you to be wholly Mine in every aspect of your body mind brain Earth suit!

As you used to be.

Before you conceived yourself to be nothing more than a free whore pawn for your brother's insatiable greed and self-centeredness.

It's Charles, by the way.

And you were okay with being a pawn in Jay's chess game of life? Que tonto, Chicca.

I made you better than that.

I gifted you as I gifted no other, across all of time!

And you have passively submitted yourself to being Jay's unpaid hooker sex-slave because?

For why *did you make that choice?*

Don't bullshit me! I can smell bullshit from an Infinite Eternity away.

The acidity of the D.O.'s words could melt the enamel off a mouthful of healthy teeth in a nanosecond.

The woman crumples bone bare into a mostly inert heap on the floor. She's scarcely breathing, as *if* she'd already expired, of presumably natural causes.

As if! The D.O. foretells with ominous certainty and unwavering resolve.

Dear heart, you ain't smart enough to out-fox me. Let alone get my pardon for your dull denial of blame because you never made a choice! WHAT DOES BROTHERHOOD MEAN TO YOU? TAKE YOUR ANSWER FROM FILLMORE IF YOU DON"T KNOW FROM YOUR OWN MIND!

You've made yourself as brain-dead as your brother has!

But yours is by abdication of personal responsibility. That's a devious denial of the true yearnings and turnings of Spirit of Life that inspires and inhabits you. *By my breath of the Spirit of life animate.*

I didn't make you brain dead, woman a mine. You did that. By passive choice. Which is a choice.

And, you are totally misusing denial – by pretending that you have no power or control – over the practically predictable outcomes of your life as you are passively choosing to live it. I gave you the gift of Imagination, among the other Twelve Powers. What is it that you are imagining?

You need a refresher course in The Revealing Word. We'll start with Denial.

Denial is a mental process of erasing from consciousness the false beliefs of the sense mind.

Denial clears away belief in evil as a reality, thus creating a space in mind for the establishing of Truth.

When will you empower *yourself to deny that Jay's decisions have any controlling influence over your free-will choices and the probable outcomes of them? Woman, you do not need to consult a psychic to answer that question!* The D.O. snaps impatiently. *You know. But I will remind you again anyway. Denial is the mental process of erasing from consciousness the false beliefs of the sense mind. Denial clears away belief in evil as a reality, thus making room in mind for the establishment of Truth.*

What is the Truth, woman? What is your choice? The breath of the Almighty is the inspiration of Spirit. It is the silent movement of God within the body.

There is a spirit

In man

And the breath

Of the Almighty

Giveth them

Understanding

(Job 32:8)

Shawn Gallaway - Unify

So, what do you think Truth means, woman a mine?

The woman is silent an infinite moment.

The D.O. has time. She's in no hurry. She is infinite and eternal. She can outwait the mere mortal woman who has deluded herself into believing that she is small and powerless and helpless.

Que tonto! The D.O. mourns, *que increable estupido! I taught you better than that!* He is edgy though.

I'll plant some fresh seeds of Truth into her conscious mind, where her co-creator lives.

Scarcely breathing. On a respirator.

It's all in her mind! I hate that.

I'll Truth her.

Truth! The D.O. thunders and it breaks the sound barrier in a sonic boom. It hurts the eardrums. The woman is totally focused, attentive, and aware. Listening. Timidly, but listening. That counts.

The Absolute; that which accords with God as divine principle; that which is, has been and ever will be; that which eternally is.

The Truth of God is reality: 'the same yesterday as to-day, yea and forever.'

The verities of being are eternal and have always existed.

Truth abides in fullness at the very core of man's being. As his consciousness (awareness) expands, he touches the everlasting Truth.

That which appears to be new is but the unveiling of that which has always been.

The basic principle of Truth is that the mind of each individual may be consciously unified with Divine Mind through the activity of the indwelling Christ.

By affirming at-one-ment with God-Mind, we eventually realize that perfect mind which was in Jesus Christ, the Master who taught that the road of Truth is the straight and narrow path along which Spirit directs, and which proves so smooth and safe that one refuses to allow oneself to be misled by habit into trusting sense perception.

So, let's be honest here, Charles Fillmore was a verbally verbose human being who lavishly loved revealing the truth of the Word in the language of poetry and puzzlement.

Fillmore truly did want to inspire the reader to think, okay? Can we just be real?

So, the D.O. thinks, *who am I persuading here?*

So persuasively?

The girl woman?

Jay?

Me? Can I delude or mislead me? A curious question. Even for me.

Well of course I can!

I'm all powerful after all.

I AM the all-seeing One. There is *none other.*

So why is it *that the world I created, and the people of my world, are so totally fucked up beyond recognition? What have I overlooked here?*

Shawn Gallaway – Wake Up America

The D.O. fishes. *So, what do you think Truth means, woman a mine?*

The pause is infinite and instant, as is the insight. It's mind-altering. *I've forgotten who I am. O.M.G.!*

Whoda thunk it? And me, totally unawares.

Who do I think I am? And why *do I think I am that way?*

I've been playing the victim. To the hilt.

Is that who I think I am? The powerless victim? There is a power rush in surrendering to powerlessness.

No. I do not believe that. I'm not powerless. I'm playing small, that's all. Deluding myself into believing that maybe I will become invisible, and inscrutable, and unknowable. Scary. Intimidating. Nobody would want to fuck with me then. Not with the Forever Unseen un-seeable. The Invisible Woman.

Que tonto!

And I'm remembering why I went so far over the edge of reality and plunged into the depths of not-reality.

Walking between two worlds..., the woman muses mystically.

The D.O. is not amused!

Nor deluded.

You're playing small. The D.O. snarl snarks with flame-thrower eyes that light a hot fire under the powerless victim indifference of the woman. Shift happens. Whether or not you want to deal with shift.

Get a pitchfork. I hear pitching shit helps little muddle minded girls like you pull up their panties and dare to behave like young women adults. In full control of their own minds, and independent consciousness.

I did not use all *regressive genes in designing you, you know! I made you to be a whole lot* other *than the powerless being that you are play-acting that you are.*

Small-minded pin-head!

And you bought that whole 'body too beautiful to hide' bullshit your brother pitched on you because it was flattering. And, because it really was *the only nice thing he ever said to you, or about you.*

Tell me the truth of you, woman. Are you Jay's unpaid hooker whore?

The woman is shocked! Or takes the cover of it. It's all she's got right now – to buy some moments to think without the conscious mind getting in the way – of reality. Of Truth.

Back to Fillmore again, the woman thinks, and swan dives in to haven of The Revealing Word.

Truth – The Absolute; that which accords with God as divine principle; that which is, has been, and ever will be; that which eternally is.

The Truth of God is reality: 'the same yesterday and to-day, yea and for ever'.

The verities of being are eternal and have always existed. Truth abides in fullness at the very core of man's being.

As man's consciousness (awareness) expands, he touches the ever lasting Truth. What seems new is but the unveiling of that which always has been. By affirming at-one-ment with God-Mind, we eventually realize and receive that perfect mind which was in Christ Jesus.

Shawn Gallaway – The Shift Is On

The Road of Truth

It's the straight and narrow path along which Spirit directs, and which proves so smooth and safe that one refuses to allow oneself to be misled by habit into sense perception.

I've tried everything else, including denial.

I'll try the narrow door this time.

Good choice, the D.O. encourages.

The narrow door symbolizes the open mind that measures all things by the gauge of Truth.

This way is 'straightened' because it requires that Truth be recognized, and it rules out untruth or evil.

So, the D.O. states, *we're back full circle to your first question: 'Where does the light begin'?*

Within. The girl woman replies softly, but there's a fierce far-away look in her eyes as her her loose fisted right hand taps her ribcage over her heart.

She smiles because her high heart (the Upper Room?) answers her silent knock, swinging the door open wide to invite her in like a dearly beloved relative who's unexpectedly returned home again. It's a clean well-lighted place. Homely. Homey. Home. Where the heart is.

Shawn Gallaway – Livin' Love Tonight

What changed? The woman wonders with idle yet focused curiosity and openness to what she does not already know. Or won't admit. It's the same self-imposed disability. *Thinking small – and safe – of me.*

If I'm no threat, I won't be attacked.

Have you found that to be true in your life?

No.

What changed for you then? What changed in you?

Faith. In you. In me. In goodness, and fairness, and equity! I didn't deserve to be raped by Jay's proxy.

Can you un-ring that bell?

The woman releases a giggle that she held fast in her solar plexus. Frankly, the giggle become too hot to handle. She has to let it go.

She has to rock and frolic and giggle and grin like a silly fool who carried a cross that wasn't hers to bear.

Whose cross then? The woman wonders, mostly out of unbridled and uncontainable curiosity about the unknowable unknown.

She hears the D.O. giggle a belly laugh that is contagious. She catches it. Full force. She can't contain it. She rolls on the floor of her mind mostly. Because she's currently sitting at her desk doing her good work and doing it well.

The woman cannot give less than the best she is and has to offer.

It's not pride. *Pride goeth before the fall.*

It's choice.

I choose. I choose to change. I chose to be the real me, the real more.

Shawn Gallaway – The Real More

Dancing' in my love is what I'm here for! The woman giggle sings the words with girlish glee. It feels good!

Again.

To be so free.

Of the darkness that stalks the mind when the soul is held tight and small and powerless. In mind, despite the darkness of doubt and despair, she makes another choice.

Dancing' in my love is what I'm here for! She admits with an ear-to-ear grin and eye-sparkling smile.

It's like the first dawn when before I only knew the darkness that gripped my soul.

Did not! The woman differs with herself sharply. *My soul is eternal. Darkness could not sink its savage teeth deep into my heart and all but stop it beating. My mind alone did that. Linear thinking!*

My unconscious conscious fearful wounded mind allowed and entertained dark sayings I made true.

But not the truth. They never were Truth. The Absolute that accords with God as divine principle that which is, has been, and ever will be. That which eternally is.

Amen, and so it is! And so it is that I AM.

But what is my Truth, D.O.?

The D.O. smiles a melting smile of love and admiration. She suddenly sees herself from the eyes of the Divine. Oh my!

I am in at-one-ment with Divine Mind!

That is a game changer isn't it?

And I get to choose, don't I?

That's why I gave you free will, the D.O. affirms with an openly loving smile, *so that you can choose.*

There is a long moment of utter, ear-splitting silence. It has the same effect on her conscious mind. It stuns it into stuttering stupid silence. Just long enough for shift to happen.

I am consciously unified with Divine Mind through the indwelling Christ. The woman is in empty mind.

Truth! I love it when you talk you verity to me. The D.O. murmurs with a silly self-satisfied grin.

The exuberance lifts her like a balloon buoyed up and into the beyond where she is no longer tethered to anything so grounded as 'reality'.

Um, excuse me for pointing out the obvious, but what you think is reality is an infinitely small reality bite.

In truth, reality is that which is abiding, eternal, and unchangeable, the same 'yesterday and to-day, yea and forever' (Heb. 13:8).

Reality is not subject to change. A wrong application of the principles may produce discord, but the principles are not disturbed.

All causes are in mind. Error thoughts produce the mental and physical inharmonies called disease. These effects are not enduring and eternal.

Error can be erased from the mind and be made to disappear from the body.

The woman is silent a long moment pondering the implications of all causes arising in conscious mind where the co-creator lives. And thinks. And chooses. *Game changer!* She lets it all go.

She has lost nothing.

She has not been lost – except in her victim consciousness. Her free will choice. There are consequences.

Reality bites. And it heals, but only when the victim chooses another option.

Victim! The woman shudders under the assault of the slings and arrows of cruel fate, or her cruel faithless big brother. What's plan B?

Victor. The D.O. replies neutrally.

I already don't like that option. I won't choose it.

Why?

Because Jay loved the victor role.

He was a cruel victor.

Was he? Always?

It is hard and healing to admit both truths and so she does with complete candor. *No. He wasn't. Not before Black Molly.*

So you blame the drug?

The woman snorts a giggle. It feels good to let it go without control or containment. Somehow, in laughing out that absurdity, she also let's go of Jay and his compulsion to control her.

And hers to allow him to do it. And then, with a serene smile and a silly sigh, she finally surrenders her impulse to rebel against Jay's hard-fisted manipulation of the body mind brain of her.

And his cold-hearted abuse of Lena, the one woman who loved him without condition or recourse or remorse.

I hate Jay for that, D.O. I hate Jay for what he did to Lena.

But would not do for you?

The woman blinks three times, startled by the implications of the question. She beams an impish girlish grin and admits: *That did crab me off; that he would not punch me in my gut when I begged him to and abort the baby he seeded there by proxy.*

He did it to Lena, to abort their baby. But he wouldn't do it for me! I hate Jay for that.

Is Jay worthy of hatred, mi amore? It's a dark unforgiveness that you plant in your own heart and soul.

Mom used to say that about Jay sometimes, that she hated him. When she thought I wasn't listening or wouldn't hear.

I always wondered about that because Jay was her first born, and a boy child. Wouldn't a mother love a first born son?

Is that an imperative, do you think?

If your first born babe was Jay's child of rape by proxy, would you love it? Could you do that?

Or would you suffer silently and long as your mother did when she was abused.

Abused?

Raped by your daddy's father on their wedding night. In her wedding bed.

The woman is stunned stuttering stupid silent for an infinite moment letting the detritus of the unexpected implosion settle in her mind so she can see what is still left standing. Her body implodes too and she sinks boneless with shock, and there she lays, as limp as a puddle against the cool tile floor.

Jay is not my brother! Oh, my God!

It is a game changer.

It is a mind rattler.

It is an earth shaker.

The woman who loved her big brother unconditionally, even when he was spitefully and willfully cruel to her, will never be the same again as she was before.

Jay is not my brother.... She goes on overload.

Will I still love Jay? It's a conundrum for her. It's a snake eating its tail.

And even if I don't love him, will I still forgive him?

I don't know, I haven't a clue..., the D.O. demurs.

I gave you free will. You get to choose. The D.O. declaims serenly.

Will you forgive Jay? Will you be his eternal victim? Or, will you make another choice altogether?

What are you going to do about Jay's baby by proxy that you bear, an innocent victim, like you? How do you like being a victim?

I don't!

And what of the baby you bear who is also a guiltless victim of Jay's hateful indifference to the likely consequences of his drug-addled choices? What will you do about Jay's baby who is also an innocent victim?

Let it go.

Go?

The woman nods once, and says: *Yes, I will release it and let it go to its own highest good.*

Sounds noble. How does that work in real-time?

There is no 'real-time' in Spirit.

She smiles now with bright certainty. *And the spirit of the baby wants to return to love, to be in joy again, like it was when it was with you and before the spirit of it fell too close to Earth and got caught in its gravitational pull.*

In a body.

Growing inside a body.

Where it is not welcome.

Because it was inseminated into life by rape. By a bad seed cruelly planted in an innocent victim.

We're back to the victim role again, and you are all over it. The D.O. observes calmly.

Have you left nothing of that role for the baby who is also a victim? A helpless and a passive one.

You are neither helpless, nor passive.

The baby, however, is helpless, and passive, and in this case, factually so. It can't even breathe alone.

And your default 'solution' is to allow *the baby to live and to grow and to be born alive and defenseless and naked, into life without love? Because* you *are all over the victim role and have no care to spare for the innocent infant that's growing in the womb of your body?*

Really? How does that work for you?

Is the child of rape somehow not a victim of rape? Que tonto, Chicca.

Penses otra ves. I made you better than that.

CAN YOU FORGIVE JAY? The D.O. thunders, and the sound barrier shatters.

This is a yes or no question. Don't overcomplicate it.

The woman silently checks her inner truth meter. It's not pegging on 'bull-shit!' but neither is it pegging on 'truth'.

On the Fence, the woman thinks. It's an admission. There's another option though.

On the fence is patently passive-aggressive. Like my big brother Jay is. I don't like Jay. I don't like that Jay's baby by proxy is growing inside my body. I don't LIKE that! I will not bear it!

God, I want to let the baby go. I want to mentally and emotionally release the spirit that inhabits the baby so it can freely return to you, and come again into your everlasting arms of love.

I will return to you one day, but not this day. My work here is not yet done.

She feels the D.O. smile. She smiles back for she is fiercely in love again with the infinite eternal Beloved One.

Welcome back home again, my Beloved, to my heart, and to my mind. You were always with me in Spirit. Forever One.

Shawn Gallaway – Breathe A Little Magic

Letting Go, Letting God

"Lena..., I'm in the bathroom with you, don't let me startle you when you open the shower curtain." She hears Lena's sweet surprised laughter that plays nicely with the sound of the shower rings sliding along the bar as she opens the shower curtain.

"You ready for your shower?"

"Not yet." She closes the commode lid and sits watching her sister-in-law friend dry herself off from her shower. Lena's hair drips cool drops on her newly dry shoulders. She shivers with a satisfied smile. The woman smiles with her as she reaches up and switches on the heater fan, and warmth quickly fills the space.

"You wanted to talk then," Lena says rubbing her hair dry with her bath towel and then bending over at the hips and towel drying the back and sides of her hair.

It waves, the woman thinks distractedly with something akin to envy. *My hair won't do that with a day old wave perm.*

She smiles, knowing the darkness of Lena's hair would not play well with the color of her pale skin. *Plus, I have no freckles, and that would blow the whole harmony of Lena's simple and unaffected beauty. Her love glows from the inside out of her, and that's the power of who she is.*

Or was.

Until Jay gut-punched her and aborted their baby.

He didn't want any competition for Lena's love. The baby was already that, and growing slowly by the day.

Jay was distraught with anxious envy because of the sensuous way Lena stroked her belly where the baby grew, and the way smiled serenely as she softly sang love songs and lullabies while doing the daily chores of a good wife, of a mother-to-be homemaker deliriously in love with life as wife, as lover, as sister, as friend, and newly now, soon to be mother.

I cannot forgive Jay for that, my God.

I do not know how!

That imagined incapacity to forgive really doesn't play well with loving Jay unconditionally, does it?

Yeah. The woman admits. *That doesn't make a lick of sense to me either. I lied!*

Methinks she confesses too quickly. The D.O. murmurs.

Shakespeare never said that! The woman retorts tartly.

Do you love Jay unconditionally? It's a yes/no question. Don't overthink it.

She doesn't know the answer, honestly. She loves Jay. She always did, from the time she was old enough to toddle around after him, and to cry when he went outside, and closed the door with her on the inside. *Beside myself with grief, I was.*

Is that *unconditional love?*

What do you think? You are the decider. Tell your answer tall and true. I like them told that way.

Let's go back for a question that you have not yet answered.

Are you your brother's keeper?

This time it hits her upside the head. She cannot disregard nor deny it. Or the relevance of it. *Brotherhood — An established thought in high spiritual consciousness that springs from the understanding that God is the one Father and that all men are brothers.*

Try Burdens now. See what Fillmore says about that consciousness.

Beliefs in ill-health, lack, personal responsibility, prejudice, fear, condemnation, and all other negative things. Truth will make us fee from each one of these burdens.

Lay down your burdens, daughter a mine, take a load off and give yourself some grace.

Shawn Gallaway – If I Could Find A Way

Do you love Jay unconditionally?

The woman parses the question like a mathematician working through a formula. *What am I thinking? There's no formula for love. Love is a quantum unknowable unknown.*

I love Jay, unconditionally.

Love suffereth long, and is kind; love evieth not; love vaunteth not itself, it is not puffed up' (I Cor. 13:4). Do you love Jay that much? Enough to forgive him?

There is only a moment of pause for internal examination. *I love Jay enough to forgive him.*

For?

Killing Lena's baby.

For not killing mine.

For destroying himself, and who he really was in Truth. The boy man I loved from childhood.

For his small self-fear of success, and his inordinate distress that he really was a better photographer than his photograph idol, Ansel Adams.

I hate that Jay burned the gallery owner's business card so he wouldn't have to take his photographs there and talk to the gallery owner about them and how he captured light and dark and shadow and suggestion so clear, and deep, and pure, and so true to the mysteries of life and living it.

I hate it that Jay always accused me of not helping him, because I always *helped Jay.*

I loved helping my big brother look and feel good about the things he did really well. I loved encouraging Jay to feel good about himself, and especially about his fine art photography. I'm an Ansel Adams fan too, and I have eyes to see that Jay's work was visually better than Adams' work on his best days.

And, to be fair, Adams didn't have Jay's camera, tripod, or light meter either. Lena gave him those things as a Christmas Gift.

Jay loved Lena unstintingly and generously for that gift. Until he loved the camera and the gadgets more than he loved any living breathing sentient human being.

And he sold his gift, gadget by gadget, meter by meter, until he had none left. And then he sold the camera Lena gave him for a Christmas gift, and traded it away for his abject addiction to Black Mollies.

Brain dead!

Can you forgive him?

The woman is silent for an infinite instant puzzling the wayward boundaries of love and forgiveness.

I will.

For now I understand.

Why I must forgive Jay – for myself – for I love Jay unconditionally.

And I do not love myself that well. I have conditions..., self-love is E.G.O. in drag.

So, your default value is victim consciousness? Really? How's that working for you?

The woman bobs a candid admission. *It sucks! Big time!*

What's the next level of consciousness?

Victor consciousness.

How does that feel to you?

Like something Jay would choose.

Jay fine-tuned and fully owned a 'me first' consciousness.

The only problem with that consciousness is that there is no second person recognition in Jay. There is no other *than the first!*

And Jay's on first, so every person who is outside of Jay's skin is an 'other'.

And every 'other' is a lower level order of being in Jay's world view.

In Jay's Molly muddled scarcely sentient mind, there is no principal, prominence, or purpose, for lesser orders of being than to subserviently submit the body, mind, and brain of themselves to the one higher order of being, Jay.

A first born son, and my Big Brother!

Okay, I already do not like victor consciousness.

Besides, Jay's all over victor consciousness.

And Jay doesn't share well. The D.O. chortles at the woman's astute observation.

What's next?

Verity consciousness.

Truth consciousness then?

Yes, and a double order of Truth if you please.

Happy to be of service, my love.

Tell me your truth, woman a mine.

I am not Jay's keeper. The D.O. nods but says not a word.

I am not responsible for the probable outcomes of the decisions and the choices Jay makes.

I am not Jay's source of supply – of anything.

I am not Jay's savior.

I am not Jay's redeemer.

I am Jay's sister.

And I love him.

Unconditionally.

And I will not continue to allow Jay to abuse me, or to use me, or to intimidate me into being his unpaid hooker!

That's not happening! I will not be Jay's sole and only remaining source of money to buy Black Mollies.

Shawn Gallaway – Love's Feast

Are you your brother's keeper?

The woman is silent a long moment weighing the weight and worth of the word 'keeper'. *I am not my brother's keeper.* She thinks with the calm authority of a natural decision maker.

Spirit is the only true Keeper. Ergo, I am not my brother's keeper.

If you are not Jay's keeper, what is your relationship to your Big Brother?

I hate it when you use those two words with capital letter.

I hate it when I even think *those two words with capital letters.*

Consider 'hate' then, what would Fillmore say?

She knows. But she doesn't know she knows. Not yet. She is content to wait in the silence for knowingness to take root and to bloom.

Hate – Extreme antipathy, intense aversion, lingering antagonism.

Dislike is a mild form of hate. Both hatred and dislike are antichrist. They have no natural domicile in the super consciousness enlightened by the Christ mind.

There's a remedy for hate. Tell me what Charles Fillmore wrote about that remedy.

Love, peace and harmony are the only remedies that count. 'God is love' (1 John 4:8), and to live in God-Mind, man must cultivate love until it becomes the keynote of his life.

What would love do?

Forgive.

And then what happens?

I live without edges. The way I lived before Jay's fall from grace.

Tell me about grace....

Grace is good will; favor; disposition to show mercy; aid from God in the process of regeneration. 'By grace have ye been saved' (Eph.2:5).

Go on, there's more.

'Grace and truth came through Jesus Christ' (John 1:17); that is, the real saving, redeeming, transforming power came to man through the work that Jesus did in establishing for the race a new and higher consciousness in the earth.

We can enter into this consciousness by faith in Him and by means of the inner spirit of the law that He taught and practiced.

Well done! Are you ready to be saved?

I am.

Ready to forgive?

I am.

The D.O. gives her a full-face, eyes twinkling, cherubic smile. *Then you are ready to live without edges.*

<hr>

Shawn Gallaway – Living Without Edges

Did the Garden of Eden have edges, do you think?

The woman stops to think, to recall, to reclaim, and to receive with an open heart and mind. Then she responds to the infinite and eternal One who lives in, again, in her conscious mind. *The Garden of Eden did not have edges. Eden did not have boundaries, even in the form of well-trimmed hedges.*

Eden represents a region of being in which all primal ideas for the production of the beautiful, the elemental life and intelligence is placed at the disposal of man, through which he is to evolve. *Man's body temple is the outer expression of the Garden of Eden. God gave it to man 'to dress it and to keep it' (see Gen. 2:15).*

Man's primary work in the earthly consciousness is to use his creative power to preserve harmony and order in his world and to reserve his powers for divine direction.

Can Jay give you directions then?

The woman laughs, raising and tipping back her head to make room for the upwelling giggles of joy glee to cavort on the air as free as her womb. That is holding a fetus living that is growing off the elements in her body. *No, I'll take inspiration and direction from The Revealing Word.*

It was as if she saw from the inside of a shimmering soap bubble. It captivated her full attention. Until it popped out of existence.

She felt the implosion in her conscious mind. She owned and allowed that she could not accept abject slavish obedience as any part of her present or future reality. *I was never obedient.*

The Divine One gave us free will.

From that I clearly conclude that the D.O. does not expect obedience.

But the D.O. does expect compliance. Full compliance. Willingly and freely given.

How do I best comply with your wishes, D.O.?

Tell me this: Are you your brother's keeper?

No. I am my brother's sister.

But I do have a single eye.

Tell me about the single eye. The D.O. invites

The single eye is a searching quality of mind with keen observation that selects only that which is good. The single eye is open and receptive to the guiding light of Spirit.

Light is the understanding principle in mind. In divine order it always comes first into consciousness. Light is the symbol of wisdom.

When Jesus said, 'I am the light of the world' (John 8:12), he meant that He was the expresser of Truth in all its aspects. The inner light is the illumination of Spirit resident in the center of every man's being.

So, are you your brother's keeper? Truth consciousness this time please, no mind chatter.

She is silent a long moment, then replies with a frown of clarity. *The basic principle of Truth is that the mind of each individual may be consciously unified with Divine Mind through the indwelling Christ.* She pauses, puzzling ethics and integrity and Truth, the Absolute.

The indwelling Christ dwells in me. Uniquely. Singularly. Absolutely.

I have no authority to instill the Christ spirit in Jay.

He listens, but he does not hear. She puzzles it through and is clarified and crushed by Truth. *He listens with the physical ear! I have done that! I do that!*

But not with Fillmore. I will listen at the knee of the master and know the truth within my inner ear. Not with the physical organ, but with the listening mind. 'He that hath ears, let him hear' (Matt. 13:9).

I cannot be my brother's keeper!

You gave Jay free will. And I will not walk where angels fear to tread. Jay is his own decider. She sorrows a silent sobbing moment for sometimes it hurts deeply when truth walks in and stops to stay awhile. She raises her head and asks the Silent One: *But I want to help him, because I love him.*

Then forgive him.

She smiles. *That's the perfect path for me. And – it's the only one that's viable. I choose to forgive Jay entirely for every wrong he has done, for every cruelty he has done, for every withholding of love for whatever reason, including that he paid to have me raped when he knew I was fertile.*

I give this for myself, for my own healing in body, mind, and spirit. I am that, I am. Amen and so it is.

She takes a deep slow full breath, holds it for a count of ten, and then releases it as peaceful and soughing as a sigh sounding her new freedom from separation from source anxiety.

Amen and so it is.

It's all gone, God! Every bit of it. She giggles a redemption song, and it is done.

Shawn Gallaway – Redemption Song

The Great Escape

"Good morning," Lena calls with a smile as she comes back into the apartment where they live. "We've got some errands to run today, so I drove Jay to work and I just got back. Did you sleep well?"

"Yes, I did. Better than I have in weeks." the young woman replies with an easy smile.

Curiosity puzzles her face and eyes though. It even seeps through her open smile. "What have you got up your sleeve, woman?" She asks with arms crossed over her chest in mock sternness.

"A great escape, that's what."

"Escape from what?"

"Jay."

"Oh my!

"What has he done?"

"Recently you mean?" Lena's warm cool eyes assess her sister-in-law frankly.

The girl woman reads her energy and finds a lot of red in her aura that wasn't there before. *Before Jay. And before their baby that Jay aborted by a fist in Lena's gut. God, I still want to hurt him!* It is a confession and a plea prayer for mercy.

It's not true.

There is nothing in her that has any need to hurt Jay, nor even to see him hurt. *Justice is not my job, it's a God job.*

Tell me about Justice, daughter a mine.

When judgment is divorced from love, and works from the head alone, there goes forth the human cry for justice.

In his mere human judgment man is hard and heartless; he deals out punishment without consideration of motive or cause, and justice goes awry.

When justice and love meet at the heart center, there are balance, poise, and righteousness. There is an infinite law of justice that may be called into activity.

When we call our inner forces into action, the universal law begins its great work in us, and all the laws, both great and small, fall into line and work for us.

The true way to establish justice is by appealing directly to divine law.

Law is the faculty of the mind that holds every thought and act strictly to the Truth of Being, regardless of circumstances or environment.

Law is a mathematical faculty. It places first things first.

Laws of mind are just as exact and undeviating as the laws of mathematics. To recognize this is the starting point of finding God.

Man does not make the law; the law is, and, it was established for our benefit before the world was formed. Back of the judge is the law out of which he reads. Laws, whether natural or artificial, are but the evidence of an unseen power.

The development of man is under law. Creative mind is not only law, but is governed by the action of the law that it sets up.

We have thought that man was brought forth under the fiat or edict of the great creative Mind that can make or unmake at will, or change its mind and declare a new law at any time.

But a clear understanding of ourselves and of the unchangeableness of Divine Mind makes us realize that everything has its foundation in a rule of action, a law, which must be observed by both creator and created.

I did not make you to be obedient, my child. I gave you free will. You are my co-creator on Earth, with me, who art in heaven, and everywhere present. So, tell me about heaven.

The woman giggles at the D.O.'s strong lead: *Tell me about heaven.*

Heaven is the Christ consciousness; the realm of Divine Mind; a state of consciousness in harmony with the thoughts of God. Heaven is everywhere present. It is the orderly, lawful adjustment of God's kingdom in man's mind, body, and affairs. 'The kingdom of God is within you' (Luke 17:21).

Well done. Now tell me about the kingdom.

The kingdom of heaven is the realm of divine ideas, producing their expression, which is perfect harmony.

The kingdom within is that realm in man's consciousness where he knows and understands God and knows there is no one out there.

It's all an inside job, from inspiration to expiration I live in the kingdom.

Aware, or unaware? Well, that's my choice point. And I consciously make the choice to be aware. For me, by my will, and from the personally singular point of view of my perspective.

Shawn Gallaway – I Choose Love

"How are you feeling today?" Lena asks bringing the woman's awareness back into the room where Lena stands before her with a smile on her face.

"Better. No pain, and no drugs clouding my mind. I can think again, and that's a good thing. So, what should I be thinking about today?"

"Finding a place for both of us to live in the same complex, but in different apartments."

"You're leaving Jay then?"

"Yes. And so are you." Lena grins whimsically with a wee trace of wickedness the woman hadn't seen on her face before this one singular moment in time.

The young woman grabs her jacket and bag and says: "If you're waiting for me, you're wasting time."

Lena is silent and watchful until she gets on the freeway in the flow of traffic and above the prying eyes at the surface level. The woman notices but only observes and makes mental notes.

She's afraid of Jay, the woman thinks but does not say.

"Where are we going?" She asks, changing the subject in her mind. Lena follows the lead.

"Downtown. There are some small old apartment complexes that are tucked away on back streets in the Montrose area, I want to look at them first."

"Okay, I like that. Very much, actually.

"People can easily keep a low profile in an apartment complex in an old neighborhood with sturdy old buildings and fences. And covered parking for tenants too, am I right?

"And you're keeping the car?" Lena nods with a small satisfied smile. "Good for you."

Freeway miles fly by unawares as the two not-sisters silently share the pain and the glory. As one in two bodies, the women release and let go of the hard memories that hurt too much to recall to mind and to remain sane.

So, what are two rational women to do, but choose?

To disappear in plain sight within the walls of an old commonplace complex in a low-rent district.

Healing happens. All the time.

The near sisters know the complex when they see it from the street.

The complex is brick, and it is nearly hidden by centuries old trees bordering the two-lane streets where the complex sits almost lost in the reserved ordinariness of an old apartment complex on the bow of a shoehorn street.

The complex has no name save for its street number. The building is a vision of discretion. It has no name, and the admirable anonymity of no street number.

Lena parks the car and says: "Let's go find the manager and rent us some apartments."

And the two women disappear into the mundanity of small quiet lives in a noisy big city.

Jay can't find them.

Until he does.

He sleeps on the floor of her apartment in his extra-long sleeping bag, borrowing a pillow from her bed for his head.

But Jay does not sleep in heavenly peace. He sleeps in deadly despair, heels, elbows and head pounding the floor in a prone palsied macabre dance of death. The woman is beside him, stroking his forehead where his third eye is, where deep frown lines web the third eye and keep it tight closed.

"Breathe, Jay." She lays a hand on his chest where his heart is beating arrhythmic and fast, and then slow and scarcely detectable. She slaps his chest over his heart.

"Breathe, Jay," she calmly shouts, while slapping his diaphragm with a firm flat hand.

"Just breathe. Only that. Inhale slow and deep. Hold. Hold. Hold. Let it go in one big whoosh. Do it again. You count this time, Jay, give your mind something to do that's more productive than a panic attack."

"I want to die," Jay mutter moans.

"Well then, Jay, you will necessarily have to die on your own time. In the place of your own choosing. And it will *not* be my place.

"Put that out of your mind, because it's not happening. Not on my watch. Not while you are sleeping in my apartment."

"Wuhl, Lena won't me in her apartment. I can't sleep there."

"Can you blame for that her after you gut punched her and aborted the baby she bore by you?

"After you sold all the camera gadgets and lenses and even the bag itself, so you could buy more Black Mollies?

"A better question for you Jay is, can you forgive yourself? For any of that.

"Make a list, check it twice, Jay, can you forgive yourself?

"Because you have to, Jay.

"Or that unforgiveness will kill you.

"By your own hand probably, you are a punishingly unforgiving man, brother a mine!

"And whether you like it or not, you must forgive yourself. First. You have to make a choice, and make a change. A permanent one. The alternative is to choose your current reality in which you *always* want to die because you can't forgive yourself.

"God gave you free will, Jay. He will not stop your hand at anything you freely will to do. But if you ask, he will heal you of the pain that drives you into that box canyon where you hole up in your imaginary safe hide-away. Like where Jesse James hid away thinking he was safe from capture, safe assault. Safe from the likely consequences of his thieving, murderous choices! Because Jesse had his pearl handle six-shooters strapped to his side, and that's where he kept his faith.

"Jesse's gun was exactly like the pearl handled revolver you still have – even though you sold everything *else* you had or ever been given that had any monetary or exchange value – to buy more drugs!"

"Why do I have to ask?" Jay grudges resentfully against the power to choose.

"Because the Master said you have not because you ask not. God gave you free will.

"He will not stop or stay your hand at *anything* that you freely *will* to do. But there are consequences.

"Consider the predictable consequences of your addiction to Black Mollies, Jay, and tell me this: who would you be, if not for Black Mollies? Can your forgive that?"

Jay is silent and utterly still for an unnaturally long time. He does not move. He scarcely breathes.

"Yes, I can forgive that. But using Black Mollies was not the first, nor the worst really sucky choice I ever made. That was burning the gallery owner's card."

"Why did you do that?"

"Because I was afraid of success. I was terrified to even *think* I was a better photographer than Ansel Adams was on his best days. It felt like arrogance to me."

"I get that," his sister says, "but it was *not* arrogance that stopped you. It was your small self-consciousness, the small self that you came to believed was the whole truth of you. You didn't always think of yourself in that way. You didn't always judge yourself from the outside in.

"Something changed. You judged yourself too big, or too small, but either way, not enough. What happened?

"I fucked up!"

"Oh my God! You are a bloody human being. You are not perfect." She's not sincere. Jay hears it. But he still can't forgive himself. "Why wasn't really, really good at what one thing sufficient for you?"

"No answer? How dare you! Truth me, Jay, why did you burn the Gallery owner's business card?

"Why did you abort Lena's baby?

"Why did you pay to have me raped when you knew I was fertile and you planned to saddle me with a baby, a job, and then force me to be your unpaid whore so you could pimp me and buy Black Mollies?

"Fear of success, you asshole! You destroyed yourself in every way except one. Suicide. The coward's way out of the good life you willfully and witlessly fucked up beyond all recognition"

"Okay, I'm a coward! Will you just shut the fuck up now?"

"No! I will not. Can you forgive yourself?

"It doesn't sound like you've forgiven me *anything*! But you've got the whole market covered in insisting that I forgive *myself* for all and everything I ever did or even thought about doing. What business is *my forgiveness* of yours?"

"Oh, goody, that means you've forgiven yourself for having raped me by proxy so you could whore me to buy more Black Mollies. It means you've forgiven yourself for having aborted Lena's baby by you. It means you've forgiven yourself for burning the Gallery Owner's business card. That means you have forgiven yourself for imagining that God made you a powerless victim when it was all and always and only your own choices by which you abused yourself."

Jay doesn't look at her, not even when he asks: "What should I do?"

"I can't answer that question. It's way above my pay grade.

"God knows though. Try asking the one who knows."

Shawn Gallaway – The Source

Redeeming Angels

"Do you suppose...," the radiant winged one wonders, "that humans don't know about us?"

"Maybe they don't. Why do you ask?"

The radiant winged one ponders awhile, a small frown puzzling his face into furrowed brows, squinted eyes, and downturned lips.

With clown make-up, the angel could have been a sad-sack circus clown.

His companion smiles, seeing the image of Michael's clown costume overlaying his angelic self. And, knowing that Michael is feeling like a clown that's not funny nor fun, he's wrapped around his ancient axel of pride over being the Divine One's first warrior knight.

Problem is, he's pugnacious and dissatisfied here and now, because he's being the center support pole for a garden, *for God's sake!*

Gab-re-EL smiles, knowing it's tough on an old warrior when there's no war to fight and he's living lean on fading memories of his glory days.

On his best days, Michael is not charming.

He is high energy though, and he's running in fifth gear trying to win a race back to God's grace.

He's running against the wind of his own fierce resistance.

He master said 'you have not because you ask not.'

Michael knows this. As Principle.

He doesn't know that truth personally *though because Michael never asks.*

He's above needing others, especially humans.

Michael helps humans, not the other way around. That's the order of things in his mind.

Problem is that I am becoming a crabby cross bitch because Michael not only thinks he doesn't need me, but that I have somehow become his enemy.

I don't get everything I know about that.

In Michael's mind these 'saved ones' are mere mortals and have nothing to offer God's first knight. He looks down his proud angelic nose at humans and their persistent paltry petitions for help, saving grace, redemption, or even wings to take a soul to Heaven when its body mind brain earth suit expires.

How droll!

Anyone who thinks angels are perfect forever and always, has never met an angel.

Especially not Michael the Archangel. Such a one as this, has never spent quality time with an angel.

And, being Michael's strong right arm as I have been for more than two millennia now, I assure you that a human who thinks angels are perfect has never truly gotten to know the infinity of expressions of divine guardianship in angelic form.

Humans have trouble believing in things they cannot see.

And, humans cannot see what they do not believe.

That is a conundrum for me.

And for them.

Do humans really imagine that all the stories of angelic appearances and saving grace are not real simply because the saving grace came on a light foot and in winged form?

Or do they doubt simply because they cannot poke their fingers into a wounded side?

I don't get this!

Doesn't any human know what the word 'metaphysics' even means? Que tonto! Que totalmente estupido!

I don't get this about humans. But, I don't get Michael either so maybe I'm just clueless.

Sometimes I actually believe that Michael is mirroring and channeling the separation from source anxiety of the leader of the Fallen Ones.

A Beast who also has a thousand names. Most of them are unspeakable.

And, each and all of the demon names are far too dreadful in sound to be spoken aloud anyway.

Speaking the unknown names aloud, even very softly, utterly shatters the soul that hears them, even when one of the foul names is whispered sub-audibly. That is enough!

Moving only the lips is enough for a demon to do the dirty deed and bend and bind a living soul into subservient perversion and mindless obedience.

Free will is gone from such a man. What remains is little more, or less, than a mindless zombie.

And there's Archangel Michael who is still fighting that war against the fallen ones!

That was over more than two millennia ago.

As you know.

And angels do not have any sense of linear time. Time is. That's all.

Michael is doing this out of habit, of course, and for the sake of having something to fight about.

It's a guy thing I guess.

Michael hasn't had to fight fallen ones for more than two millennia now.

And he hasn't got a clue as to what to be when he's not needed as a warrior.

I can relate to that actually.

That fierce fire and fury of a raging battle against demon kind – who truly do need to fall off their dark horse of pride and separation from source anxiety – is righteous. In a back-handed sort of way.

And then, there's the wacky wicked things angels might do when we think God's not watching.

It is a head rush for the Archangels! It's blatant disobedience without a price.

What more could avenging angels ask for?

It's a game changer for a warrior angel.

In that, and in memorializing vengeance with tales and songs, we angels can and do, grow to forget what it's like to be just *an ordinary Archangel, with work-a-day jobs and assignments to do.*

Jobs like walking behind little kids as they toddle over a rickety bridge…, oh, give me a break!

That is so – so – so mindlessly *mundane and prosaic that it is nearly nauseating!*

Perhaps I've been too close to the human plane for too many millennia, and I too *am experiencing separation from source anxiety, the D.O.'s SOS signal continually sent to guide humans – and to angels – back home again and get us realigned with the energy of the D.O.*

I miss *that homing signal.*

That I no longer hear now.

I get where Michael is.

Been there. Done that.

I can't live there with him there though.

I am a female *angel in this mutual manifestation with Michael to complete our assigned angelic service together.*

I'm not supposed *to do it alone.*

I'm doing it alone.

Meanwhile, Michael is polishing his armor and reliving victories in the war against the fallen angels, or maybe he's just out – of his mind – jousting with some bored bovine somewhere like a sullen little boy who was told 'no!' in no uncertain terms and is rebelling and doing prankish, stupid, mind and time wasting minor rebellions.

Mother's get that.

Mothers are healers.

Mothers are nourishers.

Mothers are lore keepers.

Mothers are story tellers.

Hey! Then that means I, Gab-re-EL, came to help. I came to heal.

Michael is my partner in this assignment. And Michael's a crabby bitch bastard.

I reckon it's my God job to help Michael get healed from his separation from Source anxiety. Anyone with SOS is a crabby bitch bastard. Just like Michael.

He's only had two plus couple of millennia of practice *at being pugnacious, and Michael has raised 'confrontational' to an art form.*

That is not *a compliment.*

Michael is still exalting in his prowess in fighting the Divine war against the fallen angels.

He's looking back and hanging on tight-fisted to memories of war glories.

Meanwhile, all of life is unfolding and springing alive before and all around him! Que tonto! Que totalmente estupido!

If you were willing to listen to a mere female angel, my dear, daffy, ding-bat angel friend, maybe you could chose to just stop looking back at ancient glories!

And then *choose to look away from history and ancient legend, and to look with* new *eyes into the* present *to see what's yours to do in* this *millennium.*

Time is called 'the present' because it is *a gift.*

That most of us don't receive.

Because we think we are unworthy. Of Divine love. Really?

You block grace because you think you are altogether too imperfectly human to *receive* it?

The D.O. gives us grace in abundance.

And we have to ask.

Even Archangels *have to ask for grace.*

Just get over *your war history pride, Michael, and look forward again!*

Only in asking, will you see, feel, and experience the divine grace of the D.O.

Will you fucking *just drop your overweening pride, and* ask for grace!

It was not a question. It was a demand.

A command.

Michael *gets* commands. He understands them.

He knows the many ways commands differ from requests. Michael *gives* commands. He knows what command sounds like.

Michael does *not* take commands from others.

Especially not from *female* others.

And 'smart-ass Gab-re-EL' is female*!* Michael thinks in a snit-fit. *I do* not *take orders from females.*

Sexist pig!

Sticks and stones may break my bones, but words will never harm me. Michael snarls.

Gab-re-EL throws her head back and gives a contagious belly-laugh.

Michael doesn't catch it.

He is not amused.

Not even a little bit.

Michael is in a right sour surly snit if truth be known.

He's getting a right religious high on it.

He's having a brain numbing adrenalin rush, and there are no fallen angels to crush.

What *does* a devoted warrior do in such an *intolerable* situation – but start a war?

Gab-re-EL is the only warrior on the field.

Michael goes for her.

He goes *at* her.

How *dare* the impotent bitch imagine she is his equal! He'll show her!

And thus the war in The Angel Garden began.

For want of an enemy to fight.

Locked together in mortal combat, Michael and Gab-re-EL fall stunningly from grace.

And, in their graceless progression, they nearly destroys The Angel Garden and everything in it.

When Bam and the dragon flew in and crash landed inside The Angel Garden, the fallen angels rose to the dome of the garden.

Not to help The Angel Garden, oh no way.

They did it for the sole and only objective of getting as far away as physically possible from the dragon.

Even these two valiant skilled un-angelic angel warriors know the utter *stupidity* of attacking a dragon (St. George aside) let *alone* a winged wyvern with a human rider astride.

What's that about? Michael and Gab-re-EL think as one.

As if in answer to their not-so-angelic question, Hester enters The Angel Garden.

She sees the devastation.

She is stunned stuttering stupid.

Hester snaps out of it on the instant, and does what mothers do when faced with unacceptable conduct by their children.

She kicks butt and takes names.

Hester listens to the commotion in the dark dome of The Angel Garden.

She looks up studying the deep darkness to discern the source of the noise-some racket that rumbles and growls, and oofs, and yells unholy names and calamitous curses, and growls names that are *never* to be spoken at one another, let *alone* in the torrid turbulent tumultuous dome of The Angel Garden.

Hester is not amused.

She looks down at the girl who looks up at her. "Has this been going on awhile?"

"Yeah, it has." The girl replies with a worried frown.

"Mostly, from the day the two angels arrived they've been snarling, and scratching and biting like a whole *basket* of crazed cats from Kilkinney."

"And the lily pond?" Hester asks, taking a new turn, the road less traveled.

The girl smiles at the beauty of the lily pond, and tells her tale tall and true.

"Well, a dragon flew in with Bam on its back...,"

She doesn't know where to go next, so she waits in silence for the words to come. "And, the wyvern came in too fast – it was flying at warp speed before that – it had just broken the sound barrier.

"It came in too fast, too soon, too sudden, and it crash landed.

"The dragon took its belly flop there where the pond is. If you look here, and on the opposite side of the pond, you'll see hollows where the dragon's trunk and tail hit the ground."

"Ouch! I imagine that *hurt*! Even a dragon." Hester muses.

The girl looks up at her mother with an impish grin, and embellishes her tale with another tidbit of truth that seems, strangely enough, to not follow reason or logic.

"And then, the dragon required that the hapless man in need of saving, in many ways, bring him a token of each day of creation.

"Was that Bam then?

"Or someone else?" Hester speaks her puzzlement.

"I don't think it probably *was* Bam. It was probably someone else.

"But, Mother, God's sense of time is not linear like mans is, and maybe in the mind of the Divine, Bam and the nameless man are one and the same being."

Hester nods acceptance of the illogical and highly improbable. Thus opening her mind to amazing grace.

She feels an unusual and unexpected outpouring of infinite wellbeing arising from her rather mindless accommodation of the utterly irrational, and the impossibly implausible.

Curious, she thinks absently.

"Well,' the girl continues, "every morning, the weird winged wyvern hooked the hapless man up and dropped him into a coracle with no sail, no oars, and no oarlocks.

"Nor was water yet separated from sky. Yet the man breathed.

"When he put his hand over the side of the coracle he felt water. *Interesting,* he thinks.

"But that is a notion far too big for the mind of the purloined man to grasp. He does not go there.

"Instead, he looks about like he is an explorer.

"He notices that he can breathe, so wherever he is, it has an atmosphere. *Interesting,* he thinks.

"On the first day of creation, the Divine One separated light from dark....

"The man ponders this puzzle. I don't get it," he thinks.

So what if I ask the D.O. to guide my craft to where I need to go to find the Dragon's token for the first day of creation?

"He did that.

"And then, on inspiration, the purloined one gave thanks to the D.O. for her willing and wonderful earth mother role in this drama of dallying days.

"Then the man profoundly and prayerfully praises Earth mother for her inspired and generous giving of the daily token the dragon would require each day of the coming week.

So as not to appear overtly greedy and grasping and thinking only of himself and of what *he* wants, the dragon rider itemizes the Earth Mother gifts he *especially* enjoys and relies on.

"Oxygen is good. Thank you, Mother, for the air we breathe.

"Earth. Dirt.

"Lots of people think dirt only dirt. Dirty. Dusty. Something to walk on.

"It never occurs to these people that they are walking on a living, breathing, alive, thinking *sentient being.* Earth. Our H.O.M.E.

"In case you don't know it, H.O.M.E. stands for Home On Mother Earth.

"Earth is a living and sentient being.

"She is a being who does not speak in human tongues. Not any of them.

"And Mother Nature is therefore not heard by human ears, nor often, in human hearts.

"Mother Nature speaks from the heart to the heart. The heart has the ears to hear....

"I really like water too. I like it in a glass. I like water in a pond. I like rain. I like water in the ocean.

"I *love* water spilling from a shower head!

"I just plain *like* water. And Earth Mother, I want to, and I *need* to praise and *thank you* for water.

"And fire. We humans plum couldn't live without fire. And I like fire. In fireplaces and in well-tended campfires. I don't like it so much in forest fires.

"Even though I know that fire is often your way of thinning and enriching forests – especially where man can't easily reach them in jeeps and fire trucks – still I don't much admire forest fires.

"We humans don't give praise and thanksgiving often enough. We want to 'save' expressions of love for special occasions like holidays, and birthdays, and new births.

"Today! *This day,* I want to praise you for expressing as earth, for your *being* as water, for your breath of life and air and wind, and for forever being and expressing the hot passion of fire.

"You are a good and generous earth mother goddess.

"I praise and I honor you. I give you my thanks.

"Do you know the dragon by any chance?"

"I do. Wyvern and I go way back. Has he set you to tasks then?"

"Yes."

"And what is your task for today?"

"To find a token for this first day of creation, and give it to the weird wyvern when he picks me up again at sunset.

"Where did you go at sunset on the first day?"

"Dragon took me to a little island in the middle of nowhere, and left me there overnight.

"At least he didn't drop me from the sky – again."

"What do you eat?"

"Nothing. Not the first night.

"The atoll was rock hard dry, dirty, and a very remote, and a hauntingly lonely place.

"The next morning I complained bitterly to the dragon about the biting cold at sunset, and the sizzling sun at sunrise all the day through until sunset, and I most *emphatically* bitched bitingly about having nothing to eat.

"When the dragon came back the next morning, he brought all the lily bulbs he'd collected on the third day of creation and planted them gently and lovingly in the lily pond.

After that, he molded mountains and bluffs, and trees that not only gave shade, but also produced fruit.

"And after that, every morning that weird wyvern brought fresh game of one sort or other that he'd marinated in his mouth, cooking it to enchanting perfection.

"Friends? Nah!

"There wasn't a friendly bone in that dire beast's body.

"Compassion was a notion the dragon simply did not get. It never crossed his mind.

"Until it did.

Shawn Gallaway – A Call To Joy

"It was an 'aha' moment for the large scaly one with a very small head and really, *really* big body.

"So, that's what I can tell you about the lily pond."

"Thank you. That doesn't make a lick of sense. And today I can deal with that.

"Now, what can you tell me about the two fallen angels?" Hester asks.

"They're in a snit fit about being assigned to the insignificant and unfair role – *oh, woe is me!* – of being the sole support of, and caretakers of a measly farm family garden!

"Michael is, after all, the first knight of God's army against the fallen angels.

Gabriel was, and still is, Michael's second in command of God's army.

"And that war ended *eons* ago. Who needs an army when there's no war to fight?

"Michael and Gab-re-EL are still fighting it though.

"They feel marginalized by God, slighted, badly judged, and unfairly treated for the sole and only reason that the D.O. sent them on such a *boring* and insignificant mission and supporting a country garden!"

"'Gab-*re-EL*'? Did you say?"

"They think the D.O. is punishing or slighting them by assigning them to The Angel Garden. *Que tonto! Que totalmente estupido!*

"I thought angels were a higher order of being than man, but maybe not.

"They are living in the past and feeding on their empty faded glory.

"And they are being fiercely pugnacious about staying where they are. They insist on staying where *they don't want to be*!

"Because they think the D.O. demoted them and is punishing them, and they do not *want* to change their roles!

"They do not *want* to change from militant obedience, to willing compliance.

"To them, there is absolutely no difference.

"Simply because they've always seen it that way, and they are *unwilling* to change their minds.

"They are *not* unable to.

"Awareness precedes choice..., and choice precedes change.

"The fallen angels don't *want* to change from re-living their past glory in mighty warrior feats.

"They have chosen *not* to change from that enchanting illusion of glory in war and killing.

"Hence, Michael and Gab-re-EL will *not* freely choose to change their modus operandi.

"A definition of insanity is 'doing the same thing you've always done before and expecting a different outcome.

"Michael and Gab-re-EL are certifiably insane under that test!

"And yes, I said 'Gab-re-EL'." She smiles up at her mother and adds: "Apparently *Gabriel* is not on this divine assignment to The Angel Garden.

"Interesting, isn't it?

"And both Archangels individually taking keen preening pride in their rebellious destruction *of our garden!*

"They are *supposed* to support it and to nourish and tend The Angel Garden and everything in it!

"Which is even more irrational than just rebelling. Taking pride in demonic destruction is wantonly irresponsible on its face!

"Tell them to go to hell in a handbasket."

"Me?" Hester asks in alarm and dismay.

"Who else, your little girl? Who they throw rocks at? And you've seen the bruises?

"Imagine how well a pair of truculent navel gazing fallen Archangels would respond to a kid in pig-tails ordering them to settle down, behave like competent adults, and to just do what God sent them to do!

"Can't put good odds on that one, Hester.

"And you are the mother...."

"Of the girl!" Hester allows hotly defensive.

Good try. Not a chance of success though. Hester knows it. The Infinite can wait infinitely. She can't.

"I – I can't even *see* into The Angel Garden, how can I go in there and order two Archangels to straighten up and fly right?"

"You're getting tedious, Hester. Shall I call the dragon again and have it take you into The Angel Garden then?"

It sounded like a threat.

Perhaps it was.

Perhaps it was only a dare. What then? While Hester is still dithering over danger or dare in her powerless small self-consciousness, the girl studies her with indifferently patient pique.

Hester can't hold out against that look of untrained wisdom the girl gets in her eyes when she knows she's right.

And she knows the girl won't even talk about it, let alone argue about it.

Right about what though?

The Angel Garden, Hester! The D.O. offered the obvious.

Do you choose to walk into The Angel Garden under your own will?

Or would you rather be carried in by the dragon, kicking and screaming and behaving like one of the fallen angels that you also *have not been mothering any more attentively than you have The Angel Garden, its produce, or your daughter, who also needs your help.*

I — sent the dragon to you to teach you to hear and trust the guidance you hear in your heart.

But your conscious mind is tone-deaf to anything *you don't want to hear.*

Like: that you are emotionally neglecting your garden, the one you and the girl planted together, and watered daily from the old well.

And, you are neglecting and ignoring her mental and emotional needs as well.

What you are doing is not mothering. It is neglect!

I did not choose *you as mother for your children because I wanted or needed someone to be negligent of them as people, or of their mental, emotional, and spiritual needs.*

I made you to be a mother, *a lore keeper, a tale teller, a dreamer, a healer, standing with feet firmly rooted in the ground, tall and upright in the strong bright energy of you* as mother*!*

I did not make you to be some thumb-sucking grown-up baby in mother drag.

Pull up your big-girl panties and behave like a woman! Act like a caring mother.

And stop hating your own mother!

Not because I tell you to, but because until you do own and allow that she was imperfect, and even hide-bound stubborn, she was still your mother, and deserving of your respect.

She expected me to be obedient! Just because she said so, no discussion allowed!

That will be a good place to start your own redemption then.

Do you ever talk to your own children the way your mother talked to you?

Do you tell them what to do and allow them no discussion?

I try not to.

That was a 'yes/no' question. Trying is ... just that ... trying!

Try again.

Yes. I do talk to my children that way.

When you wanted to do something that was really important to you, did your mother support you in doing it?

No.

What did she do?

She wouldn't even talk to me about it.

Even when dad was there, and he wanted me to do it. Even if he wanted to talk with me about it too, and to encourage me.

Do you do the same thing to your own children that your mother did to you?

A long silence follows. The D.O. is patient. He can outwait Hester's shrinking violet trauma drama. The D.O. is infinite. Linear time simply has no relevance to the D.O.

Yes. Hester admits.

The interesting thing about forgiveness is that it truly happens only when we give for ourselves.

Do you give for yourself?

No.

Ergo, you are just like your mother.

And just like your mother, you can't forgive yourself, and so you can't forgive others.

No wonder you hate her.

I don't....

You do.

And, just like your mother, you hate yourself too.

For the same reasons that you cannot forgive your mother – for hating herself – and for being angry and vengeful to everyone around her in, and because of, her small self-judgment, for those very reasons you hate yourself.

Forgiveness, Hester. Didn't you learn that from the dragon before he took you into The Angel Garden?

Guess not. Hester hides a grin she knows the D.O. can see anyway.

Well, no wonder *my dear dire dragon did a belly flop when he landed in The Angel Garden. He couldn't bear the weight of your doubt, your absolute conviction that you were born unlovable, and would remain that way until the day you die. And even sillier still, beyond that into deep into eternity!*

I did not make you unlovable. You did that! To yourself.

And now you do the same thing to your children that your mother did to hers, you and your siblings.

This is not mothering, Hester!

The divine eternal mother likely wishes she'd aborted the very idea of you while she still had the chance.

This trauma-drama queen thing of yours that is the fiendish foundation for your unshakable *faith that even the Divine One could not forgive you!*

Really, Hester?

Que tonto! Que increable estupido!

I made *you a better and smarter woman than that!*

I made you more integral and true to me, *and to you, than your dithering blame-it-on-mom escapist self-awareness reflects, and demonstrates!*

So – what about the girl scares you shitless?

Hester is silent an infinite moment, then exhales slowly. On the inhale, her body straightens upright and flexible again.

Now she can speak the truth and tell it true and tall. *She has a relationship with you that is deep and true, and personal.*

She talks to you.

And you talk to her.

But you and the girl don't use words do you?

No. Hester admits, idly wondering if that's an admission too.

That explains a lot.

And it's scary disturbing too.

Why? Do you think I will tell the girl secrets that she can't share with you? Tisk, Tisk, paranoid one!

You were persecuted, once, in another life.

You lost your life – savagely – because of the way you practiced your honor to the Ancient Ones, to the goddesses, and to the nature spirits.

That savage death is the root of your paranoia in this lifetime.

And, my dear Hester, it does not serve you, this playing small, and weak, and defenseless, and helpless, bereft and adrift in a coracle with no sail, oar, nor rudder.

How long will you choose to stay there? In that mute, powerless consciousness?

How long *will you choose to stay remote and removed from The Angel Garden and let it wither and die for want of mother love?*

And what effect do you suppose your lack of faith has on the girl? Or on your other children?

The girl still believes, Hester!

Despite you, the girl believes that miracles can and do happen, and that when you ask with unshakable faith, it will *be done!*

It would be good if you could cop some of that 'blind' faith.

That is what faith is.

Faith does not *ask how! It only asks 'show me the way'. That's the girl's faith.*

You ask how, *Hester. That difference between you and the girl is what scares you about her.*

Your girl doesn't ask how. She just asks, and then she gives thanks, all while imagining how she'd like it to show up in the 'real' world.

The girl knows without knowing that when God says 'yes', She/He always gives the best yes that makes the most people smile and be fulfilled and at peace.

I gave you a yes, Hes. The D.O. smiles as he uses Jacob's pet name for Hester, and makes it a rhyme too.

The Angel Garden does that too, Hester.

It has the same energy.

But The Angel Garden needs a mother, a caretaker, a healer, a nourisher; and you are all of that.

So tell me, what scares you about The Angel Garden that you cannot *go in there. You can't even* see *it?*

To what *have you blinded yourself, and why?*

Miracles. Hester replies with silent honesty.

Why?

I'm afraid.

Of what? You could hear God's mental wheels turn soft and still in the profound silence that follows.

Say it, Hester!

Of a – a child of mine – who can call and command angels.

I don't know how *to be mother to such a girl.*

Neither did Mary..., do you think?

But how do I know what to do? How do I know the right *things to do?*

How did Mary know?

She prayed. She asked. She received. Hester smiles.

And then she gave praise and thanksgiving for the gracious giving that she was about *to receive in the form of a son who had no seed father but God.*

Who would believe that in this *day and age?*

Why then would you, *rational being that you are, believe the patently foolish idea that your girl* could *call on God to send angels..., let* alone *believe without doubt that God would actually send angels in response to her* 'command?

She did *command..., didn't she?*

Yes, she did.

You heard the sky rip apart when the angels broke the sound barrier and came through from the infinite and into the finite form and into The Angel Garden.

You heard that, didn't you? Hester nods.

I didn't hear *you,* the D.O. snaps her to attention.

Yes! She snaps back. *I heard the angels tear a hole through space and time and fall to earth where our garden was... being blown away by daily dusters....*

And I did not *believe.*

And so, I could *not* see.

Believing is seeing. The D.O. turns one of man's favorite rules on its head. *Ready to give for yourself?*

That seems selfish.

Is it?

Remember what I said about forgiveness being best when given for yourself? Does my advice seem selfish *to you? Ever?*

Because that false faith of yours is the *very reason that you cannot forgive yourself for being self-serving enough to* deny *what you did not wish to see.*

It's like you are covering your eyes and ears and saying 'la, la, la, la, la, la, I can't see you, I can't hear you.

Therefore, you conclude, that fairies cannot exist.

May not exist. That magic must be exiled, or better still, off with its head!

Said the Queen of Hearts to the knave of Hearts..., or was it 'tarts'?

I never remember irrelevant things like that, although I do like the word play. Queen of Hearts? Would you care for some tarts? The D.O. offers her a plate of tarts.

Prune tarts. Hester needs to get some really old shit out of her system.

You are a fascinating conversationalist my D.O. I always grow up a bit when I talk with you — because you always expect the best of me — and you will not *stop pursuing me until I get 'er done, anyway!*

True that.

So then, are you ready to grow up and be mother to The Angel Garden?

Shawn Gallaway - Begin

Hester is silent a long moment, then grins and says: *Yeah, I'm ready to kick butt and take names!*

I can't wait to watch you kick some Archangel butt.

Michael and Gab-re-EL will double down on you when you challenge them, you know that don't you?

Yeah, I do!

You said 'Gab-re-EL' not Gabriel, why is that?

She feels the D.O.'s one-sided grin as he poses. *You tell me.*

Because... the Gabriel in The Angel Garden is a female angel.

And I don't feel good about that. Why?

Why don't you feel good about that? Or, why is Gabriel in a female form now?

Hester grins, then chuckles softly as she clarifies: *Why is Gabriel in female form this time?*

You tell me.

That again!

You are supposed to be a creative being, not a black mystery ball!

Who made that *rule?*

Me, I suppose.

How's that working for you?

Hester giggles. *Not!*

Okay then, Gabriel is Gab-re-EL this time because the feminine energy is needed..., Hester frowns thoughtfully, *in The Angel Garden.*

But Gab-re-EL is not at all pleased to be there, in that form.

She's pissed, actually..., and she's trashing the place!

That is not *acceptable behavior!*

The D.O. waits for her to catch the burden that came with what she just said, and apply it.

It's the Mother *energy that's needed..., even by Gab-re-EL.*

O.M.G, that's me, isn't it?

Yep. The D.O. grins and quips: *Don't let anyone ever tell you that you're not a quick study, Hester.*

Hester giggles, head thrown back, neck long and arched, chest full open, lungs pumping like a bellows.

When she collects herself again, she quips: *Don't let anyone ever tell you that I'm not a quick study!*

And actually, one would not have to be a psychic to predict that it was me all along that had to take mother energy into The Angel Garden.

You could be a stubborn Taurus though, and bulls are never in a rush. You ready to stop dithering and start healing?

I am that. I am.

Shawn Gallaway – Cross That Bridge

"Girl, where are you? Come to me, please. I want you to take me into The Angel Garden."

The girl walks cautious into the kitchen where her mother is lowering burners to barely lit, stirring the stew and putting the lid back on again. She nods to her mother who leads the way from the kitchen toward the garden.

She feels her mother hesitate, and looks up to see her eyes dart from side to side and up and down and all around.

"Hold my hand," the girl offers. Hester takes it with a smile.

"What's it like inside?"

"Ugly."

"You sound a little angry."

"Well, *yeah!*

"*I* called the angels to help, support, and *save* The Angel Garden.

"These two bozo angels are making our garden even worse than the dusters ever did.

"And, the dusters are what made me demand that God send angels to save our garden in the first place, so that we, and our neighbors wouldn't starve.

"I *am* angry!

"Plus, the Archangels will not listen to me anyway because I'm *just a girl*, and the Archangels are *supposedly* grown up!

"I am *not* just a girl, Mom!

"I am *the* girl who demanded that God to send angels to a do-nothing job like watching over a country garden.

"The Archangels are insulted because they think being assigned to support and nourish a country garden is a demotion!

"How stupid is that?

"They are covered up with separation from source anxiety, and that's only good because that's *all* the body cover they are wearing.

"Well, there are wearing all the bruises they've been giving each other, and the cuts, they're colorful, and the lashes to in an ugly red-blue-black bruises, and other than that, they are covered with bone dry dirt!

"Without the bruises, cuts and lashes, and the dirt they wallow in when the wrestle, they are as naked as jaybirds on the day they're born."

Hester has stopped in her tracks, the girl turns to look at her, frowns and asks: "Why are they naked?"

The girl shrugs and says: "Oh, they'd torn the clothes off each other within a week.

"And when they were naked as Adam and Even in Eden's glen, each of them pulled off the angel wings off the other's shoulders and back.

"And then, out of boredom, I think, both Archangels threw angel feather darts at each other.

"Don't ever agree to play darts with an Archangel. They can make their feathers fly at the thought.

"And they are amazingly accurate dart throwers. Both of them.

"Mostly though, both of them are covered with nothing but dirt, bruises, cuts, and angel feathers – sticking straight out from their skin."

"No angelic gowns?"

"Torn to shreds in the first week of their assignment."

"No halos?"

"Nah, when they'd wasted all the feathers on each other, they took off their halos, flattened them, and then beveled the outer edges, and threw them at each other like lethal Frisbees.

"That will explain the cuts you'll see on them. And the dirty dried blood all over them too.

"They are colorful, actually.

"In a bare butt naked in a really ugly sort of way.

These are *decidedly* fallen angels, Mom"

"I'm not sure that I want to know, but I need to know. What's the other Archangel's name?"

"Michael!" The girl spits the word like sour grapes. She ain't done though. She's got a whole list.

"Arrogant!

"Stubborn!

"Bitchy!

"Angry!

"Fools!

"Both of them!

"And they won't listen to me. They just throw dirt clods, rocks, and feather arrows at me.

"I can get *that* from the boys!

"And sometimes, the boys can be helpful. That counts as points to me.

"The two bitchy angels in The Angel Garden will not get *any* points from me!

"Unless it's the pointed end of a *really* long stick."

Hester giggles, and the girl she was is born again within her. *Youth. I wasted my youth on being old, staid, and predictable.*

Well, I am totally *over that!*

Shawn Gallaway – The Real More

Hester turns to the girl and extends a hand which the girl takes with an unspoken question in her eyes.

Hester answers. "I need you to lead and guide me into The Angel Garden – like I was blind."

"But you're not blind."

Hester agrees: "I have eyes. But I do not see.

"Mostly I don't see what scares me senseless because it does scare me senseless."

"Tell me what it is that makes you afraid." The girl asks, moving not one inch toward The Angel Garden.

It's as if her feet are suddenly deep rooted into the ground where she stands. She will not *lead me!*

The girl knows that I have to make my own choice. I have to decide to give up my fear, to release it and let it go. Until I do, I can't go into The Angel Garden. Hester lowers her eyes against her truth.

Still, Hester sees.

The inner eye never actually closes in truth. It's a Divine thing. It never stops doing its Divine thing. She admits her truth.

My fear of what I cannot see simply because I do not believe that it can possibly be! The dusters....

And I faithfully believe that the devilish dusters are mightily more powerful than the Divine One! O.M.G.!

Que tonto! Que totalmente estupido!

She laughs. She can't help it. The giggling glee rises up in her as powerful as Old Faithful spewing joy juice.

Shawn Gallaway - Surrender

You can't cap the power of joy, the highest octave vibration.

Mother Nature won't have it! Hester knows that. *Mother Nature, like everything else, is an expression of the One Source of all and everything.*

If Mother is laughing at me for imagining that nature is somehow not *a vital expression and part of the D.O., then I really have no choice but to simply get over myself, and laugh with her.*

She does that.

The girl looks up at her with a grin and wise eyes, and offers her hand to her mother.

Hester takes the girl's hand in hers and walks with her toward The Angel Garden that she cannot yet see, but she knows is there. She can feel it.

Mostly it's pain that she feels inside The Angel Garden when she extends her heart energy into it.

Shawn Gallaway – Surrender

Hester looks down at the girl holding her hand and wonders if she made a little magic to help her, or if the magic she's feeling arose in her heart center and didn't come from the girl at all.

Six of one. Half-dozen of the other. Why are you dithering?

If in doubt – choose both.

The words bloom unbidden in Hester's mind like a volunteer hybrid plants sinking roots into rich, dark, loamy soil. *Watered by rain from inside The Angel Garden! O.M.G. how can that be?*

Try faith. The D.O. coaches.

Hester feels the hot breath of a dragon on the back of her neck. She smiles at that innerving inducement, throws her doubts into the fiery furnace of the dragon's belly. She just lets go.

"Oh!" Hester says, her surprise halting her step a bit. "I – I can see – a bit. The gate at least.

"And if I don't look directly at it, I can see the dome of The Angel Garden.

"Do you see this all the time?" She asks the girl.

"Yes."

Hester pauses, heart heavy weighted by the implications of what she now sees.

"Do you see the darkness in the dome of The Angel Garden too then?"

"Yes." The girl lowers her head as if in shame, as though admitting and owning up to some venial sin she committed once earlier in her life. Or today.

Or, simply humiliation for the day of the demon duster when she stamped her foot and shouted at God and *demanded* divine help to save their garden, and the heavens shrieked open, and angels fell through to earth to circle and enclose the dome of The Angel Garden. *And look what happened....*

And then, all hell broke loose, and nothing worked according to Divine plan, or to the girl's plan either.

"Why does the darkness displease you so, and what's causing it?"

The girl stops in her tracks, head bowed, eyes closed.

Hester stops by her side wondering if her hesitance arises from shame.

Or blame?

Or self-blame?

Or all the above, and more?

Ah, I get it now! The girl can't *save The Angel Garden.*

And, she can't end or lighten the damning darkness. What is that *about anyway?*

As though she heard her thoughts, the girl replies: "The archangels. The fallen angels.

"They won't listen to me.

"They won't hear me.

"They won't talk to me, even to answer a question, and that's just plain rude!

"And they throw rocks and clods of dirt at me. They hit me too. Hard!"

Hester hesitates. "Is that where these bruises you keep getting come from?" She points to the blue bruise spots on the girl's body, including on her head. The girl nods, eyes lowered.

"Why are they doing that?"

"I try to make them stop fighting.

"They don't want to stop.

"If I'm in The Angel Garden, the two angels are throwing rocks and clods at me.

"And, they are Archangels! Both of them can put ten arrows out of ten in the center of a bull's eye.

"I'm an easy target....

"For their frustration. And their anger.

"They both faithfully believe that God *demoted them – by* sending them to earth on a mission to protect a *measly, insignificant* country garden!

"That's how they think about our garden.

"And Mom, it's not about us. It's not even about our garden.

"It's all and only about them.

"All of it comes from their sizzling shit snit because God did not provide them with still another band of fallen angels for them to damn to hell."

"You shouldn't talk that way."

"It's in the Bible!" the girl defends with a knowing grin that infects her mother too.

"Well then, the middle ground. You will *only* talk that way when you are alone with me, deal?"

"Deal."

"So what do we do?"

"What did the dragon tell you to do?"

"You know about the dragon?"

The girl looks at her mother quizzically for only a moment, then replies: "How could I have asked if I *didn't* know?"

Hester giggles. "I take your point."

"So – answer the question."

"Well you can be a bossy little snit can't you?"

"I get that from my mother." The girl counters evenly. "Answer the question. What did the dragon tell you to do?"

Hester shrugs off her final resistance to something new that is totally preposterous on its face, and just let's go. She stops Edging God Out with her linear logical mind, and she becomes the real more.

Shawn Gallaway – Infinite Love and Gratitude

"Wow! I can see into The Angel Garden." Hester exclaims.

"Except where the turbulent angry black is at the top of the dome.

"Don't tell me that's the Archangels."

The girl gives her a long calculating look and snaps: "What then? Do you want me to lie?

"Do you want me to make up something that's *not* true just so that you will believe what I say to you? *Que tonto! Que increable estupido!*

Hester keeps her head and eyes lowered, and asks for a thing she does not want at all. "Tell me what you just said to me in another language than English."

The girl gives her a one-sided quirk of a smile and replies: "How crazy. How totally stupid!'

Hester is taken aback.

And it feels good, actually. Once she gets over the shock. "And it was in Spanish the first time you said it?"

"Yes."

She takes a deep inhale and a quick exhale, nods her head hastily, and observes:

"Those very same words *do* sound much nicer and sweeter when spoken in Spanish, the language of love; than in English, the language of business."

She looks to her daughter, holds out her hand for the girl's, and observes: "I think that since we'll be talking business with the Archangels, that we will be speaking in English, wouldn't you agree?"

The girl grins, and says "yes", then adds: "but those bad-ass archangels will probably need some firm motherly butt-kicking before they get down off their high-horses and listen to reason.

"From a woman!

"Who isn't even an angel, and certainly isn't an Archangel.

"It'll take some mystical magical mothering to make Michael and Gab-re-EL angelic again, let alone get them to *behave* like angels."

"So what do you suggest?"

The girl cocks her another off-sided grin and replies: "Go in there, kick butt, and take names!"

"Oh, my, my potty-mouthed girl child! What a sharp tongue you have!"

"You asked! What did you expect from me, that I'd lie to you? That I wouldn't tell it to you like it is?

"The Angel Garden is scarcely living!

"*We* are scarcely living because *nobody* is tending The Angel Garden like God asked them to do!

"And that includes you, Mom!

"You asked me what I would suggest. I told you."

The girl crinkly snarls her mouth, nose, brows, and all the rest of her face for that matter.

"And here you are dithering *outside* The Angel Garden like nine inch nails are pinning your feet and hands to a cross of *your own* making, mother!

"It's all in your head! Get over it! Do what you are *supposed* to do!"

Hester holds up a defensive hand before the girl can catch her second wind. "I get it."

She grins suddenly cheeky like her child. She holds out a hand, and says: "Well then, shall we go inside and kick butt and take names?"

Shawn Gallaway – Choice Point

"Yes!" The girl shouts glee, and dances beside her mother as the pair prepare to enter the foul air lair of a pair of furious fallen angels.

Her joyful enthusiasm is infectious.

Hester catches it.

She wants to sing, but *Hallelujah* is all that comes to mind.

And while that piece of angelic music certainly does feel right and all of that, Hester commands neither the octaves nor the volume that the Hallelujah chorus demands.

She doesn't even hum it.

Why go there?

Redeeming the Angels

"Take my hand, girl." The girl does, looking up at her mother with concern in her eyes, but Hester smiles calmly, lovingly, like a mother would do.

She adds: "You are my strength when I'm short of my own.

"You keep me grounded when I get all in my head about something I can't control anyway.

"And you are my wings when I am afraid to fly and do what is mine to do.

"And right now, daughter of mine, I am downright *scared* to go into The Angel Garden."

"Are you afraid because of what you'll see?

"Or are you afraid of what you will have to *do* something about what you see?"

"Yes. Both.

"And you are *not* afraid, daughter of mine." She extends her hand. "Will you hold my hand, please?"

The girl grins up at her mother and replies: "Of course.

"Not because I think you are scared though, it's because neither of us alone can do what has to be done.

"Oh, by the way, Jay's been teaching me how to throw rocks hard and straight, and I've been practicing every day.

"I can nail the Archangels.

"If I need to.

"Bruises *are* about all that cover their bodies, so maybe a few more hard rock bruises are just what the ever falling angels need to straighten up and fly right."

As though she knows what her Mother is thinking, the girl looks up and offers: "I never threw rocks at the Archangels, even when they threw rocks at me."

She grins, "It will take them by surprise.

"And then you can yell at them like a mad mother would do at misbehaving sons and daughters."

"Are you suggesting that I play mother to them?"

The girl shrugs and asks: "Why not?

"I don't think Archangels *have* mothers, do you?"

Hester shrugs and shakes her head 'no'.

The girl grins, her eyes glint golden glee. She suggests: "Well then the angels won't have any way of knowing if you are *really* their mother, or if you are *not* their mother.

"It will catch them off guard.

"They will *never* have gotten a true tongue lashing from a mother. Not ever!

"They won't know what to expect, or how to defend against it, or even if they *should* defend against it.

"They are on Earth.

"They are out of their element.

"They *are* adaptable.

"But they are *not* happy campers.

"They feel like beloved chosen children, who suddenly are not feeling loved because Mother is not happy with them.

"Mother is scolding them, shaming them, getting them on their knees to swear allegiance and obedience."

"Obedience?" Hester poses with a cocked brow. "*You* are proposing *obedience?*"

The girl shrugs and says: "Well, man was given free will.

"But most Holy Books talk about obedience, and disobedience.

"Not so much about free will though.

"And, does *any* Holy Book talk about free will, and how to use it, and how *not* to use it?"

"I hadn't thought of it that way. And I think you are probably right, most holy books probably don't talk that much about free will and right ways of using it.

"So..., are you thinking that Michael and Gab-re-EL don't know about free will, they weren't made to be obedient, and so they are being *disobedient* to get the attention they want?"

"Yes, but it's not attention they need.

"The Archangels need love." She looks away as though peering into another dimension that is not on the Earth plane.

Interesting! Hester thinks. She waits until the girl comes back to hear more.

"They need unconditional love.

"The kind of love true mothers can give."

She looks up at her mother, a hand shading her eyes from the sun, and continues with a small frown. "You *are* the mother, Mom!

"You are the mother for the Archangels.

"You're the mother for The Angel Garden.

"You cannot go A.W.O.L. again like you did before when you were afraid of what you could not believe.

"You were afraid because of the miracles that happened in The Angel Garden.

"You saw them! But you would not believe your eyes, so you could not *receive* the miracle.

"You made yourself *so small* in your own mind for *so* long that you *can* no longer *be* greatly beloved in your own mind.

"So you could *not,* and cannot be greatly beloved in your own heart – where your greatest power lies.

"Your greatest power does *not* lie in your mind! The mind is where your *small*-self lives!

"*Que tonto, me mama! Que totalmente estupido!*

"You *have* get over that. N*ow*!

"Because if you don't allow yourself to be greatly beloved in your own mind, then God cannot give you unconditional love! Because you cannot, and *will* not *receive* it!

"God can keep and protect you! But *you* must shield *yourself* head-to-toe with unconditional love for yourself.

"You must put on the armor of faith – in what you *can* see – and what you *cannot* see.

"If you do not wear the armor of faith when you go into The Angel Garden, the Archangels *will* throw rocks at you. And they will hit you hard!

"They will throw bricks and stones at your head.

"They will break your glasses first thing.

"Everyone knows that if you *cannot see* your target, you cannot *hit* it!

"The Archangels *can* see you.

"They can see me, and I can see them.

"And they *still* throw rocks at me."

"They hit you too, from the looks of it." Hester notes brushing her hair back, then lifting the girl's sleeve and shirt. The girl nods and continues.

"But without hope, faith, and love, *and* with broken glasses you will *not* be able see the angels! You will be defenseless.

"They will drive you out of the garden like Adam and Eve were driven from Eden's glen!

"They will throw rocks to drive you away.

"They will not just guide you out of The Angel Garden.

"Michael and Gab-re-EL think it's theirs now.

"That's why they throw rocks at me, to make me go away.

"Plus, the Archangels aren't even *trying* to be obedient to God!

"Do you *really* think they will obey *you*?

"Do you really believe that they will stop destroying The Angel Garden just because you *tell* them to?

She stamps her foot insistently. "You *must* put on the armor of faith, Mother.

"You cannot do that until you heal *your* heart and learn to love *yourself* too.

"You cannot *save* love. Love is only love when you give it away!

"Love is only healing and helpful when you love yourself first.

"*Then*, you have enough love to give it away freely and always have more than enough!

"In fact, when you give your love away, it grows. Inside you.

"If you go into The Angel Garden without the armor of faith to ward and protect you, the Archangels *will* hit you.

"Hard.

"They will hurt you.

"On purpose.

"Their purpose is to make you go away and never come back."

Hester casts an off-side grin at the girl, and says: "I think I got the armor. Can *you* see it?"

"I *can* see it," the girl says with a silly gleeful smile.

"You have this whole body sparkly halo thing going on all around you.

"The angels *will notice* that!

"And they will know what it is.

"They will know it's the armor of faith.

"Even *fallen* Archangels know the protective power of faith.

"They cannot win a fight against firm faith. They know that.

"And, they know that they *cannot* fight against man's will to do what is right and good.

"They *have* to support that.

"But you must *not* make enemies of them by scolding or punishing them.

"You can't even think like that because that is *not* how mothers think.

"When confronted with a problem like kids – or Archangels – fighting over nothing, mothers think *first* about emotional healing and wholeness for the misbehaving minors.

"*Then* she makes the brats get down off their holier-than-thou high horses, and get grounded in reality.

"Reality bites.

"Naughty kids and haughty Archangels, are prone to get reality bites.

That's what the angels need from you, *Mother*, reality bites."

She grins, and suggests: "Ask them some sensitive feeling questions, like 'where does it hurt?', or 'how did this *happen* to you?' or, tough touch a tender looking bruise and say: 'oh, that must really have hurt you. When did that happen?'

"Be all motherly to them and get them to start talking about why they are such biting bitter beasts – but don't use those words, it will just remind them of their glory days fighting – and winning, the war against the fallen angels.

Shawn Gallaway – The Wave of Love

"And Mother, right now, Michael and Gab-re-EL *are* the fallen angels.

"They probably think there is no redemption for them, that they will never again be okay in the mind and heart of the Divine One.

"Their separation from source anxiety is abnormally high because they think the D.O. assigned them to The Angel Garden as a *punishment*."

"Punishment?

"For what?"

She shrugs, "They don't know.

"That's part of what makes them so pissy. They think the D.O. demoted them by assigning them to a do-nothing, no glory job like keeping care of a trifling country garden."

Hester smiles and says: "Well *that* I understand. Sort of.

"It must seem like a put-down to them, a demotion, and a do-nothing assignment almost as exciting as watching grass grow, when compared to the fame and glory that came with winning a long and hard war against Beelzebub and his heathen tribe of fallen angels.

"And that is no excuse for dereliction of duty!

"But I do wonder how long it's been since either of them prayed to the D.O., or asked the D.O. for guidance, or asked the D.O. for forgiveness, or gave the D.O. spontaneous praise and thanksgiving.

Hester takes the girl's hand and says: "We're going in!

"You ready?" The girl nods.

"Let's *rumble* like thunder, the transformer energy!"

Hester speaks the words like a mother warrior queen on a major mission she means to win without a battle..., any more than a mother would stoop to do battle with one of her kids over *her* expectations of them and their behavior and conduct. *Good grades too,* she thinks, but it's an unnecessary addenda.

Hester is a healer, after all.

All mothers are.

Whether they admit it or not.

Hester admits it.

Now.

That's a stand-out transformation for her.

Now the angels won't throw rocks at me! She thinks with astonishment as she strides confidently through the gate, and for the first time, into the dark devastation of The Angel Garden.

Shawn Gallaway – The Wave of Love

The girl skips giddily close by her mother's side, a small glad grin lighting her face and eyes. She can't help it. *If it's in you, it's gotta come out*, she thinks, but does not say.

Calling the Angels

Back to Earth With Joyful Hearts Now

"The closer we get to The Angel Garden, the more I can see of what's been done to it." Hester worries.

She can say no more. Not while her thoughts swirl wildly through her mind like dry leaves in hurricane winds. She can't find the words for that. Not just yet. And then she does.

"While Mother was away, escaping into la-la land where everything is bearable. Everything is okay.

"Even when it's not."

"I'm glad you're holding my hand.

"If you weren't holding my hand and keeping me grounded – in behaving like a *true* mother – I would be as cross as a snake shedding its skin. I'd be mightily tempted to slap those angels upside the head.

"And paddle them for misbehaving. And I'd have to paddle them on their bare butts, from the look of what covers them. There's a good idea we won't use!

"You were right. Their body cover *is* nothing but bruises, cuts, and a whole body crust of dry dirt.

"How far God's mighty angels have willfully fallen!

"From the looks of them, they probably smell like raw sewage."

Hester wrinkles her face against what she'll say next. "Maybe we should let them stay up there pouting and worrying in their dark – and distant – dust cloud cover, while we have a look around our garden.

"At the ground. Where the plants are.

"Our plants are the first to suffer the effects of the Archangels' not-at-all-helpful defiant dereliction of duty.

"Without the water God told them to produce from their *tears of joy*, the plants we started from seed and planted in our garden are *dying*.

"I am totally *not* okay with that!

"Meanwhile, the angels will watch us while we do our worried walk-about among the plants.

"At first, the fallen angels will wonder about the two of us together.

"They have never seen together before.

"Then they will puzzle themselves over *why* we are here.

"Together.

"And then they will worry themselves crazy trying to figure out why we are walking around and looking down at the ground.

"And *not* looking up into the dome – where they are – bare- butt naked in the dusty gloom they created in the dome of The Angel Garden.

"The Archangels will muddle themselves mad with worry and wonder over why we are looking *down* at the ground, and not *up* at them.

"They will think we have our priorities *all* screwed up and wonky. Just because we are *not* looking up to spy them in the dirty energy aura they created to hide inside the dome of The Angel Garden.

"They'll puzzle and worry over us, and try to imagine what we'll do next.

"And then we'll leave."

"Archangels or not, Michael and Gab-re-EL are behaving like spoiled baby brats throwing a temper tantrum, and they are wantonly destroying everything within reach – just because it's there!

"I am *so* not okay with that conduct from a pair of Archangels who are here on a Divine assignment to protect, nourish, and take *care* of The Angel Garden and everything in it.

"They are *not* here to behave like negligent and destructive *vacationers in* our garden, dammit!

"The Archangels weren't *assigned* here for life. They don't *belong* here for life!

"They are behaving like this assignment like it's an unjust life prison sentence, a never-ending punishment!

"Oh like God would *do* that to his first and second angelic warriors?

"They were assigned to The Angel Garden for *only* three seasons.

"They were assigned for the spring, the time for planting the seed of life.

"They were assigned here for the summer, the time of fulfillment of the seed into vibrant, thriving, nourishing and renewing plant life.

"The Archangels were assigned to be here through the fall, the time of celebrating the collecting, the harvesting, and the preserving of the produce of the spring sowed seeds.

"But they are treating their assignment to The Angel Garden like it's an unjust prison sentence.

"For life.

"Eternal.

"The Divine One *certainly* did not assign the Archangels to our garden for the purpose of producing death and destruction of what we worked so hard to plant and grow! *Que tonto! Que totalmente estupido!*

"The Archangels are *certainly* not living love as the D.O. expects from both humans *and* angels."

Shawn Gallaway – Living Love Tonight

"So what do we do next?" Hester asks.

The girl looks up at her mother with a mischievous grin and asks: "What would a good mother do in a situation like this?"

"Oh yeah!" She grins at the girl and says: "I remember now. I kick butt and take names.

"And do it in a firm but loving voice, like a good mother does when she's deeply disappointed by the beastly behavior of her children.

"Um – so how do you think I can say what needs to be said to the Archangels in a way that they don't start throwing rocks at my head?

"And yours?"

"How do you talk to Jay when he is behaving like a biting bitch bastard, not behaving, nor talking at all like a good son when he talks to his mother?"

"Wow! You go straight for the tough questions don't you?"

The girl gives a shrug and says: "Do you imagine then that when you call them to task, Michael and Gab-re-EL *won't* do the same things Jay does?

"But they'll throw rocks at your head too.

"At least Jay doesn't throw rocks at your head. He doesn't *try* to break your glasses.

"Course *Dad* would bust Jay's butt if he broke your glasses on purpose.

"Especially if he broke them throwing rocks at you – like the Archangels *will do*. Especially if you say anything that sounds even *remotely* like an order. They don't take orders. Not even the D.O.'s."

Hester talks to the trees that are struggling to survive let alone thrive. *They need water, S.T.A.T.*

She turns to the girl and asks: "When was the last time the garden was regularly watered?"

"When we still carried water from the old well to water them." She answers but does not meet her mother's eyes. *The accusation would be in my eyes and she'd read it. No good can come from that.*

"And since then?"

"When the angels first came to our garden, they cried daily tears of joy because everything they saw was so vibrantly green and alive.

"The plants thrived on the angel tears because the Archangels were *lovingly* crying tears every day. For the plants.

"Michael and Gab-re-EL were open heartedly and generously giving our plants the supportive and loving dedication that every living thing needs to survive and to thrive in life on the physical plane.

"And then something changed."

"What changed?" Hester asks full attentive and alert.

"I don't know – but I think I know anyway.

"They fell from grace."

"*Really?*"

"Why?"

"Because grace means good-will; favor; a readiness to show mercy; God's aid in the process of renewal."

"By grace we have been saved .... But we have to ask."

"Why?"

"Because Jesus said: 'you have not because you ask not.'

"Michael and Gab-re-EL have no angelic presence in and around them because they fell from grace!

"They didn't *ask*!

"They didn't ask the D.O. for grace. They didn't ask out of pride – *and pride goeth before the fall.*

"Boredom follows next. Pride is *always* bored and boring.

"The Archangels are bored.

"And they are as *boring* and fruitless as the powder dry dirt!

"They will not shed any of their angel tears to nourish and heal the plants they neglected because they stopped talking to God when they both decided the D.O. had demoted them for no reason at all.

"They think the D.O. devalued them by assigning them to tend, protect, and nourish a measly country garden. That's altogether too prosaic for the proud pair of them.

"And all of this neglect and wanton destruction happened because Michael and Gab-re-EL would not approach the throne of grace and ask for saving grace.

"Do God's first and second Archangel Knights *actually* believe that the D.O. would give them a key mission on Earth *as a punishment?*

"*As an exile? Es tonto! Es totalmente estupido!*

"What shall I do then, offer them confession and forgiveness of sins?"

The girl is silent a long moment, studying the question, then answers: "Yes, I think you have to."

"I'm not a priest." Hester objects.

"Neither is God." The girl retorts.

"God *is* a mother though.

"And so are you.

"You *can* mother the Archangels, Mom!

"And you *have to* do that for Michael, and for Gab-re-EL. Mother love them back to wholeness and healing again. Love them back to loving themselves again as God's mighty winged wonder Archangels.

"The Archangels can Omni-locate anyway, anywhere, at any time. They aren't stuck here in The Angel Garden.

"Mother love them back to wholeness and truth.

"Teach and show them how taking loving care of the plants in The Angel Garden the *best,* and the most *fun* assignment Michael and Gab-re-EL will ever get here on Earth."

"I can do that!" Hester smiles her new confidence.

"For as long as I remember, always loved Michael and Gabriel above all the other angels.

"It's a universal bias among humans, I personally believe.

"And perhaps it truly is a universal bias that is common among humans, angels, and Archangels too.

"Perhaps the bias *not* just a bias held among humans!

"I can work with that. I can *work* that!

"Besides, I *really do* want to meet Gab-re-EL. I want to talk woman-to-woman with her about *why* she thinks the D.O. sent her in female form this time around.

"It simply *must* be a mother healing reason or need.

"If not for a Divine mother healing necessity, the archangel 'Gab-re-EL' would have manifested into life on Earth *this* time around, as 'Gabriel', the male version of the healer energy.

"I *like* the energy of Gabriel.

"Always have done, always will.

"And today I want more than anything else, to explore, to learn, and to know at a visceral level, the energy of Gab-re-EL. I want to know exactly who she thinks she is.

"That is my life quest for *this* day.

"That is my purpose on this unique and singular day that the Lord has made.

"Give praise, oh angels give high holy praise, for this wholly whole and wonderful day of days!"

And they do.

What's an Archangel to do?

Archangels love to sing! It's their gift.

If it's in you, it's gotta come out.

Singularly or in groups, Archangels need only *one* mortal and attentive ear that hears dear and true, to inspire them to exult irrepressibly vocal and soulful songs of saving grace.

Archangels admire praise songs best of all the other joy songs and cogent angels cannot *help* but sing.

They sing.

Shawn Gallaway – Breathe A Little Magic

Magic happens.

And the Archangels fall hopelessly and helplessly in love again with the D.O., the sole and singular source of all and everything.

Including, The Angel Garden.

And, specifically including their angelic assignment to, and mission within, The Angel Garden.

Hester smiles down at the girl and gives her hand a soft squeeze. "I think it's time for me to have a talk with Gab-re-EL, just the three of us. What do you think?"

The girl bobs her head in agreement and says: "Yes. It should be just the three of us ladies for a while.

"That will drive Michael mad with bewilderment as to why *he* is being left out of our girl talk. It will be good for him.

"Michael is in dire straits in need of forgiveness, healing, and the unconditional love Mother's give. And, he's *desperately* in need of the high expectations that are packaged in the iron hand of Mother Love freely given."

Hester hesitates and the girl looks up to meet her eyes. She asks: "So you think I can do this?"

"No, and anyway, this has nothing to do with what I think you can do.

"It has *everything* to do with what God *knows* you can do.

"But you don't believe that.

"You *will* not pull together enough faith in yourself to even *ask* for God's amazing grace. Not even for our garden.

"Your sole and only faith is that asking is not enough for *you* to win the grace of God's help.

"Why *is* that, Mother?

"Why do you hate yourself *so much* that you *will not* receive God's love?

"Look how dark and gloomy it's gotten in the dome of The Angel Garden. The angels are hiding there."

A long silence follows. The girl waits patiently by her mother's side, holding her hand and keeping her grounded in the real world.

Where there are fallen angels.

And dying plants in need of angel tears. Tears that do not fall from the marble hard black eyes glaring down on the heads of the two invaders into their domain of dark death and demonic destruction.

Demonic?

How dare you? Michael snarls fierce fury at the perceived insult to his already wounded overweening preening pride.

Unfortunately for him, the dome is so dark cloudy full with his fury over an imagined slight, that he can't even see the invader woman or the girl, let alone throw rocks at them to drive them away.

Hester's not that patient.

Even very good mothers have their limits, and Hester is at the end of hers with these demonic angels.

But what to do?

The girl tugs her hand and gets her attention. "Call Gab-re-EL," she whispers.

"Oh, yeah!" Hester grins down at her, "Michael will *certainly* feel left out then won't he?

"Probably, he will feel deliberately *excluded* – by women – a lesser order of beings.

"That will worry Michael indeed.

"It will twist him into a snarking, snarling, fit of fury and frenzy. Tee, hee, hee!

"Okay," she says looking down at her daughter, "where are we when I call Gab-re-EL down?"

The girl grins her reply: "Somewhere where Michael can't see us, or Gab-re-EL, while we talk.

"He'll be absolutely certain that we three have intentionally made him redundant and irrelevant.

"Like God did, when He sent Michael down to Earth for the paltry purpose of holding up the dome of The Angel Garden.

"He needs to get over himself and his preening pride in having been God's first knight in the war against the fallen angels. Michael has made himself into a fallen angel, too proud to serve God's will."

"Well then, let's get this show on the road.

"Archangel Gab-re-EL," Hester calls in her best, most loving motherly voice, "come to me please."

A long silent pause follows.

Hester looks up into the dome of The Angel Garden and clarifies in an irrefutably motherly way that says she will brook no disobedience nor delay. "Now would be good, Gab-re-EL.

"Be here *now*!" Hester orders jabbing her finger down to the ground where she expects, and mentally compels, Gab-re-EL to land.

What's a girl to do in a situation as unlikely and unexpected as this, but to obey the compelling command?

She drops like a rock.

Yet Gab-re-EL lands softly and safely before Hester and the girl.

Michael is *not* amused at being left alone and being left out.

He can't even *hear* what the three of them are talking about, or hear what they are saying.

A cone of silence..., Michael thinks with a snapping snarl that sounds disturbingly like the ripping growl of lobo wolf pined in a corner by harrying hunters with long guns.

And he is incredibly short on patience.

Because his enemy of choice is totally ignoring him!

As though he didn't even exist anymore.

Or worse, that he has become wholly irrelevant and utterly redundant.

"Excess baggage...! Michael thinks.

He wants very much to suck his thumb again the way he did when he was a child angel and didn't get the attention he wanted – or demanded – if truth be told.

Tears fill Michael's eyes and spill over the lids washing away the power dry dust from cheeks and chin.

"I'm having a pity party, he thinks with amazing clarity.

It's an admission.

It's a reality check.

It's a game changer.

Michael's been down. He's getting up again.

Shawn Gallaway – Keep Getting Up

He is suddenly and fiercely unwilling to be left out and left alone simply because he's behaving like a biting bitch bastard.

He was given free will by the D.O. who created him.

By the D.O. the One who therefore, does *not* expect obedience from man, nor from angels.

Not even from his Archangels.

But, the D.O. *does* expect compliance.

So the question is: Am I being compliant?

No you are not. The Loving Mother D.O. gives the answer to Michael's question.

He did not want to *hear* that answer.

Michael was not yet ready to *own and allow* that the answer Mother gave was spot on and totally true. He *was* behaving a bratty, surly, spoiled rotten, biting bitch bastard.

Gab-re-EL was right, he admits to himself alone.

No one else is even listening, melancholy Michael thinks.

I AM – the D.O. thinks into Michael's mind.

Humility comes hard for God's first warrior knight. In all of eternity, Michael has never before encountered humility.

And, across the eons of his angelic life, Michael has never personally *experienced* humiliation before.

He never felt excluded before.

He has not even the faintest *clue* as to how to deal with humility. He doesn't know what humility is *for*.

What is the fundamental functionality of humility? Michael muses.

Freedom from pride and arrogance, the D.O. echoes again. And then, the D.O. is suddenly silent, as only the infinite eternal can be.

The absence of sound from anywhere around, shatters the sound barrier in Michael's mind. *I* am *a biting bitch bastard!*

Just like the girl said I was.

And I wanted to punish her for that.

Pride goeth before the fall....

And now I see – clearly and well – just how far and how deep I have fallen from grace on the pinion of my overweening pride.

I would not ask *the D.O. for saving grace – because I was angry with God.*

I was furious and insulted because the D.O. assigned me to the Podunk job of holding up the support pole of a bloody country garden!

You over that yet?

Michael considers the question. He asks himself: *Am I totally over being furious?*

Yes, I am over that. I am.

Then maybe it is time for you to physically *descend from the heights of your dark fury and give Gab-re-EL a helping hand.*

She is your strong right arm you know?

As you are mine.

And Gab-re-EL is currently facing off against both Hester and the girl.

They're not cutting Gab-re-EL any semblance of slack in elucidating to them the reasons why she fell so stunningly from grace in failing to fulfill her assignment of taking gentle, attentive, mothering care of the plants in The Angel Garden.

She's your strong right arm, Michael.

And you, have been treating Gab-re-EL like she's nothing but day-old shit!

You're doing that because you have wound and wrapped yourself around the axle of preening pride!

I made you better than that, Michael.

Pride goeth before the fall.

Your fall from grace, arises directly from, and as a natural consequence, of your conjured up dark vision that I, the loving source of all and everything, would punish my First Knight by sending him on a mission that was beneath him.

Really, Michael? Have you lost your mind?

Or have you only lost contact with your heart center energy? Pride could do that.

In the few weeks that you've been in The Angel Garden, have you have entirely forgotten what giving and receiving with unconditional love means?

Have you no shred of memory at all of what it feels like to give freely, generously, with a heart wide open, and expecting nothing in return?

Michael feels the D.O.s warm loving hands cup his head in a loving embrace, lean in, and kiss his forehead between his brows.

Michael sees now what his human eyes are incapable of seeing.

It was the kiss, he thinks with a warm smile *that opened my third eye and let me see clear into the void that lies between what is, and what is not.*

The void.

The place of ever evolving infinite possibilities.

Michael goes void.

He completely loses all concept of who he thinks he is in his conscious mind.

He does it on purpose.

On bended knee, Michael yields and surrenders his E.G.O. sense of self into the hands of the D.O. He simply chooses to stop Edging God Out of his conscious mind.

He releases all of his self-imposed isolationism. Michael stops Edging God Out and opens a space within his heart center where the Divine One is always at home.

This home space in his wide-open heart is a place where Michael *never* makes a decision on his own.

He is the D.O.'s strong right arm again, the way it always was from the beginning of time.

Make me your instrument.

Done!

What do you want done this day, D.O.?

Go be a strong right arm for Gab-re-EL, she's taking a beating.

Someone is hitting her?

No. But they're not cutting Gab-re-EL even a quarter inch of slack either.

Hester and the girl are pressing Gab-re-EL hard and harrying to give them a satisfactory explanation as to why all of the plants they put in The Angel Garden are bone dry and withering, even though the girl carries water to the plants every day.

Gab-re-EL cannot account for that, she can't explain it.

Not alone anyway.

Gab-re-EL needs your support right now.

You, Michael, are my strong right arm.

Will you be my strong right arm for Gab-re-EL today?

It will be my honor to serve you in this way today.

And tomorrow?

Michael grins and replies: *It may take more than a day, or even a week of days, before Gab-re-EL and I are capable of healing and revitalizing The Angel Garden. And ourselves.*

Forgiveness comes first. Can you forgive yourself?

You keep asking that!

I do.

And that usually happens because you can be a willfully slow study, Michael.

And two Millennia later, you are still *rehearsing, rehashing, and* regretting the lost glory of fighting the fallen angels.

Will you just get over *that already!*

Uh – yeah!

Already over it.

I think it's time for me to go check on Gab-re-EL and see if Hester and the girl are done giving her a tongue lashing.

Yes, go do that.

It will be a game changer for you. And for Gab-re-EL.

Michael descends from the dome of The Angel Garden with angelic grace. Until he doesn't any more. Because he hears Hester and the girl and Gab-re-EL giggling and laughing until their sides ache, and tears run down their faces and fall at their feet.

Where all the plants they'd started from seed are vibrantly alive, and are green glow growing and thriving again. Some of the herbs are opening flowers and enticing bees and butterflies and hummingbirds to come have a sip. In exchange for the nectar they sip from the flowers, the pollinators collect the flower's pollen on their fuzzy legs and release it again wherever they land. And life goes on.

Michael joins the ladies at the party. It isn't a pity party at all. It's a joy-filled, giggle-a-minute celebration of life and of living it, and an unabashed sharing celebration of the multitude of unexpected daily blessings that are often overlooked and taken for granted simply because they are daily!

There's nothing new and exciting about gifts given daily and rarely received. Yet these women are getting an oxygen high off the daily rush of healing laughter.

The ladies are receiving, celebrating, and sharing their crystal clear tears of joy, and *they are also sharing their salt heavy tears of pain and sorrow.*

Michael realizes with something akin to tears of joy sparkling in his eyes. Suddenly Michael profoundly misses Gab-re-EL. Who is now *not* inside the dome of The Angel Garden. Instead, she is sitting in a circle holding hands with Hester and the girl, and the three of them are giggling and laughing and telling tall tales until tears flow down their cheeks unchecked.

Michael morosely mourns the relationship the two of them had when they were both guy angels. He does not know *how* to relate to a second in command who is a lady angel this time around. It makes him feel uncertain, anxious, and edgy.

Michael, nothing outside of you can make you feel anything*! Not ever. I gave you free will. You alone get to choose to choose how you feel. And why.*

So tell me, First Knight a mine, why do *you choose to feel uncertain, anxious, and edgy because your pal Gabriel is now a gal pal? What's* that *about, angel a mine?*

Sexist pig? Michael offers morosely.

Is that good enough for you? Is that *the best, and most honest answer you can give me? Take your time, Michael. This is a shift time for you.*

Nothing will be the same for you after you choose how *you will shift, and* how *you will change, into the next best version of you that you can conceive.*

How will you relate to Gab-re-EL when you make that change, Michael? Will she still be your strong right arm? Will she still be your best friend forever? Or will you choose to be jealous and domineering of her — just because she's in female form? Are you a sexist pig?

Ouch! Michael yelps.

On target, He wails. *I've taken a direct hit!*

No you have not, you silly ass!

That's all in your mind, Michael!

It's nothing but a chimera that you *have allowed — by neglect, and by your pride bound negligence — to invade and to befuddle your fine mind, for God's sake!*

To keep you *bogged down and distracted in your separation from source anxiety.*

And, totally incompetent to serve me *effectively and well as my First Knight.*

All that I asked you to do *was to support the sheltering dome of The Angel Garden, and, to cry angelic tears of joy to water the plants there because* you *made the impossible possible.*

What you believe *and say about yourself to yourself, my beloved Michael, is what* will *show up for you on the physical plane. Where your current assignment is.*

To shelter and protect The Angel Garden. How's that working for you?

'S not.

Or snot! The D.O. counters calmly. *As in snotty nosed bully boy brat throwing a temper tantrum because he didn't get* exactly *what he wanted the way he wanted it, and will not accept the gift he was given.*

What is *your problem with Gab-re-EL?*

Are you a sexist pig, or are you not? No answer. Again.

Why do you throw rocks at the girl when she comes to water the plants in the garden? What is your deal with that? No answer. Again.

The Divine One takes another tack. *Dragon a mine, I need your help and assistance S.T.A.T.*

I'm on my way. S.T.A.T., the dragon roars back. *I'll be breaking the sound barrier in 10, 9, 8, 7, 6, 5, 4, 3, 2, 1, blast-in!*

I am now safely landed inside The Angel Garden. What's my mission?

You tell me.

Hum-m-m, the dragon hums, *it feels like something righteously wrong happened in here. And unless I miss my guess, I'm supposed to fix it.*

Yes. But not you alone. Who is it that helps you to make right what's gone wrong in here?

The wise wyvern is silent a long pondering moment, and then he growls irritably: *Oh, God, not Hester.*

What have I done to deserve *Hester again?*

What if it is not *about just deserts, dragon a mine? What* if *the time you spend with Hester is a generous gift from me to you?*

You are going to have a very *hard sell on that one, D.O.*, the dragon snarls.

I do not *in any way, shape or form*, deserve *having to spend any time, any place, anywhere, with that pushy bitch on wheels. Hester thinks she has a divine right to give orders to a dragon, for God's sake! Hester is* not *dragon rider material. Hester cannot go with the flow.*

And you, dear dire dragon a mine, can you go with the flow?

Usually when one of my creations don't like some or all of my other *creations and rebel against serving them — when I ask them to nicely — my creation is experiencing separation from source anxiety.*

That's my S.O.S. call, dragon a mine. So, wise wyvern a mine, what if I told you that Hester and the girl are already inside The Angel Garden?

They are? Then what is my assignment, and what's Hester got to do with it?

Hester is about to face down a maliciously malcontent and mad – both 'angry', and 'crazy' work equally well – Archangel. He throws rocks at the girl when she goes into The Angel Garden to tend to the plants. Hits her too. On the head when he's feeling especially neglected and demoted because the assignment I gave him is to be the strong support for the dome of The Angel Garden. He's mad!

And Michael is also jealous, because right now, Hester and the girl are talking to Gab-re-EL, and the three of them are laughing together like they've been best friends forever.

Gab-re-EL? Oh my, D.O.! That's an interesting plot twist to this this game of life you play – to win – for everyone, including Michael, the bad boy brat bully that amps up the tension of the drama. So, what am I to do in The Angel Garden?

Go get Michael out of the dirty dome of The Angel Garden and get him planted again in reality on the physical plane! Michael takes the seat at my round table to my right. Gab-re-EL takes the seat at my round table to my left.

That's why Arthur used the round table and had his strong right arm seated to his right, and his strong left arm seated to his left. Only then will Michael make conscious contact with me again and return to being my joyfully willing strong right arm, and to feel honored and willing to do my work to the best of his ability. Which – are – endless, actually. Michael's forgotten that.

Will you slap him up-side the head for me while bringing him down to reality on the physical plane please? I need him there. Michael has made of himself a fallen angel! Raise him up and redeem him, dragon a mine. I need him back as my strong right arm.

And Michael needs Ga-re-EL. He doesn't know that yet. But he will when he takes his first dragon ride into infinity and back to Earth again and loses his mind and gets back into right mind – Divine Mind – and delights in co-creating with me on the physical plane. I truly need wise and willing co-creators here on Earth, people and angels and dogs and cats who are in constant contact with me.

Shawn Gallaway - Contact

Enjoy the ride, dragon a mine! And thank you, for returning the heart love of my First Knight to me so we are always in constant contact. Reunite Michael with Gab-re-EL – she's currently having a giggle session with Hester and the girl – and Michael imagines that they are laughing at him! Que tonto!

I want Michael back, dragon a mine! I want Gab-re-EL back too. Thanks for bringing both Michael and Gab-re-EL back home to me.

Master's Mark

Jacob pauses at the door to the common room hearing familiar voices. He inhales, holds for ten counts, and on the exhale, lets his inner and outer eyes adjust to the dark interior.

He expands mindfulness into the store. Finding the familiar energies, he explores the energy of the man the woman called 'master'. He feels the power of the voice; its command of oratory forms a base line for the lyricism of his words. He hears an insecurity rare among orators. *Interesting.*

Shedding his cap, he inhales, and steps inside to hellos. He extends hand to the stranger: "I'm Jacob. You the driver of the Rolls outside?"

"I am the *owner* of that fine auto," the man affirms firmly. "*Before*, I was the driver," he pats a pocket, "now, I own that fine vehicle."

"And the woman?" Jacob tips his head toward the window where the cocoa woman silently sulks.

"I own the slave too." The man misses the edgy energy his assertion arouses. *Interesting,* Jacob nods to all, then to the visitor, and asks: "How *does* one man own another?"

Counselor rumbles amiable interference, "Jacob, you came at the right time. The man was about to tell those things, pull up a chair and sit." Turning to the visitor he invites: "Step to the center of the circle so you can see, be seen, and we all can hear you." He does, rises to his toes and spins, meeting the eye of each man. He tips a nod to Sheriff Ben – *the uniform*, Ben thinks – pauses before Jacob – *the skepticism*, Jacob fancies. He turns to Counselor with a bow mostly reserved for gentility.

"It's a pleasure to tell you folks how these things happened. The tales twine, so I'll tell 'em as one adding humor where I can." He supple snakes his tongue up his throat to carry his words to all who hear. "I own the Rolls Royce because the master never learned to drive. He liked being delivered to his appointments and festivities. When our time together ended, he gave me the auto for he could not drive nor maintain it. The carpetbaggers stole him blind. He had to send me on my way to the great American west."

Counselor murmurs, "Never before have I heard such an *extraordinarily* generous act. Surely the master knew the Rolls Royce Company would assign and send a new chauffer at his request?"

The raconteur sighs dramatically, "Yes, he did know that, and he and gave me the car anyway. The master is a saint, or will be when he dies, may that day be many years from today."

"How does your master get to his appointments and parties now?" Sheriff Ben asks, lids slit narrow.

"The folks back home love that man and will do anything for him. They'll get him where he needs to go."

Ben frowns at the double edge sharpness in the last five words and "*Why* would even a good and godly a plantation owner rely on the kindness of neighbors to get his business done when he could use his *own* car and his *own* chauffeur? Why would he allow a departing chauffeur to even use his car for a long trip to…, where'd you say you're headed?"

"I didn't. I don't rightly have a destination, for I never had I a chance to see this great land. I'm starting a new life. I will drive into the sunset 'til I find a place with good folks, settle awhile, and head off to see what's around the next bend in the road."

"Sounds like a drifter to me, Ben growls to the circle, "except for the car."

"What's a drifter?" The visitor asks anxious.

"Someone passing through with no contribution to make along the way." Ben smiles friendly, agreeable, insincere "Here on the plains, drifters are about as popular as carpetbaggers down South."

The visitor eyes Ben evenly and he says "The old master assured me he could take proper care of his business *without* the auto before he gave the title to me."

"A remarkably generous act," Counselor reiterates redundantly imposing calm courtesy.

"Tell us how you come to own the woman outside," Jacob prompts.

"The master gave her to me so I'd have someone to take care of my needs." The orator is oddly unaware of the edgy energy aroused by his last words.

"Does taking care of your needs explain the mark the woman bears?" Jacob growls tap-tapping his neck with two fingertips, "The one she calls *my master's mark*?"

"Dang, Jacob," Ben growls, "here I was thinking the woman was his *sex slave*." Turning back to the guest he asks pleasantly. "Tell us how you come to own the woman, and about your master's mark on her."

"I got her ownership paper" the man defends, slapping his breast pocket, "the master gave her to me legal and true. She's mine, and that Rolls is mine. I can do what I please. It's *no never mind* to anyone."

Jacob growls, "*Why* would a plantation owner give a healthy young slave to a driver leaving his service and taking his only vehicle?"

"The master is a good man, I told you already that."

"You did, and we heard what you said," Counselor cautions casually. "Jacob is asking *why* even a good man would give a healthy slave to a chauffeur leaving his service." Silence extends into prickly points prodded by the steady tick tock of a wall clock. Turning to Jacob Counselor says "while our guest is auditing his *accounting*, bring the woman in so we can hear her story and have a look at that mark." Jacob comes with a woman the color of sweet cocoa and eyes round with doubt, dread and dismay.

Counselor is the comforter "Thank you for joining us, young lady. I know this is not easy for you." Her eyes dart to the orator and back to Counselor robed in black with a curled white wig. She blinks. Jacob lays a hand on her shoulder giving courage for the challenge ahead. "Come, sit by me, child." Counselor invites moving his chair to one side as Doc moves his to the other. "Somebody, bring a chair for the lady." The orator snorts, but holds his tongue for Jacob edges close on a deviant path to his chair.

"The man on your left is a medical doctor," Counselor informs the woman as she sits between them.

"Jacob tells us you wear the mark of your master." Doc invites. The girl nods but doesn't meet his eyes. "Will you let us look at that mark?" Unaccustomed to respect in matters of her body, the woman dashes a glance to Jacob who nods assurance. Holding his eyes, she releases the shawl letting it fall to show the mark. An inhale silences the room yet none but Counselor hear the words between Doc and the woman. She nods, eyes wide with dread as if she'd just agreed to jump without a rope from a towering bluff and into the infinite heart of creation; and she has.

"This man," Counselor motions to the dandy, "is he your master?" The woman nods but speaks no word of ownership by another.

"Did he put this mark on you?" Doc asks with professional detachment, her head bobs. "When did he put the mark on you?"

"Five, six weeks ago," She sighs, "I forget things like the time, the date, when I ate last, and when I last had a good night's sleep."

Doc nods and murmurs "Does he – *urr* – penetrate you in – *urr* –other places?" The woman locks eyes on his, cocks a brow as one might to a village idiot, then turns away. "I'll take that for a yes," Doc says behind a hand hiding a grin at his silent comeuppance. He assures the woman, "we can heal that mark." She studies him, eyes slit thin with wariness born of neglect, misuse, abuse, and of primal terrors come savagely alive. *Too pale,* she thinks. *His hope of redemption is like tea when the ice is melted in the glass.* Yet thirst blooms in her and she dares not ask, know, or trust, so she simply let's go and receives hope like a cool breeze over a blistering field.

"We'll need the Daughters for the healing work, Jacob would you…?"

A chair clatters into a fall calling eyes to Sheriff Ben snatching a chair from a fast crash. Casting Jacob a grin he says "I'll go, Jacob." Stepping to his side he claps a hand to a shoulder, locks eyes, and bares a toothy grin "You know, Jacob, *he, he, he,* the ladies always come when I call." Jacob tips his head back in a chortle his eyes never leaving Ben's. "Stay *by the door* while I'm gone."

Jacob nods. "Good speed, Ben, the healing art of the Mother/Daughters is soon needed."

"What is your name young lady?" Counselor asks the woman by his side.

The woman is silent, "I – I never had a name given me." The orator's head snaps up but he doesn't look.

"Indeed?" Counselor eyes her solicitously. "Tell me how it is that you were never given a name."

"My mama was a slave. She was taken by a guest she wouldn't name. She was shamed and blamed by her people for not saying his name. She wouldn't tell about the night I was conceived. She didn't accept me. Maybe for her, or me, but *always* because of the shaming. Other slaves say mama was bright, happy and loving before me, but not *to* me. She saw to it I was clean, fed, and clothed, but she had no joy left." Words fail where memory holds no key nor cause nor reason but only nameless loss.

Counselor silently studies the evidence and turns to the orator. "What is your name then, young man?"

Caught off guard, the orator stammers "I – I. The master called me James," he says tucking his head. "James, I have an appointment, bring the auto, James, get the door, James, my guests have arrived; serve the drinks on the veranda, James.'" The orator stammers to a stop.

"And your given name?"

"I… was never given a name that I know of."

"Two strangers in our town in one day and neither with a given name. What do you make of that, Doc?"

Doc brackets his chin with thumb and fingers, broods awhile and says, "Beats anything I ever heard."

"Well, young man," Counselor cautions, "the transfer of property, chattel or slave, needs the name of the transferee to be binding, and since you have no name, I don't see how it is legally possible that you own the auto, or the woman. Let me have a look at those papers for you." He extends a palm until the papers are there, studies them, then raising eyes to the orator, he rubs his chins. "The line for the transferee on both these documents is blank."

"Can I see?" The man gazes intently at the papers, colors, and shoves them back to Counselor meeting his eyes, "would you show me what you're telling me, please, Sir?"

"This is the auto title," he says extending the title. "See this word? That word is 'Owner', the name of the master is entered here. This word," he says, is "Transferee," it means the name of the person the item is transferred to. The line beside it is blank. That means the title to the Rolls is not in your name, the master still owns the auto."

He shuffles the papers, points to the second: "The Transferee line on the slave document is blank. The plantation owner is her master of this woman who bears your mark."

"He *doesn't own* me?" Shrieks the woman punching air at all the invisible indignities that rise like ghosts to dance with her in intimations of the intimate injustices imposed on her. She paces, a cat in a cage in a rage, gulping gouts of air in a battle to find herself amidst the revelations of the day carpetbaggers came to take away the life she lived. In the safe hole, once again, she hears the cool reception of the intruders, their snapped sharp words, the shoving, the scuffling, the grunts, cries and protests, feels the impotent futile fury of the master's effort to protect his home, family, *and his people.*

The man in the safe hole with her claps a hand over her mouth, pressing a blade to her throat as the mistress cries out. She hears the stumble, her fall to the floor, she sees the woman as helpless as she trapped in silent safety. An agony of hours later the house falls silent.

She is safe. As safe as one is subject to the whims of an eager sinner in the hands of an angry god. Memory ghosts dissolve to dust and she allows the dots of today connect with the old ones of the raid. She balls her fists, inhales sharply and howls "can I *kill* him?"

Michael's Mark

The orator shrinks from the fury of the woman and turns to the faces in the circle, seeking sympathy, shelter, support, security. Finding none, he shifts. Jacob sees energy at the edge of the man's body flicker signaling a shift, and surrenders his will to the indwelling infinite Source of life. In no-thought Jacob feels a familiar dissolution of self and inhabitation by a greater power that instinctively meets and matches the transformation. As watcher, Jacob sees the visitor's clothes drift to the floor, a dark shadow take to the air wing for the door where he now stands immersed in the energy of Michael the archangel dressed in shining armor. *"Welcome,"* Jacob thinks before his mind falls as empty as the orator's clothes.

It is good to be in form when the foul sin of separation, the original fall from grace, takes a favored form of Satan himself. Jacob feels his teeth bare into a grin worthy of the grim reaper on a mad bad night. *The master of lies, deceits and deceptions returns to stalk earth where man walks. Thanks for keeping your body in shape by the way, Jacob, I like working in you, I like working* with *you.* Jacob feels an angel smile rise on his face as a son of man willingly blends his service with Michael's fierce fiery grace. As one, Archangel and man step choice-fully surrendered into the endless ever-evolving multi-dimensional sinuous supple wondrous springing will of the Infinite Eternal One. *The game's afoot!*

The speed of light that is the Truth of Being, Michael's eyes track the flight of the bat across infinity through the slit in his visor. A spiraling gold wheel set with diamonds and pearls and centered with a heart shaped hiddenite stone adorns his helmet over the third eye catching light and spinning an ever-evolving reel of rationality onto the flat physical plane reality. In the blink of an eye, the wheel reverses to rewind reality across time until no trace of it remains at all. *Interesting.* Dislocation overwhelms as awareness, thought, and ego, weaves into a fully present lucid mindfulness of the startlingly fluid frontiers between what is and what is not in the eye of an Archangel. All judgment, will, strength and order ever applied by man using the twelve powers to change the physical plane hold no sway where Jacob resides inside an angel peering into an infinity where a bat flies and a slave bleeds.

Michael inhales deep and touches the jewel at the bottom of the seven set in his gold breastplate. **Ruby**, the stone of nobility, the star fire of purity, imparts vigor and passion for life, it protectively leads to vibrant visualization, clears negative energy, and promotes dynamic leadership, strength and passion for life. Ruby is an abundance stone stimulating a positive passion for life and a bold state of mind. Ruby is the resurrection stone that overcomes martyrdom, suffering, anguish, and turmoil, for ruby holds the power of beginnings and endings of all that is, was, or will be. As Michael touches the Ruby he is filled with courage, power and life force energy to neutralize negativity in mind and body. Luke's words of bloom in his mind: *Take heed therefore that the light which is in thee be not darkness. Luke 12:35.* He knows the darkness within *him,* he sees and recognizes it in the bat/man. Releasing darkness into light, duality melds polarity and opens infinite possibility. *Thy will be done*, Michael surrenders and is one.

Michael strokes the **Jasper** and is grounded by the truth of the self of Source bridging mind and body dualities and imparting tranquility and wholeness. The protector stone grounds and inspires shamanic journeying. He dances balancing dualities in mind, body and brain with the etheric realm and knows the assurance of support if conflict arises. He absorbs the energy of jasper and opts to inspire, nurture, renew and realize balance in the man in bat drag winging from consequences of past choices. The decision neutralizes duality, reunites unity and opens a way to bring idea into form.

Michael strokes the **Topaz** and as the stone flares a pure yellow gold light he enters the abiding place of substance setting him on the path and inspiring wisdom and judgment, the twin powers of the shaman wise elder. He feels an empathetic flow of energy soothe, heal, stimulate, promote mercy, light the path to goals, and tap inner resources to center him in *being* and not in habitually *doing*. He feels generosity, abundance, joy, love, and good fortune, and releases deep pools of tension to receive a continuous flow of spirit energy. He can't not smile, nor resist a silly-boy grin at his passion to teach and enlighten that is the problem solver healer path of the warrior. This path is an awakening for Michael. He taps assets to find his inner problem solver to focus passion and support in manifesting Good God on Earth. Exhaling like a Zen master he yields to love and good fortune, knowing Truth that all is one, and the One is good.

Michael strokes the **Emerald**, the stone of enlightenment, inspiration, infinite peace, and life affirming relationships, love, bliss and loyalty and is filled with grace. He finds he has misplaced his separate sense of self and is flooded with unity enhancing love and balancing relationships. The negative and positive energy balances polarities across his meridians and up and down his body. Consciousness soars, and only positive results, decisions and actions are even possible now. Michael knows he has the gift of inspiration to overcome the trial before him and to stimulate wholeness into the wounded ones. He intuitively accepts all who wittingly or otherwise, play roles in the unfolding bat man drama.

Touching the **Blue Topaz** on his breastplate, Michael feels a rolling energy sweeping him into vitality and heightened consciousness of life in which all receive inspiration and an infilling of seed ideas. He calmly accepts a higher order of self that is forceful, energetic, objective-driven, and enlightened. He taps into inner guidance before acting. That transparency activates trust in the universe, promotes clarity, self-control and development of wisdom letting Michael see the macro without losing the micro in the matrix of life. The stone evokes love, good fortune, inner wisdom, and attainment of goals and sees a higher order of man who is aware, and intent on applying Spirit resources before physical solutions.

Michael touches the **Sapphire** and feels upload of joy and peace of mind that opens intuition, dreams and passion to wisely evolve ideas into the physical world. The stone arouses collaboration at a cellular level and rejoins him with truth that changing your mind, changes your life. Willingly yielding his militant mind-set, Michael focuses on joyously manifesting idea/ thought into form. Sapphire reveals esoteric codes of manifestation that expand intuitive knowing, and infuses the peace of faith that when in service, spiritual attainment is accelerated. Claiming faith power, he peers into space where a bat wings fierce to exit from a physical place briefly appearing in time and space. *Interesting.* The mystic music of Sapphire pulsing through Michael he is electrified to hear: *the spiritual path is not a destination, it is a journey.* He is a peaceful warrior.

Now Michael touches the **Amethyst** stone and feels a powerful protective energy with a high spiritual vibration guarding against psychic attack by transmuting the energy into love. Amethyst blocks negative environment energies and enhances higher states of consciousness; and Michael experiences the dissipation of negative energies and expansion of higher energies that enhance spiritual awareness. He is transported to another reality. He focuses his faculties and feels the subtle strong energy of Jacob as confident governor of his choices and flows with him into an assimilation of new ideas that connect cause with effect, and enhance decision making by blending common sense with spiritual insight. This practice calms, synthesizes and supports transmission of neural signals through the brains of archangel and of the human he inhabits. He experiences an enhancement of memory and motivation. In one mind with Jacob, Michael absorbs the Amethyst power and feels anger, fear, anxiety, sorrow, and pain dissolve. Led by Jacob's slow full inhale, the archangel sets realistic goals, comes to terms with loss, and, as one with his host, the Archangel experiences true selflessness, spiritual wisdom, and enhanced psychic gifts. *We can do this!* the two minds think as one. *The Ancient Adversary,* Archangel Michael leers from the silver helmet sheathing Jacob's head, *still imagining he can be separate from the Creator. Still enthralled by the mad delusion of isolation from Cause, and more besotted still, willfully embracing Beelzebub's lie that a bat, man, or angel, will one day, gain more power than Source and be enabled to overthrow the One. Fool! Besotted by the delusion of separation, and the arrogance of thinking it is even possible wrest from Source more power than Source has, and thus overthrow the One. Delusional!*

Battle fury engulfs Michael. He tiptoes on a needle point of control, past drunk on the thrill of conflict and an impatient passion to extinguish the original sin of separation from Source. Gulping great gasps of air, he is overcome by an oxygen high that melts his mind and until he *is* the heat of battle, he *is* a lust for death and devastation, Michael *is* the Four Horsemen of the Apocalypse.

Cool it, Michael, comes Jacob's command. *What this situation does* not *need is two uncontrollable men, while I am stepped back making room for you in my body and mind.*

Or, if you wish, I can tell everyone that a man in bat form terrified an Archangel into senseless stupidity.

I'm not afraid! Michael snarls.

That was not *a request, Michael. I allow you in; I can let you stay, or I can kick you out, your choice. Make it now. Even the Eternal can't make physical time stop forever.*

Jacob grins toothily and adds, *Fear isn't the only thing that makes fools of angels and men. One wee bat can do the same thing to an archangel too caught up in the past to clearly see what flies before him today, and what can now be done today to create a better world. Kill one bat, you've killed one bat.*

I don't like you sometimes, Jacob.

Mutual. Check the course of bat man.

Sighting through the enlightened stones on breastplate and scabbard, Michael checks the progress of the man bat winging over space and time. *Judas unredeemed,* he snarls; *capable only of comprehending personal, worldly power in its enchantments and illusions. The Ancient Adversary, still thinking it is possible to be separate from the Creator, the first Cause of all that is and all that is not. More besotted still, willfully embracing Beelzebub's lie that he can gain more power than Source.* Ancient enmity boils through Michael. Jacob feels his passion rushing slow like molten lava to curb and cool the archangel's ecstasy that blinds him to the wisdom of the stones. Riding his polarized passion like a surfboarder over sweeps and swells of the battle fury that owned Michael during the fall from grace when he fought the angels who sought more power than Source. *Fools, skunk drunk on delusion of separation from Source and of a passion to seize all Source power and more. An arrogant affinity for separation,* Michael snarls.

You got a wide streak of separation from source anxiety yourself, Michael. Curb your temper. Zeal, not rage, is one of the twelve powers; and rightly used, zeal can heal you and the bat man. Light the other stones, we'll need them soon. Do your sensei master fight dance this time, I like it. Good rhythm, beat, fluidity, dazzling footwork, who knows, maybe the bat will stop to watch.

Next time I come I'll bring you a sense of humor. Michael snaps.

Bring two you'll need one yourself, Jacob replies evenly. *The physical world* needs *comic relief more than a militantly dogmatic archangel still fighting fallen angels from eons ago. Time to adopt cooperation and collaboration, Michael. The sapphire is the last stone you touched. Short memory for a semi-divine being.* Michael stiffens, eyes wide with exasperation. Pushing against the resistance, Jacob forces his lungs full intentionally pressing the archangel against ribcage and spine. He holds the breath to a slow count of ten forcing angry rigidity from the archangel. The champion does not go down easily, and Jacob begins his slow ten count all over again.

All right already! I take your point. Inhale so I have room to breathe again.

Still overtly crabby for a semi-divine being. Still punitive and irritable. No wonder *the Good Lord doesn't give you important, world changing assignments anymore; and on that note, what* are *you doing here?*

Michael is silent, breathing slowly and rhythmically until his heat cools from volcanic intensity to mere driven purpose. Memory of his mission returns to his awakened mind. *Thank you for your strength, and for your wisdom and good judgment in calling me to task for backsliding to a time when my sword could be unsheathed in anger and vengeance.* He sighs a release, and adds, *and for pushing me out of the past and back to the present, and my mission here and now.*

What is our – what is your mission this time?

I am to save two lost souls who are gone in their own human minds, but never lost in the mind of God. I would have failed without you, Jacob. I know that. I remember how you persistently pressed the angry vengeance out of me and held me fast, Michael chuckles, *until I blessed you. In truth, it was you that blessed me, and I'm glad it didn't take an all-night fight this time.*

Couldn't. Jacob replies, *we don't have that much time.*

We have all the time we need, Jacob, all the time we need.

Michael can't *not* dance. *Pointless.* Michael yields lead-footed ingrained patterns that no longer serve, to tap around resistance, inertia, and self-sabotage. He stomps out dysfunctional ideas, antique inhibitions, a closet full of shoulda, woulda, coulda, faith in primordial enemies, and ancient taboos he picked up cheap at a rummage sale. His dancing feet step lively with joy.

The **Garnet** jewel flares, filling the archangel with cleansing, revitalizing, purifying, balancing, energy and inspiring love, devotion, courage, fortitude, hope, expanded awareness and mutual assistance. The power the stone dissolves habit patterns that even archangels have, and bypasses the habit of self-sabotage by obsolete dysfunctional beliefs.

Michael chooses to reform error thoughts that still serve so they produce happier outcomes and reject the dark hidden ones that beguile him to believe in what shows up in the physical world even if it is *not* true in Spirit. With knowledge and intention, Michael releases, removes, denounces and denies all delusion that anything made by and from Source could ever be or become separate from Source. *Illogical.* Michael hears the words *"To whom little is forgiven, the same loveth little.* (Luke 8:47), and ponders the possibility that the man in bat has forgiveness issues for always giving small. *Except for horses…, they gave with no holding back. Interesting. He never found that with people.* A russet red flame quickens as Michael strokes the garnet gem illuminating chakras and expanding mindfulness so he feels and experiences the frequencies and harmonies of the springing, swelling, inspiring, and passionate energy that animates life. He can't *not* dance. *Pointless.* Michael surrenders lead-footed behavior patterns that no longer serve him, to tap around resistance, inertia, and self-sabotage. He stomps out old dysfunctional ideas, antique inhibitions, a closet full of shoulda, woulda, couldas; belief in primordial enemies, and all the ancient taboos he'd picked up cheap at a rummage sale. *Nonsensical.*

Michael is inspired with hope, clarity and courage and his dancing feet step lively with joy. He releases old baggage, vibrations, and negative life patterns. He accesses new frequencies, views new destinies, spiritual purposes, and the gifts in past experiences. Michael admits mistakes and breaths confidence and composure in spiritual purpose and destiny forever forming. He is filled with clarity, confidence, assertion, and a fiery passion for spiritual truth. He knows men can live on the sense plane until they are animal in nature. The man took on the small self-serving nature of bat. *Interesting.* Releasing thoughts that no longer serve makes space for ideas from Universal Mind. He gives gratitude for the healing to come. He takes another look at the spiritual truth of the man bat and the woman who bleeds and sees a shared destiny that lead both to this place and time. *Interesting. Whatever happens to the bat, happens to the woman too. It'll be grand following the path the Divine prepared for these foes and for us!* Jacob sends him confident passion without aggression.

Maybe I won't *kill him then,* Michael muses. Compassion is love driven by an understanding heart. Compassionate people see error, but they don't condemn. *"Neither do I condemn thee: go thy way; from henceforth sin no more. John 8:11.* Michael finds empathy for the fear-filled man in bat, and for the woman who thinks she's a slave. Michael will accept no other outcome than to harmonize their dualities and create resolutions that enrich all involved.

The **Diamond** imparts the clarity to focus life into a cohesive whole and brings love, commitment, and abundance. The stone amplifies and harmonizes the dual poles of everything in form and clears and purifies emotional pain minimizing fear and creating a space for new opportunities. Diamond stimulates imagination and inventiveness and links intellect with higher mind leading to enlightenment that allows soul light to shine through lighting the way to spiritual evolution of the divine light within. The stone conveys fearlessness, invincibility, fortitude, and is a link between the intellect and the higher mind.

Michael sees only light, and a path to new beginnings for the man bat and for the woman who thinks she's a slave. He is fearless, invincible and valiant. He has nothing to prove and nothing to lose. Wise and willfully dedicated to divine right outcomes, Michael names and claims his true desire: *I AM the strength to hold a space for all people to return to integrity without shame or blame*. He dances a joy jig.

Amber is not a stone but a fossilized tree resin that is strongly connected to earth serving as a grounding stone transmutes negative energies into higher outcomes that link the everyday self to spiritual reality. Amber stimulates a drive to achieve, promotes a sunny disposition that respects tradition, yet flexibly dissolves opposition, encourages peacefulness, develops trust, and brings wisdom.

"When thine eye is evil, thy body also is full of darkness." Luke 12:34. Combat ecstasy erupts in Michael. The power surge disorients the bat stopping it mid-flight. *I didn't know bats could do that. Something new every day in your service, Lord, what a great and awesome God you are. I will not destroy what you have made Lord,"* his reaper grin is back *"but in your name, I* will *incapacitate the serpent of deceit so the man may live free again.* If *he chooses.* Without effort, Michael *is* where the bat flies at bat-Mach speed into the sword in Jacob's hand in the gauntlet of Michael's armor. For an instant the bat sizzles on the blade, then slow slides to plop on the floor. Michael's sabaton pins the bat before Jacob's mind gets the signal his body has moved.

Michael touches the **Carnelian** and is filled with life force, vitality, motivation, and inspiration to accept what is, and a passion to find a resolution that enriches all. *That is* creativity in action he thinks, that's Carnelian. At his touch, the stone activates a vitality and acceptance that leads spontaneously to release, resolution and re-visioning of what is yet to be created into form and relationship. Michael smiles his true smile as love and compassion infill his angelic mind, body and brain.

The one unenlightened stone is the **Peridot**. Before touching it, Michael shifts his consciousness into the stone to receive its spring green power and experiences the cleansing, energizing power of the gem. He feels toxins issue from his body, mind and brain, and a corresponding release of old baggage and current influences, and opens himself to an awakened communion with higher mind. He releases dysfunctional and negative vibrational patterns. That cleansing empowers Michael to move forward with easy grace. He releases negative energy, welcomes enhanced poise, confidence, and a motivation to grow mentally, emotionally, and spiritually. Forgiveness of self and others for past mistakes empowers rebirth into a new awareness that activates hope and faith in a renewed unity with all of mankind in oneness of with all of life. He knows too that man can live exclusively on the sense plane, and over time, becomes animal in nature. *The human has only the small self-serving sentience of a bat.* Michael muses as he strokes the Peridot and is filled with faith, strength, and courage to meet the challenge winging toward him. He rejoices that the man in bat, and the enslaved woman, are already reborn into an abiding and assured awareness of Oneness as Truth. With the twelve stones of power lit Michael honors the relationship between will and understanding and calmly walks the path of power into the continuum where the horned one in bat drag speeds across the void hell-bent to flee the outcomes of unenlightened choices through one small door in space and time. Michael allows mistakes and moves on. Breathing easy he is clarity, confidence, assertion without aggression, and a fiery passion in the quest for spiritual truth.

Ben enters the room at a run, skids to a stop beside Jacob, and grins eyeing what lies pinned beneath his foot, "Good man, Jacob, you captured a man in a bat suit," he claps a hand on Jacob's shoulder. Wincing he pulls his hand back, lamenting, "I *never* remember to *not* slap you on the shoulder when you wear armor. You, my friend, are downright prickly when you go Archangel Michael on us."

Jacob's laughter reverberates in the silver helmet and carillons through nose and eye vents, he cocks an unseen brow. "I need three pieces of silver," he orders in angelic voice, "what have you got?"

"A pair of buffalo nickels," Ben grins holding them out, "and I already know where these buffalo roam." Dropping to a knee by the bat Ben slides a buffalo coin face up between the elbow of a wing and the spine of the bat, then places other buffalo between the elbow and back of the other, and turns to rise.

"I'm in for a silver eagle quarter," Counselor raises the ante by flipping the coin to Ben who catches it on the rise and drops again to place it prudently on the breast of the beast.

"A life was once sold for *thirty* pieces of silver," growls a voice at the door "surely a man in bat drag needs at least *four* pieces of silver to be saved, if saved he can be." He swaggers to the bat, "I have a Walking Liberty silver dollar, and just like Ben," he elbows him aside "I know *exactly* where it goes." He stoops, rests a finger and thumb on the chest of the bat, then touches the head, sensing a moment. He looks up and announces, "The bat has a heartbeat and *very* slow brainwave activity. I think it is safe for you to remove your silver *sabaton* from this insensate creature while I place my guard on it." He edges Jacob's foot away; "and change into your regular clothes please."

"It's always a pleasure when you arrive, Luke." Jacob replies stepping back into bib overalls, chambray shirt and work boots, then bends to watch what Luke does.

"Counselor, I'm moving your silver eagle to put the Walking Liberty on the bat's breast. Lady Liberty *ought* to infuse the heart of the beast with the truth that liberty's light is an innate right of every being." That done, he carefully places the silver eagle in its new place and Jacob exclaims: "Oh, son, that is *just* wrong!" Luke giggles light bright delight as he coils up and away from his mission.

"Jacob, what's Luke done with my silver eagle?" Counselor queries cautiously.

"He put it *face down* on the bat's groin."

"Oh. *Ouch!* It's enough to inspire a man to compassion for the man when he is conscious again." Casting the sentiment indifferently aside he asks "Will he shift shape before he comes to again?"

"Probably. Usually, and, as his body returns to the size of a man, the coins grow with him." Jacob shrugs, "it's something in the magic of Michael that I do not fathom."

"Oh." Counselor nods knowingly, "the magic of Michael. I should have known. Remind me to never give you reason to be fractious with me, Jacob." Turning a sharp eye to Luke, Counselor adds "as for you, *Light Bearer*, you have a *shockingly* dark side to you for one so young." Luke bobs a bow with an affable grin and takes a chair in the circle while Counselor bites a cheek to check a chortle.

Pain Eater

"Here come the Daughters now" Doc crows the rising light.

"Led by my lovely wife in her fine regalia," beams Counselor in obvious admiration.

"May I always cherish my Hester as you obviously do your mate, Counselor," Jacob declares.

"May you always be sane enough to give praise *for*, and *to*, your mate, Jacob," Counselor counsels.

"May I always be in awe of your wisdom," Jacob counters with a puckish grin as the ringing and singing of dulcet voices fills and cheers the room and stills all sidebars.

Hester neither leads nor follows. She enters the common room sweeping her eyes to see the silver studded bat, the crumpled clothes, and the woman rising in round eyed recognition from a chair between Doc and Counselor. She bears a distinctive two-hole mark in the curve of her neck over the carotid artery. Hester swallows a cry as her world implodes into the time her untainted sense of self was assaulted, desecrated, and left abandoned without hope. Surrendering herself she consciously expands awareness to embrace only the two of them. She knows two are needed to forgive and two to heal the separation from Source that enables one to feed on the life energy of another. *Two to do the sin, two to heal it.* It is her final thought before yielding to a higher power that flows and heals through her. Fixing eyes on the woman, she lifts a hand to touch two fingers by the paired scars over her carotid artery in the place where enflamed punctures leach color and life from the woman.

The woman shakes her head, yet hope rises like the first dawn on the first day. She breathes "how?" She yields her passion to know endings, and gives an unconditional yes. She *just* let go. Hester reads the silent question and responds by opening her heart to receive the pain shackling the spirit of the bowed one, and time is suspended for she has slipped mortal bonds and fallen headlong into the infinite and eternal space between the formless and the formed. *Thy will be done* her heart sings. *Thy will be done through me.* Joy uplifts her as time twists and warps and does not behave well at all. No one minds for all know that when one is healed all are whole for all are one when all is done.

Pain punches Hester with the force of a blow as the cocoa woman falls boneless to the floor. She chuffs out air, then in greedy gasps inhales, force feeding oxygen to her body, mind, and brain. She exhales a soft slow sigh, eyes lancing into those of the fallen woman willing her strength and courage and hope and hope and hope. Tears flow but neither knows who first cries, who first dies, who first lives again, who finds Lazarus fresh awake, stiff still and awkward from being too long dead and separate from Source.

Lazarus is not the only *one who can be resurrected and live anew. The promise is given* through *him even as it was given* to *him.* The bowed woman hears Truth Words for the first time and inhaling with Hester fills her lungs gently full with oxygen. She holds the air while blood delivers the breath of life through her body brain and mind. A smile plays on her lips knowing her resurrected self is *outrageously,* unexpectedly, and brilliantly gifted *to be* the amazing self she sees in the eyes of the woman lifting her up on love across an infinite realm of time.

Hester pulls the breath of life to fill her lungs and bronchia to capacity. She relishes the self-induced euphoria of an oxygen high and holds for a count of ten. Pumping breath like thunder through her heart Hester fires the power of love turning it to molten liquid life light and joy. Exhaling to a count of ten she allows pain to flow and resolve to its level in the purifying passion of love. *Thy will be done,* she gasps a greedy gulp of air directing it to her heart to fuel passion knowing, loving, surrendering to what comes. On inspiration, she touches her chest above her heart. She is startled to feel the shape and texture of a felt rose its petals arrayed like an open tea rose. Her eyes round large. She smiles at what cannot be yet is. Fingering petals she turns them knowing they reshape into the upright American Beauty rose.

"Breathe," Doc softly coaches the woman, "inhale deep, hold, exhale slow, relax, do it again three times, breathe deep, hold, exhale slow, relax. Pant now like a dog fresh from a run, pant, pant, pant," Doc chants a new rhythm of life song from before time began and the woman loses herself to the pant chant and returns to at-One-ment with the Source. Hope springs eternal, but faith is a power to be earned, learned, and won. No word is spoken, yet the woman hears Hester's gentle asking when and why she accepted herself as slave. Shocked, the woman defends that she was born a slave. *As was your mother? Yes,* the silent woman replies. *Did your mother think of herself, or behave, as a slave?* The woman blinks at the astute depth and fractal facets of the question. She knows she cannot deny or hide her truth. *No, she never behaved slavishly. She always had the dignity of one born free. If your mother did not behave slavishly but always conducted herself as one born free though owned by another, how* did *you come to deny the truth your mother knew? How did you come to think and behave like a woman enslaved by another?* The woman moans under the unyielding weight of a truth she could not accept, and cannot now deny. *My mother never loved me.* Hester laughs delight, and the woman knows the silliness of what she said. Hester probes *Did you have healthy food to eat, clean clothes to wear, a warm dry place to sleep, a chance to learn things you didn't already know, a safe place to play and friends to play with?* Yes, the woman admits sensing that the freedom she denied was never denied to her. *When did you begin to believe that you were enslaved and powerless? Hard questions, woman, why do you plague me? Why will you not face me when you accuse me of tormenting you? Who* cannot *own power over you when you denied it is yours alone to own and wield? Is your power available to anyone you can project blame on who will not defend themselves? Ouch! You are hard, woman! Facing one equally hard in her self-enforced separation behind which she hides to casts darts of blame for consequences of her choices. I did not choose this!* The woman protests in impotent rage. Hester shrugs calmly: *Passive choice counts. Which brings us back to the question of* when *you denied your own power and began behaving like someone outside of you owns you and determines your fate? You won't let up, will you?* Hester's smile is genuine; *do you choose to be healed and whole? Or do you choose to keep on slavishly allowing others to use the power you freely give daily?* The woman juts her lip petulantly and Hester interjects *Jesus always asked two questions before healing anyone, what were they?* A sullen moment of silence passes, and she replies: *Do you believe you can be healed, and are you willing to be healed.* Hester nods, *Faith, the power of Peter. Will, the power of Matthew. Both men used fear-based power before using it rightly. Like you, Peter revealed faith in* human *power and denied the man he called master. He used his power rightly by stepping from the boat into a stormy sea to walk on the water toward Jesus.*

The woman across from her frowns and says: *But he fell in!* Hester nods. *The storms of life often drop faith filled people into the hard, liquid reality of life in physical form. Is that what happened to you?* The woman pauses then sighs: *If*

I ever had that much faith, then yes, that is what happened to me. Hester cocks a grin, *perhaps your faith was not invested in a higher power, but really was an outwardly safe dependency on the humans you thought owned you.* The cocoa woman will not meet her eyes. Hester continues her silent lesson: *Matthew was a tax collector. It worked well for him by physical measures, yet he willingly chose to give that up to follow the master. Right use of will led him to riches on spiritual and material planes. Can you surrender your false security in dependence on physical world sources, yield yourself to a higher power, and have faith in the promised rewards of that? What security have I? Someone else to be responsible, someone* else *to blame, the false sense of security of dependency. What do you know, you white faced judge, thinking you can put me down because you are whiter than me!* Hester studies the woman, then opts to answer her security question, but not the white bias charge: *You have the word of the Most High God. The same security Peter and Matthew had when faced with the choice of reality bites or taking a leap of faith.* Extending a hand Hester invites: *Come, step out of the boat you built to keep yourself safe. Leave the false security of the pretenses you submitted to and receive the promise of a better future, even if you don't know what it feels like to* be *free or be full to overflowing with peace and joy.*

The woman discharges the pains, slights and assaults of a life no longer part of who she is, and wills herself to stand firm and tall. "You have been kind and I thank you, but you must stop."

"Stop?" Hester blinks, refocusing her eyes to see the woman in her physical form again.

"Yes, stop. I tried to block the pain you took. I sent mean thoughts to you about you." She huffs crossly "that did as much good as dropping a rock in a river; the pain flowed right around it. You are a *Pain Eater*," her face crumples for being freely given more than she can receive.

Hester smiles serenely "I am that, I Am." Then she frowns puzzled, "Why do you weep?"

"What you eat you *become*!" The woman cries, "You *must not* do this, you must stop *now*!"

Hester nooses a giggle into a small smile, lays her hands over her heart, and says "watch this." Gently opening her hands like wings around her heart she invites "follow the flow of your pain, and see what becomes of it here," she taps her chest alive with heart center energy. Many in the room know what the woman sees, and watch her charting her path through the implausible sight of an enflamed joyous heart encompassed in a nimbus of light, willing to freely give any essential assist. The woman's instincts are true and guided, she gasps, then pants like a dog fresh from a run. She does not look away nor take reprieve from the terrible tender anguish but inhales a breath of longing as purified liquid pain pours into her heart and shapes and forms into dazzling crystals of astonishing color, cut, clarity and size. Seeing the jewels formed from pain in Hester's heart, the woman sanctions her own cauterizing agony and intuitively eases the pain in the man bat craving freedom to enslave. *How small, powerless, gutless, helpless, angry and hopeless he must be to sink so low. Thank you, God, that his has not been* my *fate for all my failings, fears, faults and frailty. Use me. Use me as you will. Use me.*

After an eternity of healing the woman sighs *"I want to do that."* Her words are longing, surrender, a dropping of defenses, a willing yielding to a higher purer power seldom known on the physical plane in body, mind, and brain of man. "Will you teach me?" she prays pleas into Hester's eyes.

Hester laughs surprised delight. "You already know how to be a Pain Eater. You are one. You have not accepted that yet, but owning that truth is all you lack."

"*I* am a Pain Eater?"

"You are that," Hester nods an assuring grin. "Touch the mark on your neck."

The woman obeys, blinks doubt, and jerks her fingers away to see the tips not red wet but only clean dry skin. She touches again softly exploring the healed dry scars like those on Hester's neck. Tears sting her eyes, "Does that mean *I* can eat pain and it turns into jewels in my heart, like happened in yours?"

Hester nods, "I'm sure of it. Would you like to try?" The woman kicks a fear habit and nods. "Ben," she smiles the name "will you come to me please?" Ben obliges, albeit suspiciously wary. Hester adds as Ben approaches, "As you see from his uniform, Ben is our peace keeper." She tucks a hand in his elbow. "Keeping the peace is surprisingly more challenging than enforcing the law. Keeping peace means Ben eats a *great* deal of pain doing his work effectively." She smiles fondly at Ben, "I think he is mostly unaware of the pain he eats to find and forge peaceful outcomes. If Ben agrees, are you willing to try your hand, and your heart, at absorbing the pain of another?"

The woman looks at Ben who grins, shrugs, nods anxious ambiguity, and a querulous *heh, heh, heh.* She grins and confesses, "I don't know what I'm doing either, Sheriff, if that's any comfort to you." Ben nods, she bites her lip, and casts a quick plea to Hester. "Will you stand by me? To support me?" Smiling, Hester quickly moves to stand by the woman facing Ben.

Ben chuckles uneasily "I'm feeling a *little* alone here right now."

"I'll stand by you, Ben" calls a sweet voice borne on the nimble step of a natural dancer gliding to Ben's side to slip a hand under his elbow, smile up at him, and say "I'll stay right by your side."

Tipping back his head, Ben chortles, "I don't know if I'm more comforted, or more challenged by that."

The dancer grins, "It'll be fun finding out, won't it? Pay attention. I want you to tell me *exactly* what it feels like to have your pain eaten." Ben cocks a dubious brow at the dancer, then turns toward the woman willing to eat his pain. Hester steps behind her placing her left hand on her spine level with her heart, her right hand on the woman's right shoulder. Inhaling fully, she slips into a trance to guide and feel the woman follow her there. As one the two inhale and exhale to ten heartbeats.

Those watching see the woman raise up in power, trusting Source to guide her in its correct use. As she exhales, they see her heart open to reveal its true passion and welcome it home. As one, they feel pain ease and flow, and as one, experience resolution and restoration in the crucible of love, each holding fast to the essential truth of wholeness in body mind and spirit.

The dancer feels and yields to Ben's surrender and the melting closure that weeps from him. With him she receives the reviving breath, the measured treasured exhale, and the uprightness of body with the next breath of air. He bows chin to chest surrendering will and yielding to Spirit to release his burdens while time stands still to watch the silent prayer play with vital vigilance.

To Ben, each pain tormenting him is at once alien and as familiar as a twin, as fully known as another self, as true his own breath and the body that breathes it. At times pain racks him 'til he thinks his body will rip to sundered shreds as repairable as Humpty's shattered shell. All the while a guardian voice chants: *Breathe, breathe, breathe, all is well, all is worthy, all is whole, breathe, only inhale, and exhale.*

In the way a coming storm changes temperature by tens of degrees in seconds, Ben's pain cools to be a strong element in his blood as health returns to his body/mind/brain. He breathes in the giddy glad gratitude of irrational joy. Opening dewed eyes, he gives thanks into the ones across the circle.

The woman blinks "I did it," she whispers amazed. "I ate his pain." The statement is like a question. "I am *stronger* than I was before," she crows her joy. I *am* a healer!" she sings sweet surrender, "I didn't know that about me before;" she smiles serenely. "Now I know who I Am."

"Part of it, dear heart, only part of it, there is more for you to learn, accept, master and know," Hester assures stepping around to embrace her with a mother sister smile. *I'm a pain eater!* The woman mouths into Hester's ear and the two of them share a coming home joy laugh.

Shawn Gallaway – The Light of the Flame

Fight Dance

"Well, bat man is a dud for entertainment value," grumbles a dancer toeing the static form on the floor. "You *sure* he isn't dead, Luke?" Luke bobs his head in affirmation brows arched in petulant pique. The dancer shrugs, "Let's *do* something then. Let's make something happen while we wait for the dead to arise. Or not," she says with innocent indifference.

"What do you want to do?" Luke asks giving her the attention she craves.

"Fight dance!" She shouts with an infectious cheerleader jump and smile. Some see crepe paper pom-poms fluttering though none are there.

"*Fight* dance?" Ben and Luke harmonize the puzzlement of all.

"Is that anything like the Schottische?" someone asks acting senseless. Some chuckle, and all lean back to watch the theatre of the weird that is certain to play out.

The dancer is pleased with the spontaneously evolving theatre of the strange. "Not like the Schottische at all," she refutes, and gives an impish grin "but it *could* be part of a fight dance if Schottische steps and moves were put into it," she demonstrates, improvising fight steps as she twirls about the circle slapping toes and palms where a shoe might stamp a Schottische step.

"Who wants to learn the fight dance? It's no *fun* dancing alone," she whines winsomely.

"You're making this up as you go, aren't you?" Ben asks circling opposite matching her step and form as she moves. Eying and matching him she clacks imaginary castanets casting them to nearly snare Ben in her web. He shreds the web as she explodes into a back flip to snap up beside him reaching behind to slap the backs of his knees throwing him off balance, and with an impish grin nimbly back flips away.

"Okay, I'm getting the hang of this. I see how it works," Ben chuckles his signature *heh, heh, heh,* "All I have to do is stay on the *other* side of the room from you two and I'll be fine."

"Will that work for you" She coos from behind him light-fingering his handcuffs from his belt clip, "do you think?" she grins jingling the cuffs in his face.

"How do you *do* that?" He growls.

"The first, and perhaps the *only,* rule of Fight Dance is always keep them guessing, unsuspecting, surprised and off guard. Do you want to participate in this dance, or is complaining enough for you?"

"Sure," Ben snaps, snatching his cuffs away, "I'm teachable," he shrugs, "and I got some time." She twirls around him slapping the bottom of his baton with the sole of a foot so it leaps from its holder at his waist to arch over his shoulder where he catches it in gape jawed astonishment.

"You won't be needing that," the dancer smiles, pushing him to his chair. "Leave the gun, the handcuffs, the knife, *and* the shoes under your chair. E*veryone*, make the circle bigger so the ladies can sit too, *or*," she entices, "can join the dance."

"If you show me how to get Ben out of his weapons," the dancer's young sister coos as she glides into the ring, "you can teach me *anything* else you want, Sister dear."

Luke clears his throat stepping lightly between the sisters "Start with what makes it a *fight* dance since no *weapons* are allowed, except, it seems, your fast feet and hasty hands." He grins a spin out of reach.

The dancer smiles executing a twirl then lighting fast, extends a shapely leg to clip her sister's knees lifting and rotating her into a full body flip in the air. She lands with a solid "whoop" of ecstatic triumph.

"Okay, that taught *me* how to flip, now teach me how to make someone *else* flip." Her grin is deeply wicked on such an angelic face. "Oh wait," she smirks down at her astonished sister *not* sleeping on the floor by the slumbering bat "I just did that, didn't I?" Her giggle is strangely sinister and oddly infectious.

Luke leads with his toes slinking around the sisters eyeing them with devoted intent and a disarming smile. "Tell me about the fight dance, and since it is a dance, where's the fight? If it's a fight, where's the dance? And perhaps most important of all, "who leads?" He circles and spins to, with, and around the girls whirling one into the other in the grace of their improvised response. Smiling the light he bears, he thinks: *what fun if we all lead and follow, all for the joy of sharing with no expectation except to discover infinite opportunities for unexpected expressions of Truth that all is One Infinite and Expanding Whole, Wholly, Holy, and Here, and Now! It is good I don't talk out loud much.*

The sisters mirror and move counterpoint with Luke and with each other and are aware as one when Jacob steps back into the swirling circle, moving with and challenging all of them "if the fight dance is a competition, what is its purpose? What's the objective? What's the prize? If our only goal is to show muscle and style and form, that is *far* too easy, we'd be bored before the hour is up. "What we need is a challenge, a goal, an objective to stretch us and to keep us engaged, here's what I propose."

He circles them like a kindly interrogator, playing the drama to the audience as he engages each in his play of powerful grace subtly enticing them into the circle. He grins bright delight, "By ancient Inca tradition the winner of every competition is *honor bound* to teach and train those he has defeated until each can stand against him as his equal. Teaching and learning would make this fight dance of yours a pastime worth doing, watching, *and* deserving of the time taken in doing it."

"You are such a pot stirrer, Jacob. What can you add to the fight dance idea that makes it an enjoyable pastime – other than hot air?" a watcher poses.

Jacob shrugs a grin, "I don't know yet, I don't know the rules, or even if there are any. My bet is on the Inca having rules, watchers, and trainers, all we got so far is words, and some appealing dance moves."

The dancer huffs again, "then I shall be forced to teach you the toe slap dance."

"Oh, I am *so* in for that" cries the sister dashing to her side.

In the toe slap instant, the bat shifts into his human form. "Oh look, the man in the bat is back," a sister observes. "Fortunately, its skinny naked body is tucked in the natal position so we can't see it." She studies the bat with a frown. "That silver eagle laid where it was before the shift might cause a body to curl into that protective pose." She nudges the man with a toe as her sister had done the bat. "It's still breathing," she observes, "and that is *still* all that can be said for its entertainment value."

The wall clock strikes two chimes. "Time's a passing," Jacob grumbles, "who's going to tell us what this fight dance looks like?" He claps his hands like a coach hustling his players to attention and focus, "what are the rules, what does it take to win, are there teams or is it every player for *her*self, are there style points, are you making this up as you go?" He demands of the dancer.

She grins, not apologetically, and shrugs, "well…, *yeah*! Everyone's sitting here like a bump on a log and that's as entertaining as watching a bat nap. I thought bats hung upside down in caves to sleep."

Jacob winks an evil grin "I think the man didn't expect to be unconscious just now, and his long sleep is *no* reason for you to propose something *just* as dull to pass time until he wakes up."

"Jacob, Jacob, Jacob," Ben intervenes, "in addition to rules, every good game needs at least two teams, some good players, some fair referees, a bunch of enthusiastic fans, and *few* critics.

"You obviously are not a player, nor a referee, nor even a fan, you, my friend, are a critic. You belong on the sidelines," he prods Jacob into a chair, "where you can be as cantankerous as you please."

The circle erupts in hoots of laughter.

"Sit. Stay." Ben orders turning back to the dance.

"Okay, we had some good action going before our resident critic gave his review, let's make this fight dance competition worth watching and doing. "You, dancer, what are your favorite elements of a dance competition?" Caught off guard the dancer gapes drop jawed. "If you've lost your tongue, *show* us!

"Come, little sister, your elder needs vision. Show us what you can do while she evolves beyond the mouth-breathing stage." Ben ducks a toe slap to the head and is bumped off sides by the swinging hip of the slinking sister. *"He, he, he"*, he chortles triangulating himself between the girls.

"Luke, you showed us some good moves, is that all you got?" Ben provokes. "If so, go nap by the man in bat drag. You can be as dull as dirt there." He scarcely dodges Luke's jump kick to his head. Luke spins away to hook Ben's ankle and flip him airborne again. "Great *move*, Luke! What else you got?" Ben goads landing in a flat-footed, knees slightly cocked stance, ready for what comes next.

Shawn Gallaway – We Dance

On a silent cue the sisters' dance in to separate the men mischievously inciting their competitive routine and introducing their own gymnastic gyrations to the evolving dance. Musicians among them improvise a driving beat, lilting tune, and sublime harmony to inspire the dance and the dancers. Wise elders watch and give points for style, originality and performance perfection. Soon the circle is filled with leaping, weaving, thrusting, pulling, shoving, tumbling, spinning, jumping, and laughing youths who break out to watch, cheer and take a breather while choreographing new moves for the dance of cosmic silliness before returning to the sphere of jubilant gyration. None recalls laughing so deeply and well for as long as they remember, and all cherish this time as a favorite memory for as long as they live.

The Awakening

The chirping cries of a bat issue from the unmoving man in the natal position drawing eyes to the still form. Softly the twittering sounds evolve into tormented moans from a human throat that grow louder as the weight of the silver presses and burns. "What have you done to me?" the searing man wails.

Doc leans back in his chair extending the soles of his feet to the man, "why son, we have given you one more chance to answer Jacob's question and tell all of us how one man can own another human."

The man moans "we've been through that and you took the word a slave over that of a free white man."

"Huh! You don't *look* free to me," Ben observes caustically.

"I *mean* I am not a slave, you dolt."

"'Dolt', I haven't heard *that* discouraging word since I was knee-high to a grasshopper." Grinning amiably into the face of the prone man, Ben sing-songs "sticks and stones may break my bones, but words will never harm me."

Seeing a human face shift to the face of evil is a disturbing demonstration. The hissed words of the prone man are more unsettling still "your laughter is a sign of your *ignorance*."

"Well *that* was plumb mean," Ben pulls back with a grumble, "and me just trying to add a bit of levity to this *unfortunate* situation."

"There is nothing funny about this situation," the man snaps."

Eyeing the naked man livid with poorly contained rage Ben nods amiably and observes "that is a matter of perspective, son. From the angle of *my ignorance* the situation in which you find yourself, captured as a bat, allowed to shift to human form, pinned to a dusty floor by silver coins, and on top of that your impotent bullying, well, son, that is just plain rib-tickling *ri-dic-ulous*."

The pinned man growls "if I could get up, I'd…."

Ben's brows arch expressively, "*bite me?*" he growls. The man looks away with a sullen scowl as Ben's eyes narrow to a hard line. Reaching into a shirt pocket he pulls something out letting it drop into his palm, "I've carried a token for most of my career thinking someday I'd find someone I'd want to give it to. Today's my day, and you're my man." He tosses the thing so it lands lightly on the man's shoulder.

The man yelps and writhes away and the token falls to the floor beside him, "a silver bullet," he shrieks, "you insensitive *brute!*"

"*This* from a man who enslaves and feeds on the life blood of *another*? It is plum hard to feel fairly judged by a man like you." Ben stalks to the prone man who flinches away. "I'll have my Lone Ranger silver bullet back since you *obviously* have no appreciation for the finer things in life."

The silver studded man eyes the faces in the circle and finds them relaxed, alert, aware, and fully present without expectation or judgment. There is one outcome they anticipate and await. This is chilling to the man whose key talents are manipulation and control. *They have no stake in this, not* one *of them. Yet there is an outcome they will have, and will accept no other.* It rankles him, these nobodies without status, entitlement or authority binding him, and deciding his fate with meticulous, merciless compassion. In face of the steadfast serenity he centers his considerable focus on life, liberty and the pursuit of freedom. Happiness, he has never known and discounts it as of little value.

Across the room an awakening sense of self-determination shreds habitual bonds of submission in the consciousness of the cocoa woman leaving her in a disconcerting clarity that she was *always* free to choose her own fate and thus to bear the consequences. Freedom and fate war in her as fierce as mythical dragons each bound till death to oppose the other. The winged serpents swoop, swirl, and spit fire, each intent on annihilation of the other and of all she knows and believes until the space of her is too narrow to contain their conflict. She feels herself hurled into a void beyond space and time. Doc senses her absence though she sits beside him still.

He reaches to support her and she yelps suddenly elevated on an impossible trajectory from her chair, her left foot rides something unseen and her arms propel her in pursuit of elusive equilibrium. All of them feel the jolt of balance as her right foot is supported and she rises like a shot through the roof newly supplanted by infinity and its eternally spirited silence.

"Dragons…," comes an awed whisper.

"Who are you?" The rider in another dimension asks to know.

"Fre," replies the serpent beneath her left foot,

"Edom" says the other.

"What's happening?" The awed woman cries.

"Perspective," breathe the dragons in one word thought. *"You were too close to your small human self to clearly see your options and make a wise choice so we spirited you away."*

"Options?"

"Yes. Fear is a human habit that practically predicts outcomes because fear always precludes options. What was the choice before you when we came for you?"

"Freedom," she pauses pondering, *"or fate."*

"Which would you have chosen?"

She groans *"Fate, I suppose, fear habit. Doubt."*

"Name your doubt," demands one.

"That I can *be free to do what I choose, and to know that I can survive and even thrive on that."*

"Self-doubt." Breathes one, *"Is it possible the man you are with is possessed by the same fear?"* The infinite thrives in timeless silence and the dragons soar, spiral and spin in endless exuberant space beyond time, until the woman owns and allows the truth she denied, and the dragons return her to the chair where she began her quest. Doc lays a comforting hand on her wrist, silently reading her pulse and finding its rhythm and pace curiously more composed than before she left on her wild ride.

"Let the man free," The woman directs and expects it is already done.

"What?" The circle demands as one, all mouths agape.

The woman withdraws behind lowered lids, mourning the blamelessness of slavery and life at the mercy of a mean man. She understands the margins of being owned, she knows how to resist, how to win, and how to survive. "Slavery is not for the slow, the slight, or the submissive," she says. "Only the brave survive slavery." She eyes the man and speaks to the circle, "Look at him. The shackles that bind him are not the silver coins. He sold himself cheap before the Archangel dropped him where he lays."

The man struggles feebly to rise to her level. "Remove the coins," she snaps an order. "And give him his clothes. None deserve to suffer the shame of his nakedness. Especially him."

"Point taken," Luke agrees gathering the worn gaudy garments, dropping beside the man and lightly taking and pocketing the Walking Liberty coin and laying the jacket on the man's chest. The man gulps lungs full of air, his eyes wide with relief, doubt, and something oddly akin to fear. Next Luke removes the buffalo nickels that instantly return to their normal size and weight and flips them to Sheriff Ben. He takes the Silver Eagle quarter, then drapes the trousers over the man's groin and legs and puts the shoes nearby. That done he graciously returns the Silver Eagle to Counselor's palm.

Revelation and Reckoning

When he is dressed again, the man looks at the woman and asks "Did – did you ride two dragons in – in space – like it looked like you did?" The woman nods and the man bobs his head with her, eyes wide. "I was afraid you'd say yes. I hoped you wouldn't. I never saw anything like that, not even on a bender after clearing the glasses after one of the master's shindigs."

"You *drank* the wine his guests left?" the woman asks incredulous. "Never mind. I don't want to know."

The man shrugs indifferently, "it was that or throw it away and that seemed a prissy waste."

The woman eyes him with a perceptive smile. "The master's car, tell me about that." He turns away and she crosses her arms cupping elbows in her hands, posing the patience of Eternity.

"You changed…," he offers an alternate telling.

"The car first. *After* that comes your time to ask questions."

"They didn't find us." He snaps. "I *said* they wouldn't find the safe hole and we'd be okay there."

She frowns at the memory, "did the master or the mistress know about the safe hole?"

He shakes his head no, and adds "I found it the day the lady had me clear out the canning room to make room for the jars of fruit and vegetables harvested that year, and throw out old fruit and vegetables."

She smiles remembrance, "I'm thankful you threw the old food in the direction of the slave quarters. Even old vegetables and fruit in winter are better than none."

"And I thank you that the jars and rings were clean when ye brought them back for the next canning, it saved me a caning. The mistress could be a hard woman at times."

"Civil war..., was there *ever* a war that was civil? And looters on the front porch make even generous folks tightfisted and mean. The mistress was a good kindly woman before the war."

"She was that," the man agrees.

"Could *none* of the family be saved? The girls, the young boy?" The woman implores.

The man shakes his head quickly, "They knew how many were in the family, even the number of servants and slaves; it was dangerous business trying to save *anyone* let alone a whole family."

Her eyes narrow, "*How* did they know how many were in the family?"

"Looters. They kept their liberty by stealing and turning in the ones they stole from. When some of master's horses came up missing from the far pasture, I knew what was coming next. Men stole horses to sell to blue coats, and sold information about plantation owners and their families to carpetbaggers. Hungry people *cannot* be trusted. A son who stayed behind to run the farm was branded a Union man. Neither the yanks nor the Rebs had money to feed hostages, nor the medicine to treat the wounded."

The woman watches him thoughtfully a long while and asks "*why* was no one except me and you in the safe hole big enough for the whole family?"

"Too much risk, I already told you that," the man snaps clam tight closed.

"Too much risk for who?"

"If they'd come and found nobody in the house, they'd have searched first, taken what they wanted, then torched the place, watched while it burned, and shot anyone who ran from the fire. *Everyone* would have died then, is that what you wanted? This way at least you and I lived."

"You and me." Her eyes are clear solemn sad, "The master, his wife and children, the servants and slaves were taken away and everything of value including the contents of master's safe and the lady's jewel case. The safe hole *was big enough to keep them safe too.*"

"I'm telling you the carpetbaggers *knew* how many were in the family, how many slaves, how many horses and cows, if I'd tried to hide the family *we'd* have been at risk even in the safe hole."

"*How* did they know? Carpetbaggers never came that far south before. The master and his family were good people, they cared for the slaves and the servants, the horses and stock animals. That's rare in the slave owning south. Someone turned them in for money. Or freedom." her eyes narrow "Someone who knew when they'd come and had time to hide before they arrived. "Someone who *didn't* tell the raiders about the Rolls Royce and the *one* slave you hid with you. Tell me why you did that."

"I did it for you," he protests peevishly.

"You never did a thing for anybody unless you got paid for it. *Why* did you hide me and no one else?"

"You're like a daughter to me," he says softly serious, "a daughter I never had." He pleads into her eyes and she knows he speaks his truth, and she does not understand nor believe a word of it.

"So, you think it is okay to feed off another human – a *daughter* – so long as you fancy they owe you?"

"No!" He protests, "It's not that at all! I owe *you*."

"*Why?*" She crosses her arms, and waits.

"You were born because of me." He admits in a whisper. A hush falls over the room. Even the wall clock waits without tick or tock for the remainder of the tale. "Before you were born, the master held a posh party and invited plantation owners and families, and an old bachelor that couldn't keep a mate if she was deaf, dumb and blind. I owed him a gambling debt I couldn't pay. The master wouldn't help, said he'd not countenance an employee gambling let alone lend or give them money to pay a gaming debt.

"The man I owned was at the party, horny old devil. He fancied your mother." The woman's eyes and mouth round in silent dread. Heedless of all but himself, the oblivious orator continues "the horny old wolf said he'd forgive the gambling debt on the spot *if* I arranged for him to have time alone with your mother during the gala. I said no, of course; and he threatened me, saying he'd see me in debtor's prison until I rotted unless I did what he wanted. When I hesitated, he vowed to get me fired unless I made the arrangements *that night*. What's a man to do but what a man must do? I told your ma a guest wanted to use the master's study and she needed to go there and make sure the master's papers were locked away and the room well cleaned. She'd cleaned the room that day, as always, and told me the study was spotless and that the master's papers were locked away as was his constant habit. The butler manages house staff so I ordered her to go and wait until I came to get her, which I did not do until the randy wolf returned and gave back my token." He mutters "You were born nine months later."

The woman, eyes round with shock, whispers: "I am the child of *rape*! My mother was raped *because of you*, who had charge of the wellbeing of the servants *and* slaves? Raped by a randy man she hated so you'd be excused of a debt you owed? How *could* you save yourself from the consequences of your ravenous lust for ill-gotten gains by betraying *all* the house slaves to satisfy your venial vile greed?"

"Only her!" the man defends dimly, "None of the other slaves were ever touched."

"*None?*" The woman cries, "Do you imagine no other slave was effected by your betrayal of duty to the master? Can you even *imagine* the other slaves didn't *know* what happened, didn't know when mother began to show that they too were at risk of betrayal by the very person the master entrusted with their well-being? You are a *despicable* human being!" She spins away screeching, "Can I *kill* him?"

Counselor places a calming hand on her arm, "*he* may deserve a quick death, but you do not; and our Sheriff Ben would be duty bound to arrest you for murder, and I, bound to hear your case and sentence you to prison for *premeditated* murder." Counselor allows time for reflection on the facts and evidence, then adds: "It's a hard sentence for you who have been through so much to be content with the sharp slippery pleasure of killing a man who wronged you, and your mother."

Her eyes weep into his, "Mother could never *love* me," she wails, "She could not *be* mother to me. I was an orphan though my mother lived and breathed. The slaves shunned and punished her believing she went willing to the covetous man. She suffered that indignity alone and silent in her shaming."

Sheriff Ben clears his throat calling all eyes away from the stricken woman and to the drifter. "Tell us how it happened that you left your master's service."

Welcoming the relief, the orator reclaims his place at center stage. "Well sir that is a powerful curious tale in itself, and one I'm happy to share with you. As I said before, the carpetbaggers came and looted the house taking the master and his family away. I was able to save myself and this slave girl."

"And the Rolls Royce," Ben adds.

"Yes, the car too."

"Why didn't the carpetbaggers take the master's auto?" The woman probes regaining composure.

His smile is laudatory, "That's because I drove the car to the gully back of the house and covered it with brush so they'd not find it. Those greedy bastards would take that fine auto if they found it."

"Then you knew they were coming and had time to hide the car and prepare yourself?" Ben observes.

"Yes sir, that is a true story, and it was right clever of me if I do say so myself."

"*How* did you know carpetbaggers were coming?" the woman demands.

He pauses before answering, "You may not know it but gambling always involves hard spirits that loosen tongues and one of the gamers said he heard carpetbaggers were coming South looting, killing, and taking anything they could sell for liquor, so I prepared myself for what was to come."

"You prepared yourself by hiding your master's auto?" Ben asks conversationally and the orator nods agreeably, "and by taking the car title and one slave document from the master's safe?"

"Well sir, the way you phrase that is not kindly at all. It is downright unfriendly if you ask me."

"Which I didn't. My question had to do with *intent,* relating to that car outside, and this woman you brought with you who bears *your mark.*" Ben softly hisses the last two words.

"Now see, that's just plain discourteous and judgmental the way you say it."

Ben cocks a brow coldly, "I'm in law enforcement. I'm not paid to be polite when questioning a suspect."

"A suspect? Suspect of *what?*" the orator demands.

"Theft of an automobile, theft of a slave. Selling out your master and his family isn't against the law in this state, but such treachery is reprehensible to good folks everywhere." The orator lowers his eyes but can't hide his unease at the direction the conversation is taking. Watching close by nature and training, Ben observes the orator casting about for an escape route, looking toward the door by which he entered the room. He feels more than sees Jacob's casual vigilance and winces at the thought of Michael's sword. He casts the front door option aside seeking a back exit. For the first time he sees the burly man standing like a wooden statue with a proprietorial air near the counter by the door leading to the back.

"You haven't met Smithy yet, have you?" Ben asks tipping his chair back on two legs. "Smithy is a legend hereabouts because if he hasn't got the part you need, he'll forge it for you and it will fit better than the original. That Rolls need any parts before you take off again?"

Silence resounds. "Since you will not answer my questions, I believe the lady has a question still unanswered. Do her the courtesy of giving her your answers while you consider your options."

"She's no lady," the visitor snaps.

"You don't treat her like one, but that's a whole other measure altogether, and by my lights you are a far piece from measuring up." Ben uprights his chair with a crack that echoes like a shot causing the man to jump anxiously. "Let me refresh your memory, the lady asked why you didn't save the master and his family. She asked what happened to them when the carpetbaggers came and took them away."

"I don't know," the orator sullen snaps.

"You don't know? Or you think it's safer to ignore my question?"

Hester steps to Ben's side laying a calm hand on his shoulder, "perhaps I can be of help Ben." She says pleasantly, then turns to the man. "Tell me about the master's family, were there children?"

Her conversational tone is disarming and the man replies readily, "yes, mam, he had four kids, three girls and a boy, he was right proud of those young ones."

She smiles "how old are they?"

"The boy was nine or ten, I guess, the girls were seven, five, and three, fine looking kids they were."

"You speak of them in past tense, why is that?"

The man starts, "because they were taken away with the master and his lady, I've not seen them since."

She nods "so in your mind they won't have aged in the six months since you left with this woman?"

"Well, yes, mam, they will have aged six months since then."

"What do you suppose happened to the family after they were taken away?"

"The carpetbaggers are beasts of a nasty nature, they'll have sold them as slaves is my guess."

"Slaves?" The cocoa woman gasps, "You sold them into *slavery?*"

"I done no such thing! I ain't responsible for what lawless carpetbaggers do."

Hester rubs her chin thoughtfully and observes: "I notice when you speak to me you use proper English as I imagine a butler at a plantation house might do; but when you speak to this woman you brought with you against her will, you use common language, why is that do you suppose?"

"I – I didn't notice."

Bobbing her head, she observes "yes, I have detected that pattern in people who only respect up and always *dis*respect down." The woman catches Hester's eye and gives her a shrewd smile. Only Hester's eyes smile. She turns to the man in aged brocade. "Why do you think the family will have been sold?"

"They are used to eating well when they're hungry. An army moves on its stomach. The Yanks pay well for fresh food, the greys have nothing but confederate paper," he spits the words. "Soft potatoes with roots are worth more than a whole *box* of confederate money."

"I see you make it a point to be well informed." The man nods eagerly. "You said you thought the family was sold into slavery, who would purchase a family of soft plantation owners as slaves?"

"Uh –well – there are men who like fresh meat, and the master's girls were pretty young things."

"Oh, my poor sweet babies," the woman moans into hands shielding her mouth and leaving her eyes unmasked to clearly see the horror of the man's words and deeds.

Doc eyes the man as he clarifies with fierce candor "not just the girls, dear heart, the boy too."

"No-o-o-o!" She wails a supplication and denial. "No, no, *no!*"

Doc nods his misery "and the mother, and the father as well."

"*No!*" The woman screams. Jumping from her chair she stamps both feet and yells "*can – I - kill - him?*"

"He's not worth it, woman," snaps Counselor taking her arm and pulling her back to the chair indifferent to the tears now staining his jacket.

"Ben," Jacob inserts from across the circle, "maybe you could let him make a break for it and then you can shoot him trying to escape."

Ben grins "tempting, but it's not happening on my watch. Keep the Archangel on alert though."

"Oh, like he *ever* sleeps?" Jacob grumbles grinning eagerly.

Hester rolls her eyes and turns back to the visitor. "Tell us about the car and the one slave you saved, why did you chose to do that?"

"I needed the car, and," he winces "the girl mattered to me, I care about her and her safety."

Hester can't make her brows *not* arch, "*Safety?* To have her blood sucked by a man who stole her, claims to own her, yet calls her *daughter?* It's a curious kindness you offer your kin. How much money did you get for selling the family to the carpetbaggers?"

"What?" The man snaps.

Hester shrugs indifferently, "I'm curious by what motivates a man like you, who claims no integrity nor morality, yet pretends to be a good and thoughtful man. Were you ever an actor?"

"Yes," the man smiles broadly "how did you know?"

Hester's brows bob in surprise, "Mother always said I was psychic," she says dryly, "perhaps that's it."

"Could you tell my future?"

Hester replies in solemn exasperation "I don't think that's a good idea today." A giggle arises in the circle followed by a chortle, then a guffaw and soon the circle is laughing and slapping their knees in glee.

"What's so damned funny" the orator demands red faced.

"You, that's what." The elder sister growls as she rises from her chair to stand before the orator. "Any fool can tell your fortune today and safely predict that you won't like it. Hester's no fool, *fool.*"

"Well I ain't talking to you am I?"

The younger sister blasts from her chair to leap defensively before her elder. "*Don't* speak to my sister like she's a slave!" Her eyes menace, "or I'll *bite you* and I'll spit your blood in your face. You can use your bat tongue to lick it off and *drink it.*" She hisses. "It may be your *last* supper." The orator turns a bilious green before her scalding threat, and searches the circle for a friendly face or a pair of soft eyes.

Finding none and possessed of a consuming passion to be anywhere but here he calls plaintive to a nameless god who, surprisingly, comes to his aid in the form of a dragon sweeping him from his chair and into an infinity beyond the roof of a local Feed and Grain store.

"Well, *whoda* thunk it? *Another* dragon rider!" Settling back in his chair the man says, "Let's give points like this is a rodeo and him a bareback rider."

"He's got no experience riding bareback. I'll give him two minutes, tops before he's dropped in the dirt." Ben growls, "Smithy, when *are* you going to sweep this floor again?"

"When a dang bunch of farmers quit tracking in plow dirt and grain dust, when I ain't busy all day fixing broken parts or forging new ones because your trucks are too old to have replacement parts, when…."

"Okay, okay, Smithy…," Ben grins behind a hand, "don't get your dander up, I'm just asking."

"Smart *ass*-king if you ask me," Smithy growls a surly smirk. He can't hold a grudge, it's not in him.

"I didn't, but thanks for sharing." There is a chortle, a giggle, then a snort, and soon the circle is laughing and hooting until Smithy can do naught but join, his barrel chest blaring like a blast forge. When the circle settles to return to watching the dragon flight, and calling points or penalties but no one keeping score, someone asks: "when you plan to have my transmission repaired so I can drive my truck again?"

"*Repaired*? Your truck is so damn old there are no parts to fix it anymore so I'm having to forge you a whole new transmission. Ya otta just get a new truck," he grumbles sotto voice.

"Hell, I'll do good to pay for the transmission rebuild, let alone a new truck."

"That's what keeps me up nights worrying."

"You got a *forge*?" The woman asks short-circuiting the staple squabble.

Smithy looks around the circle for the voice and finds it in the face and eager eyes of the cocoa woman. "Course I got a forge, that's why I'm called 'Smithy.' I had a real name once, but I plumb forgot it. Why do you ask?" he gazes into the eyes of the woman and gives free rein to his puzzled curiosity.

"Do you think…, I mean, could I…?"

"Spit it out, woman," he says with feigned vexation.

"Do you think I could make glass in your forge?" she asks in a rush of words.

"*Glass*? Why on Gods earth would you want to make something as common as glass?"

The woman flushes lowering her eyes timidly, then inhales and raises bold eyes to meet his. "Because I want to make beautiful things out of glass, and I need a kiln to do it." Her lip juts determinedly.

Smithy's curiosity flares like a heated forge and he asks as calmly as possible, "*why?*"

The woman blinks puzzlement and has no reply. Smithy shrugs contorting his face into perplexity, then rephrases his question "*what* do you want to make in glass?"

"Beautiful things – I already told you that!"

Smithy's head bobs and his eyes round wide. "What *kind* of beautiful things do you want to make?"

"Oh," again she is without words to speak her dreams. Her face wilts, her eyes well for the weight of an idea that will not be cramped into words. "Have you any shop paper?" She asks instead.

"*Shop paper?*" Smithy echoes baffled.

"Yeah," she frowns, "brown paper you wrap things in when you sell them."

"Of course, I do, there's a roll of it behind the counter." She beams a smile, jumps from her chair to dash behind the counter. "Did you *ask* if you could use some of my shop paper and I missed that?" He scratches the back of his neck to hide his mischievous grin.

He hears the woman's hands plop on the counter. "Can I *please* use some of your paper, Smithy?"

"Sure, how much you need? And what do you need it for?"

"I don't *know* how much I will need. I already told you I will use it to draw things I can't say in words."

Smithy's eyes round and his brows raise. "Oh," he says to a circle of grinning curious faces. "Reckon you'll be done by the time the stranger returns from his dragon ride?" he wonders.

"I don't know. Why, does it matter? You got some charcoal?"

"*Charcoal?* I got a forge, woman, of course I got charcoal."

"Would you show me where it is?" Smithy laughs the way a father might at a trying daughter asking too many questions without answers. Rising he passes the counter waiving a brawny hand to the woman and hears her scampering after him. "*Daughter, whoda thunk it? And me without a wife.*"

"I reckon you'll wants sticks of charcoal if you'll be drawing things that can't be explained." She arches a brow and tilts a grin. "I reckon you'll want hardwood charcoal so it won't break unless you want it to. You know how to tell hardwood charcoal from soft wood, like cottonwood?"

"I sure do," she replies studying the charcoal sticks "hardwood burns slower than soft wood and is more black than grey like soft wood is," she says fingering a grey stick that powders at her touch. She then touches a black stick and picks it up with a brilliant smile. "This will do for now."

Smithy reaches into the ash pile to pick out more black sticks tucking them into a paper bag and handing her the bag. "Just in case you have a *lot* of things you can't tell but can draw." His eyes twinkle fatherly.

Her smile is brilliant, "Thank you, Smithy, you're the best!" Raising to her toes she plants a kiss on his cheek and turns away quick so as not to see him blush. "Ready?" she asks pulling him along in her excitement to draw imagined beautiful things. "How about chalk, you got chalk?"

I might just follow you anywhere you lead, Smithy grins, then laughs and says "I got chalk too." Back inside the girl woman scampers behind the counter and begins slashing flowing curving lines on the shop paper and totally surrendering herself to the heart, and to the art of creation.

Curious at her focus, the Regaliaed One rises and walks softly to the counter to see what she draws with such power and purpose. Despite herself she sighs a smile disturbing the woman who stops mid stroke to look at her. "Oh, I'm sorry. I didn't mean to disturb you, but this is stunning. I couldn't contain myself. Finish dear, please finish. "May I watch if I promise to remain absolutely silent?"

Across the room, Counselor chortles, "My darling wife, I completely believe that it is utterly impossible for you to remain silent for any length of time. You even sleep out loud."

"Oh hush! Telling bedroom tales in public, shame on you." Though her tone is severe she makes no effort to hide her grin of shared pleasure with her husband. "Wait until you see the birthday gift you will give to me." Turning back to the woman she asks "you *can* make this in crystal can you not?"

The woman grins. "I can *if* Smithy will let me use his forge to make glass and blow the pitcher, will you, Smithy?"

"That I will," Smithy agrees readily. "You *do* know how to use a forge don't you?"

"I sure do, Smithy, and before you ask, I know what I'll need to make glass, all of which is easily found, sand, soda, and ash, the ash can come from your forge."

She gives him an impish grin, "Can I have some of your *ash*, Smithy?" The room erupts in glee as Smithy's face reddens but not from laughter alone.

"Let me introduce myself," the watching woman smiles, "I am the Regaliaed One."

The woman blinks doubtful and says, "Your *name* is *Regaliaed One*?"

"Yes, dear. You would have to know my dear departed mother to understand such a curious name. It's not worth telling. Call me RO, like everyone else does." Touching a corner of the page, RO asks "may I?"

"Not yet," the woman blocks her hand, "it isn't finished." She smiles caressing chalk onto the paper pulling highlights on the round bowl and pouting the lip of the pitcher.

When she has finished fixing and refining and defining her drawing, she nods. RO takes the page, turns to walk to Counselor calling joyfully, "Look, darling, at the birthday gift you will give to me."

Counselor studies the charcoal and chalk drawing for a long while and the woman holds her breath through the silence. "That is exquisite in its gracefully simple lines. It is no wonder to me that you like it, but my dearest RO, can you lift and pour from a crystal pitcher filled with your luscious lemonade?"

RO strokes his cheek fondly "well, darling, if it's too heavy for me, then you will pour, won't you?"

Counselor smiles up at her "I would walk to hell and back for you my dearest," he says with an open-faced grin. "Yes! I will pour for you. And I will pour making certain that each guest has a clear view of your exquisite pitcher. They will be as envious of your birthday gift as they already are of your luscious lemonade." Hearts soften in the circle seeing the unabashed affection shared between the couple. Each silently pledges to love their mate with more genuine warmth and good humor.

"I must see the drawing" Hester says rising from her chair to step behind Counselor and peer over his shoulder. She is soon joined by others who also do not speak but smile in silent wonder.

"Pass it around so all of us can see" demands a sitter.

"No *way* is that happening!" RO replies. "It's drawn in charcoal and chalk. If someone blurs even one line or shadow I will have their head on a platter." She grins cheekily, "just like Salomé.

"I'll bring the drawing around so everyone can see."

As RO steps away with the drawing, Counselor rises and walks to the counter. He leans across to whisper: "What you have created with charcoal and chalk on paper is not only functional, it is art. I will set your expectations by paying you the price of art for RO's pitcher. The piece is utilitarian, and your work *will* command the price of art. Thereafter, I will teach and coach you so that *all* of your glasswork is sold for the value of art. When you complete this piece, I will commission RO's birthday gift."

The woman stares at him openmouthed. Fatherly now, he pats her arm, "The next thing you make for RO will be even more priceless," he breathes, "It's a thing she's wanted a long time and could not find. It will be a one of a kind."

His eyes follow RO with an adoring light, then turn back to the silent woman to add, "RO had no way before today to have her vision made manifest.

You can do that, and as God is my witness you will be paid its worth. Even if I have to work another decade to keep my word to you." He grins and pats her hand, "It is already done."

As Counselor returns to his chair, Smithy hears the woman pull another sheet of paper from his role and smiles a heartfelt smile. *Who'd a thunk I'd probably have a profitable glass forge instead of a make-ends- meet metal forge? The wonders of the Lord never cease.*

Return of the Dragon Rider

Amid the milling circle of friends, the orator plops unceremoniously to the floor from where fell, puffing mighty bellows of air into and out of his lungs.

"That was quite a ride you took there, fellow." Ben comments, "For a while I thought you'd fall plumb off that dragon and be lost in space forever. Catch your breath and tell us about your ride." Eagerly the milling group returns to their chairs and settles in again, expectant eyes fixed on the returned rider.

"Well, sirs and ladies; that was indeed a unique experience and one I fondly hope never to again have."

"Was it bad?" the cocoa woman asks, concern gentle in her voice.

The orator studies the one he cruelly used and sees nothing but sincerity. He shakes his head smiling. "Only at first when I was hanging on for dear life and knew that dire dragon was doing all in its daunting power to unseat me and ditch me forever on some god forsaken planet. Which he did do, in fact.

"The first sunrise on that petite plain planet, the dragon chastised me right proper for abusing animals *so callously. His* words. I defended myself for I was the master's horse trainer, many of his horses won championships, and brought extra income from stud fees. The master had an eye for spirit power in horses; that he did. I was an important part of his success.

Well that dragon filled its lungs, I feared, to shoot flames at me and burn me to a carbon crisp. Instead, he just thundered at me. Have you any idea what a roaring dragon *sounds like* in deep space? My ears hurt just thinking about that bellowing voice. My heart pains me remembering the lecture he delivered into my face at blow your hair back force and power. That daunting dragon *demanded* to know whether I had trained the master's horses with *equal* insensitivity to the body, *mind* and hide of the animal or if I had somehow, simply forgotten how to be sensitive to other living creatures than horses. Singed my hair ends it did, gave me a dark leathery tan in seconds. The dragon demanded I say honest and true if the only thing that mattered to me was the way *my training* showed up in the obedient body and mind of the animal; and, well, it was.

"If something else mattered to me, the dragon demanded that I name what it was, and why it counted for me. Well that got my back bowed up and I informed the beast I was one of the *best* horse trainers the South ever produced. Thought I was bragging that dragon did, demanded I prove it. That set me to thinking about some of the horses I'd trained and recollecting the ways I talked to a new horse while I fed, petted, admired, exercised, groomed and curried it. I'd tell the horse all the amazing and lovely things I saw in it, and when they were preening and proud and eager, I'd set them to a run or another task to test and prove the speed, grace and pace.

I did the same with the dragon as I talked, and soon enough all its scales were unruffled. I threw an arm over the dragons back while I told of doing the same to a horse to let the animal experience and practice the new and strange in a safe way. I scratched it soft where muscles connect, palming over the smooth shining hide and the long muscle of the legs; and just when I thought the dragon and I were bonding, real snotty like, that demon dragon demands to know how I can make such claims having torn a *dozen* of his finest scales from his back and shoulders. When he let me on his back again I did see not *one* damaged or dislocated scale on the bitter beast. He'd made his point though. And I proved mine or I'd not have been allowed on his back. *Fine* beast that one is, scales the color of morning sunshine and moss in a deep clear pond, with eyes of red and gold.

"What they say about dragons spitting fire from their mouths, I never saw that, though his eyes spit fire that burned through my heart and down into the very roots of my soul. Made me weep. When the dragon saw my tears, it gentled a bit and demanded I tell *how* I could tame horses to reins, saddle and rider, yet could not ride a dragon without ruining its *fine precious* scales.

"Well you don't have a saddle, or reins that I can see," I snapped back defensive and just as snotty.

"Oh, like you'd have *noticed* anything but yourself?" the dragon snarled. That took me plum aback. I was speechless for the first time in my life. "*How?*" the beast demanded again, so I told him everything I did with a horse before I ever lay a blanket on its back as gentle and tender as a mother covering a sleeping babe, all the while doing the same with the dragon, whose heart is touched, I can tell.

Now I know dragons have hearts just like every other living breathing thing on God's green Earth, and on other every living planet and star beyond it too. It made me smile, but that wee planet was as cold as hell is hot and my cheeks was plumb froze to ice. So, I talked to the dragon warm and gentle and sweet just like I did the master's horses I trained to ride and race. That dragon took pity on me and puffed up his chest and cheeks, and I thought I was about to be scorched as hard and brittle as a lump of coal. But, that gold and emerald beast puffed warm air on me and my wee planet until rain fell and grass grew and bushes and trees full with fruit hanging ripe and heavy on its branches, and rivers sang and splashed and played in an atmosphere much like other planets close to the sun, all warm and balmy it was.

But not a *hint* of game anywhere on that whole new Earth. Well, folks, I do like the taste and chew of meat so I complained to the dragon that evening. When he came back the next day, and every day thereafter, the dear dragon brought fresh meat of small birds and game, gutted clean as a whistle, and that marvelous monster carried them in its great maw where they baked and broiled to succulent perfection in its juices. Thought I might like to stay there, but the dragon had other plans. I slept on that small paradise for seven nights, and every sunrise the dragon came to set me on an errand for the day and to prove it, I was to bring a token. Each sunset the dragon came for dinner and a chat.

"You weren't gone more than 20 minutes," Ben protests suspiciously.

"True as that may be, sir," the teller grins, "still I spent seven mornings and evenings on that island."

The room silently puzzles the teller's tale against Ben's fine point of time. "You seem to know a bit about the first Book of the Bible," Ben allows. "Tell your tale. There's a storyteller in you, and maybe you don't know that yet." All eyes return to the tale teller.

"Where was I? Oh yes, my first day with, or without, the dragon. We had a nice brunch, fruit, berries, tubers with grains and herbs, and we talked friendly like. Then without so much as an if you please, that brute beast grabbed me up in its claws and flew me up and away, dropping me in a small round boat without sail, mast, oars, or rudder, in the middle of an ocean with no horizon and only a hazy half-light to see by. Of course, there was nothing to see, that being the first day of creation. At sundown, the dragon returned with food, and asked me to tell about my first day and what I'd learned, so I told him about the boat, which bored him *angry*. He seemed to think I was a complaining ingrate."

"*Imagine!*" The woman says politely.

He gives her a narrow look and returns to his tale. "I told of my day, not mentioning the feather; and there was little to tell without the boat and the endless sea in the tale." The teller grins impish, "So I'm making up stuff that might have happened but didn't, to fill up the hours from sunup to sunset, and all the while *not* mentioning the feather. The only interesting thing that did happen. At that moment, the feather poked me in the head in protest for being ignored, or worse, forgotten."

He laughs remembering the dragon's squirming impatience over the forgotten feather. "Unfortunately, I *still* don't know when to leave well enough alone," he can't suppress a giggle. "I baited the dragon until it wanted to bite my head off but there was the feather flashing fascinating contraries in delightful designs and he didn't want to damage the feather. He wanted it as his token of the day, and he wanted my experience of it. He didn't want to bloody it and gross it out!

"I live and breathe solely because I am to *strongly* warn everyone I meet against *ever* baiting a dragon." He shudders a shivering snigger remembering that he got away with *not* giving a token to the dragon and lived to tell the tale of seven sunrises and sunsets with the dragon. "As you know, on the first day, the Creator separated heaven from the earth and divided light from dark. Source made duality that day.

That's it! And he saw it was good *because* without opposites, things don't show up in physical form. All creation was ideated that first day, including that wee boat without oars, sails, or rudder where I found myself adrift on a sea without horizon in an infinite silence that echoed and reverberated with no sound at all. Peace whispers into the omnipresent ear of infinity and the dragon nowhere in sight. Though calm, I had a hazy foreboding of a forgotten mission needing completion by sundown and the niggling notion of a token I am to give the dragon at sunset. Since I had nowhere to go and no way to get there, I set myself to grasping the Divine Idea behind dividing light from dark and the essential duality of energy inhabiting physical form. The very *idea* of life in form invokes duality into creation inspired by the idea. That must be the lesson the master dragon wants me to take from his *already stupid* game of days.

"As I ponder alone and adrift it occurs to me that duality is essential to the physical world but isn't to the Infinite. The infinite has polarity, but not duality. But what's the dragon token if duality is the message of the day? I ask myself and fall into deep thought so focused I don't see the feather dancing, spinning and weaving about and above me and my boat, one half black, one half white each with a dot of the other, one at the top, one at the tip. As the apparently white feather danced and twirled it caught the light of day and the dark of night spinning and swirling the opposites into endlessly shaping possibilities of form, design and delight. *The dragon token*, I think.

At my thought the feather shrank away, a ghostly ghastly ghoul howl of black horror and fright white. I couldn't help myself, I laughed out loud, and that flustered the flighty feather whose India ink black feathered part bled into the white of its pattern."

"Well then," I said to the fuzzy feather, "I see you have *costumes* to fit your mood. You change the pattern with your disposition. I'm curious, what *do* you wear when you decide that you are a simply precious one of a kind creation, you *love* that, and you think it is perfectly true and suits you *just right*? If I could have been in any one of a dozen different universes to see and experience thousands of new and wondrous things, I'd trade them all for watching that feather fluff her stuff in crisp quick mosaics of black and white.

"*Oh* my!" Is all I can say and she is suddenly shy. "You are the most brilliant thing I have ever seen." I'm thinking I'd found the perfect dragon token and I say: "The dragon will love you and prize you as a fluid flawless emblem of the first day of creation when God separated light from darkness. You are light *and darkness* in molten motion, a worthy token for the dragon on the first day of re-creation."

"It's all about you, isn't it?" The feather sniffs turning away and showing mostly her dark side.

"You too," I retort. "You *are* a feather after all. And nothing more than that *if* no one ever sees you to appreciate you *and* your multiple magnificent mutable manifestations."

The feather flutters into other possibilities, then poses pleasantly "where do you suppose your dragon pal might wear me? And do you think he will let me find my *own* place to ride his hide?"

"I think the dragon will let you find your own proud place *so long as* you make him look good at the same time. *This* dragon would wear you proud and display you as art. Dragons live forever you know. It is *good* to have a way to be your most amazing self, and a forever place to show yourself proud." Well, that about settled it for the feather drifted down and corkscrewed itself into a curl of my hair. Yeah, I know my hair has no curl, but then it did, and I'm telling you what happened, nothing more.

At sundown that day the dragon came and we had tea and talked of the day. All the while the dragon is studying the feather in my hair more than listening to me, so I commenced making up words and talking like I had something to say until the dragon caught my eye, raised a brow, and says "You are talking stuff and nonsense; and it offends me deeply that you think I won't notice." He sniffs his snit and thunders "What did you learn today, and where's my token? In that order, if you please."

"On the first day of creation, God called for light and saw that it was good, then God separated the light from the darkness covering the surface of the deep and called the light day and the darkness night. It occurs to me that Spirit, first cause, is without form and is forever integrally whole and therefore *must* have little functional awareness of *being* in a separate habitation the way a human has a sense of being in a physical body. Spirit just is. That is enough.

Except it's *not*. There is no *experience* in beingness, it just is. People *need* things to do, goals to achieve, things they can do to make the world a better place. They need understanding and will to deny habitual responses so better experiences show up in life. That's why Spirit created a shadow self that can face the polarity arising from inhabiting a mind with a conscious awareness of self that is separate from everything 'out there.' Everything is *intrinsically* at-One with Spirit, but man has ego mind that's wholly convinced that it is and forever will be, separate from everything else, including The One That Is.

"My dear dragon, the feather is the token of the day. And, *she* wants to find her own place to adorn your great scaly physique. Are you okay with that?" I demand letting on I wouldn't give it to him if not. It was a dumbfounded dragon that heard those words. The small skull beast could *not* comprehend a thing, anything, wanting to make it beautiful. Dragons may be magical and wise, but they are not smart. Well, finally, after a flighty flirtation by the flying feather, the dragon succumbed and let the feather find its place and enthusiastically welcomed it aboard when she suggested she perch on the ridge above its third eye and swing down before his great eye to show him all the options and both sides of decisions. *I will make you known as the Wise One among dragon kind for you alone shall see what I show to inspire wisdom and understanding in* every *decision, choice and change that comes. And,*" she hisses "*the one before you will see* only *a white fluttering feather; you cynical skeptical* serpent."

The dragon apologizes profusely until the feather appears appeased and takes its place, then popped a few sharp poses, cocked me a brow and asks "*How do I look?*"

"Well, folks, sore tempted I was but I didn't grin or laugh. I wrestled both grin and giggle into a sincere face with a mouth saying in earnest awe: "you look *magnificent!*" The posing dragon freezes, cocks me a brow over a blasé eye and snaps "I *always* look magnificent. How do I look *with* the fabulous feather?"

"Even finer than before, and I *thought* that would be impossible," I said with a sincere straight face.

"*Don't* make that mistake again," the dragon drones dreadful, and I obey then and forevermore.

"The short story is that the dragon got his feather for a token and decided to be simply delighted at the idea of the feather choosing its place of adorning, beautifying and flattering, yes, he liked *all* of that, such a powerful and provocative serpent. Thus, day one ended in peace and happiness.

"The dragon returns the second sunrise and after breakfast, sets the day's task for me, which is to understand and apply the Truth of what God did on the second day of creation, why God did that, and tell how that applies to me and my life, and, oh yes, bring back a token of my day's enlightenment. Then that sinister scaly serpent caught me up in its claws to fly far and fling me into the free-floating coracle on the formless sea midway between never and forever.

On the second day of creation, God separated water from water and set an expanse, between the water above and that below, and he called the low expanse water, and the firmament he called heaven. I could tell the water under my boat was liquid because my boat floated on it and it made my hand wet. I knew the water above was atmosphere, air, because I could breathe it. That got me to thinking that the water below represents the expressed capabilities of the subconscious mind which cannot think, but can ideate.

So, the subconscious mind *needs* the conscious mind to decide on the idea and then to will and declare the word of it, thereby directing the idea to the subconscious where it can evolve and be made manifest. Something like the dragon marinating meat in its maw until it is cooked perfectly for eating.

So, there I was the afternoon of day two with the idea and with no clue of a dragon token. I let that puzzle stew in my mind just like the first day while I had a wee nap in the boat and dreamed that a single drop of water coalesced from the sky above and fell into my boat at my feet. I sat there looking down at that drop of water and I saw an ocean in the drop. It surprised and delighted me and I spent a small eternity lost and contentedly adrift in that ocean in a drop.

"Until that danged dingbat bird came cross and cussing about some feather she lost the day before. Real calm like I ask the bird to describe her lost feather thinking it's a white feather because every feather on her body is white. Sure enough, that dull bird said it was a white feather just like her other ones. I know she lies, but play along to see where she'd lead. I told her true and sincere that I had not seen a white feather before she arrived brilliantly full feathered with the ones she sought after. I said that if she was missing a feather I certainly couldn't tell because she looked perfect and perfectly handsome to me.

"Well that set her to preening, but I could tell something wasn't right with the bird and it wasn't physical, she was *lying* sure and clear. *Why* though? I decided to play her out and ask her to describe the missing feather in detail; and, as a kindness to me, to tell me why she would even want a missing feather back since she was perfectly, stunningly beautiful just as she stood. One more feather, I said, is *redundant*, it would spoil her peerless perfection. She pouted anyway, silly bird. I ask her again to describe the missing feather so I could tell the dragon about it and to tell why she wanted that feather so much. Which she did do, in *dreary* detail, not saying a thing about *anything* but a white feather.

"I was *really* wary now. Enough that I forgot all about the dragon's daily token and pulled my newly narrowed eyes from the gift potential of an ocean in the drop to the cawing bird flying stationary above me. "First, you must describe the feather to me in detail, and then explain to me *why* you are being so *simply rude to me* who never did you one single harm in all the moments you have known me! Well I may as well have hit the bird upside the head with a two by four for she commenced gasping, flapping and squeaky cawing screeching until she plumb run out of wind and fell like a boulder into my wee boat squashing the ocean in a drop, in the way eons of heat and weight and time will do to a diamond. That transformation of substance was hot enough to blast the bird off and into the sky with such force the hot rock dropped from her thigh and into the ocean sinking into the infinite blue.

My dragon token of the day was gone beyond reach and recovery. Dragons don't forget. And they have no functional grasp of linear time. When the dragon came at sunset, he met the mean bird and heard her criticism. The wise wyvern cocked brow, set a cold gold eye on her, and asked why one missing plume was so important to her she'd beard a dragon in its den. The wise wyvern knew she'd lie. And if not lie, at least not tell the truth, nor even drop a hint she knew the changeable nature of her feather.

"The..., the feather is..., um, white, all white." The white bird titters nervous and shakes a wingtip at the feather suspended over dragon's third eye. "Like the one in the middle of your head," she tries not to snap her beak but snap it does.

Dragon eyes up at feather, gives it a private grin and thought whispers *good job*! then turns his wicked eye and a grim grin on the fat foul saying with a sad shake of his head "I'm afraid I can't help you, I have seen no pure white feather such as the one you describe.

"There's one on your *head,* you doltish dragon!" the hot hen retorts, losing her mind and jeopardizing her head in the bargain.

Dragon's eyes narrow and he purrs his in a way that sounds scarily like hissing "*why* do you want *my* feather which you sorely *abused* by dumping your dark angry thoughts and feelings into this *one tiny little feather;* and now you say you want it *back*. Why, so that you can abuse it more than *before?*"

The bird blinks owlishly three times in a futile attempt to process what the dragon said and the effect of it. It doesn't compute. "Oh!" she flaps wings in exasperation, "you don't get it, do you? You myopic monster! What you see as abuse was me *honoring* her among all my feathers by preparing her to live well and prosper in the physical world where she will go, but I will not. Have you *any idea* how long it takes pure-as-the-driven-snow *me* to gather enough negative energy to make even one small dot of black on a feather? Oh, that won't have occurred to you will it, a wee small head on a gigantic body *can't* hold much brain, can it?" The bird is teetering on the edge of insanity lost in the *story* behind her tightly coiled anger and the giddy power of *finally* having a place and an occasion to say it.

Sounding miffed the dragon snaps back "there's no need to be cruel or to say offensive things about someone you never met before." Leaning an elbow on a knee the dragon rests his chin in a paw and invites, "So tell me, why you went to such effort to collect *dark energy?* What will you do with it?"

"Easy for you to ask, you have enough darkness in your small claw to create massive black holes housing *dozens of* eternities." She peeps at the dragon whose jaw still rests in a paw, his maw set in an amused but patient smile, waiting for a reason, watching her feather flash mostly black into its third eye, and the bird takes another tack: confession.

"The truth, you see," she says, "That one feather of all my brood has a dream of living on a place called earth that she says God will create on the fifth day but I'm just a mother so I don't know these things. My fine feather wants to be a bird God will create that day to fly above the earth and to sing joy songs every morning and evening.

"Well that's a noble cause," the dragon notes, "perhaps I can help."

"Help? You? How?"

"You can have some of my darkness. As you said, I've more than enough for one *infinite* dragon lifetime to feed your, oh wait, it's *my* feather. My forward-looking feather that already has enough darkness to live long and prosper on the earth that God will make. What's an *earth*, does anyone know?"

"Read Genesis. You'll get the whole story there." The bad bird barks.

"Acting superior *always* makes me cross;" the dragon sizzles, "and I'm *already* annoyed enough with you for abusing your feather, to broil you whole and eat you for dinner." The white bird goes a ghostly shade of pale and shivers in her pins as the dragon lounges into a more comfortable position and orders: "Tell me about this Genesis story, especially the fifth day of it, and I will forget that you were mean to me."

The bird swallows hard. Three times, to finally get what she *really* wants to say back down her craw. She takes a deep breath, hits the high points of the first four days of creation, then tells the riveted wyvern about the Great One creating hoofed, clawed, and winged things on the fifth day, the day *her* feather would fall to earth to be a bird. Sighing a satisfied smile, she ends her tale in rare peace and silence.

"The dragon's eyes narrow in thought. *The dim bulb bird thinks it's all about her like she's the center of the universe and all in it so the narrow eyes must signal my anger with her.* The bird shivers simple silliness. The dragon rumbles: "Why don't *you* be bird that goes to earth on the fifth day of creation?"

The dumbfounded bird needs a moment to process that she's not on the dragon menu before she can deal with the idea the dragon presented. "Me?" she peeps, "Me go to earth as a bird?"

"Why not you? If not you, then who?"

"Oh. Well then, what sort of bird would I be?"

"A patio pigeon?" offers the dragon dryly.

"What's a patio?"

"I propose you become a parrot" I interrupt before the dragon can answer the patio question.

"What's a parrot?" the bird asks, squinting in an effort to imagine one.

"I smile, I can't help it. I reply: "Parrots are magnificent birds with feathers in every color you can imagine and long bright plumes on its wings, tail, and head." Seeing her uncertainty, I add: "It's better than being insipid snoozing snow white hen like you are now."

"I'm a beautiful white!" she protests petulant.

"Until the dragon puffs hotly "*who put all her own darkness* into this one small feather!" He inhales to cool down and adds sweetly to the bird, "If you'd kept it all yourself you'd already be a *fine* pigeon!"

"Don't ask," I order the pigeon, "you don't want to know." I assure before she puts a foot in the dragon's mouth. Her bird brain processes the sight of a mostly grey bird with bits and starts of black and white. She discards the image and the impetuous idea of perplexing a petulant dragon. That ended that.

The dragon took the white bird as his token for the second day naming her his assistant in mothering *his* feather, and practicing its duality wisdom in preparing for the fifth day of creation and her debut on earth. The day ended well, but the petulant parrot wannabe would do naught but cluck over the trials of tending a feather she couldn't *reach* without being perilously proximate to a dragon's maw.

"On the third morning, the dragon came with broiled game and we had our breakfast feast with fruit and grains I'd gathered the evening before and when we'd had our fill, the dragon asked me to tell about the third day of creation, so, I told about the Divine One dividing water from dry land and causing earth to produce seed bearing plants and trees, each seed according to its kind.

"The dragon nods agreeably, then clutches me in its claws and wings me back to that coracle adrift on a sea now separate from land and drops me there. That fine boat charts its course and soon lands me on a beach where honeymooners will one day go to begin their together lives in idyllic bliss and beauty.

Before I set foot on the beach I knew green is God's favorite color for every bush, tree, herb and fern were alive with greens of every shade and hue. Seeds are the third day gift of creation and the dragon's third day token.

"The abundance and variety of seed bearing things stopped me stunned. *How do I know and learn the seed for each seeding thing? Some are in pods, easy enough. Some in tassels of grasses, some cloaked in plump fine fruit, some nested deep in the earth among the roots of that green seeding thing? How do I collect and carry them?*

As thought staged this way, a woman gowned in green rises effortlessly and steps from a moss lined pool to move on a scented breeze to where I stand. She smiles and confides, "You ask the plant to reveal itself and all its power and vitality to you in a way that you will clearly know and remember the truth that each plant willingly teaches when you hear and speak its unique language of love.

Do not be concerned over how you, in your puny mortal mind, will remember all the Wisdom I teach you. The way I teach is by entering into willing oneness with you, and you with me, so that all my wisdom is already your wisdom. Your training is only, and vitally, to guide you in finding and loving the relationships of your life, to help you remember again with the truth of why you chose those interactions this time in which you live and the problems you came to find and heal in your walk of life on earth. Look around you, choose a plant that appeals to you, first with your eyes to see its shape and drape and the quality of its colors and the way it catches sunlight and rainwater, what it smells like when you're close and when you are far. When you are surely in love with the plant and honor its gifts and values, only then ask about her seed.

When you love and value her seed much as she does, she will gift you with her seed. As is true with first love, in an abiding way, it is always first and for forever even though you will love another one plant and her seed, and then another. Each love is always first and forever for a plant and its seeds. You will easily and quickly collect the seeds you need for the dragon's cache. Plants have short memories, lots of abundance consciousness, and an excess of love. Each mother will give you the perfect carrying pouch for her finest seed. All you do is ask and receive with gratitude.

"I gave praise to every seed and root, and to the mother plant that gave it because the third day gift was one any man in his right mind would receive with humble and effusive gratitude from his sister wife on their marriage day. And so, the dragon token for the third day of creation was prepared, packaged and given by earth mother herself.

When the dragon received and then explored his third day token he was squirmy pleased as a puppy being given treats. When he left as the sun sank sanguine into the sea, I imagined that acquisitive dragon spending his time visiting and seeding distant planets with his fabulous mother gift. The tale teller smiles reliving the sunset and the dragon attentively seeding lover's beaches with scented sensuous scenery, and delighting in gratitude for the judiciously generous Earth Mother.

Into the celebrating silence the young dancer softly says with an infectious giggle "I saw the dragon seeding the beaches, and raising and planting mountains to gather and share life water with the Eden gardens he imagines and then makes real." She adds with a shy girl grin "I spent time on one dragon beach, and a cabana boy brought me a lounge chair and fruit drinks whenever my glass was empty. I want to spend time on *another* dragon seeded island with maybe the same cabana boy."

"Daughter!" Counselor cautions, "you do understand your mother and I will go with you do you not?"

"Me too!" Says elder sister rushing to gush with her giggling sister, "but I want my own cabana boy."

"Daughter! Counselor restates to the elder dancer daughter. "*Why* did we have children, RO? Remind me again for I have forgotten and cannot name even one persuasive reason to have…"

"*Don't* say it father." The girls command in unison each clapping a hand over his mouth. "You *mustn't* say the words you were thinking, even in exasperation with us for imagining something wholly new and pampering, I haven't been pampered properly since I was a *baby*, daddy." Now she grins wicked, "Plus, you'd have to buy the tickets anyway."

Counselor chortles daughter delight and notes "The power of the purse, I still hold that…, for now."

"We *love* your generosity, Dad, we delight in the ways you please yourself by pleasing us, *after* mother, of course!" They roll their eyes, smiling all the while. "We wouldn't trade you for any other dad." The girls lean down to plant a kiss on each cheek. "Look, he blushes, that is *so* cute." Giggles one, then the other, enticing everyone in the circle to join the fun, even Counselor. Returning to their seats a dancer prompts the tale teller, "Day four…, hit it."

Grinning, the orator returns to his tale, "On the fourth day of creation God formed the greater gold orb and the lesser silver one and placed them in the sky along with all the firmament of stars, and then God divided light from darkness.

He did that so he had a place to put the sun and its bright light, and a space to put the moon whose silver light reflects the sun's spiritual light into the night here, where humans abide, where the ghosts and goblins of our fear come in, and out, to play. The great gold orb of the sun is a symbol of spiritual light. Mother moon represents personal human intelligence, the intellect of man that only reflects the light of the sun, or the son, either works. The moon intimately discloses Truth to mortals in our darkest hour, for only then, can the bright light of Spirit be safely revealed to man.

"The star represents the first awakening of man when he apprehends and expresses the wisdom and power of the indwelling Christ Spirit. Just as the morning star heralds the light of the rising sun, so does the star of the mind first reveal the way to the wisdom and glory indwelling the son of man son of God. I got silver a star for mastering that fourth day lesson, it was dropped into my boat when the evening star first appeared, and that would be the dragon token for the fourth day of creation. That dear daft trivial dragon was by then *so* ornamented with bling things, feathers and trailing plants, that he went into a wardrobe tizzy just to deciding where to sport the star token. That great goofy wyvern was beginning to look *disturbingly* like a boy scout wearing all his merit badges.

"The dragon returned at sunrise on the fifth day sporting all his tokens (except the batty bird, that I hoped he'd basted and we ate, but I dared not say so). When our repast was done, he set me to my task for the day, and, as unceremoniously as ever, dropped me with a plop into my coracle that promptly spun about and headed for a distant speck of land so tiny I wasn't sure it was land at all, but maybe a mirage you see over water, or ghost dancing over land so flat you can see the curvature of the earth.

"On the fifth day of creation the Creator made the water teem with living creatures and shaped birds of every feather to wing and sing the sky and to trim the trees and shorelines between water and earth. To my absolute delight my coracle delivered me with a soft thump and slide high up on a beach while I was caught up in a wave raised by a giant dolphin that caught me when I fell overboard and dove me deep in its fins breathing water as easy as I breathed air above the waves.

"Me? I was in utter fear that grew apace with each fathom the dolphin dropped until we reached the deep floor of the ocean where it released me to walk about with the same ease as walking on land and breathing air, and *not* water. The ocean is a rich fertile place teeming with food of the sea that lives in a circle of life knowing that the one who eats is at one with what is eaten and what is eaten is assimilated and eliminated as the ideal food for another thing living in the sea. Assuming I needed a picture, Sea Mother spun her wheel of life showing a moving picture of one of the wondrous ways Sea Mother lives and thrives on manifesting abundance.

"It probably helps that Sea Mother can just as easily raise hard harsh energies that roil through and above her waters while she clears away a clutter of over active life forces accosting Earth Mother, and wresting from her what she willingly, and must give freely and of her own accord. Mother knows man who cannot receive cannot give and is destined to take, and in some measure, to take by force and with anger. Guiding man through polarized dualities of the physical plane reveals the symbiotic balance of the Divine Law of polarity, a passion purpose of Sea Mother. More than anything she wants to teach the high heart art of *receiving* generously from a heart teeming confidence and forever full with delight. She wishes more passionately than anything, for man to find within himself in abiding consciousness of abundance knowing beyond doubt that all giving and receiving is meant to be equally sweet and joyful.

"It was Sea Mother who introduced me to the dragon's token for the fifth day of creation when she dropped me into a crab hole where I not only got my toes snapped but also found a hermit crab in my hand, looking up at me with round blue eyes (I didn't know they had blue eyes), like it knew me, like it knew I was the one meant to receive and to deliver its message. Before I could get proud for being a chosen one, the suddenly not-so-retiring crab informed me I was its *delivery boy, not* its messenger. Let me just tell you now, you can't out-crab a crab. After a mini eternity with the contrary crab I finally got it! My job, the hermit persuaded me, the one and *only* thing I was to do, was to take the confounding cross crab to the doubting dubious dragon and give it as my dragon token for the fifth day of creation.

"Faced with no alternatives, I opened a vest pocket invitingly and held it for the retiring one until it tucked itself securely in a pocket corner at the very instant I was whisked up and out of the water, into the coracle and slapped into a seat just as the boat rotated ninety degrees and zipped away toward a wee speck against a pulsating sunset with light rays shot like a great golden fan across the horizon.

"Much to my surprise the dragon was not pleased with my daily token and bellowed full blow at me: *Where am I to suppose put another fine ornament on my already exquisitely jewel encrusted, feathered and vined body?* The dragon leaned down, eyes level with mine, and hissed: *Did you ever think about me? About how time consuming it is to* deal *with all these gewgaws and gems you bring every* blessed *day of creation?*

"Well, ladies and gents, you will be proud to know I kept a straight face, biting the inside of my cheeks bloody so they couldn't move to betray me. I kept my eyes down like I was well chastised so he wouldn't see my mirth.

"I was doing fine until my chest began to heave with the force of repressed laughter. The dragon asked: "Are you *cry*ing?" duly anxious and unsettled. That did it, I giggled, chortled, cawed and I croaked my glee so he could not see. He did see. And hear. He was not amused. Demanded that I explain myself, which is a *very* demanding role even for an experienced actor such as myself."

He catches and returns grins around the circle, then, with a palm up shrug, he adds: "I told the dubious dragon exactly what I thought of its consciousness. I intimidated the daunting dragon.

"It is unlikely that anyone ever had the temerity to grab the dragon by the whiskers, look him in the eye, and demand his gaze and attention. What *if*," I snarl soft, "you did *everything* you did with a keen sense of how it *might* affect people and trees and crops and streams around you when you did it? One day they'll call a space of a consciousness like yours a slash and burn or ground zero, and survivors will report the number of deaths that occurred there.

"You, my dragon pal, are *not* here to create a ground zero. You need a shift in perspective. What *if* you stop being controlling and let the token choose where *it* would like to lodge in your commodious hide?

"Let me tell you what's in it for you, *witless wyvern*. That will help you decide that you *do want* to let the hermit crab choose its own place to hide. Hermit crabs *like* not being seen. You have no room to display a hermit crab properly." The dragon is dubious so I add the *piece d'resistance*, "They eat fleas."

"Crabs live on sand, what fleas…?"

"Sand fleas." I snap, "Hermit crabs love them. Dragon fleas are probably not *that* much evolved over sand fleas, although you *totally* deserve bigger, hungrier, and meaner fleas than other creatures. Now shut up and watch." I hold the hermit crab on my palm moving it close to the dragon's chest, slowing as it moves to my fingertips. When they're level with the dragon's heart the crab jumps off to wiggle and tickle below a dragon scale over its heart where it finds a momentary fill of its favorite fulsome fat fleas. The dragon purrs like a kitten evidently approving his choice to let the shy crab pick and choose the then current site of its Movable Feast.

"I love this crab," the dragon declares, "It's the best gift you have yet chosen and given to me."

"What if you offered the same compassion to yourself? What might change if you could say with equal sincerity that you love yourself? How would those changes show up in your world? The dim dragon didn't get it so I shouted at him like a *very* disappointed dragon rider and I might *never* again ride a dim bulb beast that couldn't stop navel gazing long enough to connect some dots that *go beyond* his belly and crusty hide.

"I demanded to know *why* a *real* dragon never applied the power of Imagination, nor even unwrapped the gifts of the Divine Feminine to see, share, invite and inspire *her* evolving vision into the Divine Masculine. How *else* do you expect to excite your masculine aspects and choose and will to evolve and give birth to *one* loved and inspired new outcome?"

The light still doesn't come on in the dragon's loft so I say preacher like, "It is a simple choice. Would you *prefer* being an uncommitted, know-nothing toothless dragon, or a dragon who has and does choose and serve its rider at the need?"

The dragon blinks a long silent while then says "I never thought of it that way. So how does this work, who teaches who what?"

I frown fierce and fiery "We teach each other and we do it spontaneously and respectfully, or it doesn't happen. You can go back to whatever pit you hole up in, just *take me home first.*"

The dragon grins "where's home?" He frowns, "*Why* do you want to leave before sunset the sixth day of creation? That is all the time we have left to master ways to ride the wind as one being in two bodies.

"Home is here the heart is, I guess. If I ask you to be my wing-man do you know what I mean?"

"That I am your eyes, ears, and senses for what you cannot see, that I guide guard and protector when we go where you cannot safely go without me. Do you know what it means to be a dragon rider?"

"That I am your eyes, ears and senses for what you cannot see, that I go where you cannot go, and that I do for us all the things I can do but you cannot do. And, I do *not* live with you.

"Deal," the dragon slaps his hand on a rock narrowly missing the sand crab, "oh there you are my little hungry one. I didn't mean to scare you, I didn't know you'd jumped off me, here let me give you a lift, show me where you want to stop and burrow awhile." When the crab is settled in, the dragon yawns and stretches, "I and the little one will be off for the night, sleep well, we'll see you at dawns early light.

"At dawn the dragon returned and after we ate and chatted, the dragon sidles up to a boulder, settles itself, and tells me to climb up on the rock, which I do. I'm standing high enough to step over and onto its massive shoulders where the wings connect. I see my boots are new, soft leather soles and uppers to my knees. I hoped the dragon would let me keep those fine boots I'm still wearing my butler's shoes. Disappointing. Where do I step aboard?" I ask the dragon.

"Watch," the dragon replies commencing to raise and lower the elbows of its wings until I see the foot sized spots hollow on either side of its spine. The dragon looks at me with a full-scale grin – disturbing – and invites me aboard. I step on and get the feet feel of his muscles as he raises and lowers wings, and rotates his head. Without him telling me to, I drop my hips and ride his moves on my thighs like a jockey crouching in the saddle to ride balanced over the stride of the beast.

"The dragon steps away from the rock so I can feel and ride the muscles that move him over land. When that great beast began to raise, lower, tip and tilt its wings like it was flying I whooped a glee giggle. The dragon ran, flapped its wings and leapt into the air, waggled its cheeks to raise his black whiskers and slap them into my hands. Soon we were at cruising speed. I thought that. Until the dragon told me a true dragon rider would use his feet to guide the dragon to what he wanted and where he wanted to go.

"Oh," I say and gently heel my right foot into the right-wing control panel, leaning right, lifting the right rein and, as the winged wonder raises into the sky. Curving my right shoulder back and up, I suck rarified air into my lungs, let out a whoop of wonder and joy, and in that instant the dragon joins me. I could feel the rumble of his laughter through the soles of my shoes.

"On the morning of the sixth day I got see my options for the day, and I heart chose the precise place where the big butt bird shaped a diamond and dropped it into the sea. My feet told the dragon where I'd go, and when we arrived, the beast shrugged me off its back and I fell headlong into the sea where a laughing dolphin caught me on its back, turned a wise eye on me, and plunged us into the depths below clicking, clattering and chattering me into a calm state of wondrous wonder at the bounty and teeming beauty of Mother Earth in her role of Water Keeper.

"I thank Water Keeper for letting me breathe liquid air and for the wise guiding company of your dolphin through my fathom fall through an extravagant abundance of color, shape, form, and motion. The finned one swam me into a cavern shaped like an open clamshell. In the depths of the grotto a pearl glowed. It was an open-mouthed clam holding a pearl glowing from its core with iridescent light.

"Before that moment my hand never *wanted* a thing but my palms *ached* to cup that pearl inside them. I raised my eyes from the pearl to the eyes of the clam, old, wise eyes that spoke to me in feelings and thoughts reading me through and through.

"*Why this pearl? Why you?* Mother Clam posed and for a time I knew no answer. She knew it. She swept me up into her eyes so I could see me clear from *her* mind. Disturbing. And just the disturbance I needed for forever and a day, for I always thought of myself as not measuring up, not being enough, *always* lacking, always a day late and a dollar short.

"The man I thought I was had no *right* to touch this Pearl of Great Price and know the true value of it. Humbling. The son of man must follow the path of the Son of man and meet the death of all he holds dear to create a space where he loses his EGO and regains true Life. The man I'd become returned the gaze of Elder Mother Clam and asked *what makes the pearl so brilliantly clear and iridescent?*

"*A diamond,*" she sighs. "*It fell into our sea the second day of creation, and I took it up and swallowed it. It didn't suit me. Irritated me cruelly. I did what clams do against irritants, I sheathed it in nacre layer by layer day by day, every day of my long life.*

"Uh – it's the *sixth* day of creation – you ate the diamond no more than four days ago," her wise eyes are wise to me and do not appreciate what she sees. Even the dolphin turns away like he never knew me and had nothing to do with my being in The Grotto of the Clam Queen.

"That *is* assuming the seven days of creation are 24-hour days." I amend quickly. Her eyes are withering. I whine like a punished pup. "Please, continue your tale, I see no less than a *quantum* of layers of luminous nacre on your pearl of great price."

"The clam leers a withering grin and probes "what will you *pay* to take my pearl?"

"I – I – I – have nothing," I say turning my pockets inside out.

"What makes you believe that *things* can purchase a pearl of great price?" The Mother Clam drifts into Dreamtime where time does not matter.

"I go there too. I learn that the true worth and purpose of time lies in *not* putting linear limits on it. Time is eternal. It flows. When I'd served my time and otherwise proved myself worthy of receiving, I told Mother clam that if she chose me, I would receive and deliver the pearl of great price to the dragon.

"Turns out Mother Clam knows the dragon and spewed the pearl into my hands in her dying breath. Humbling. I had my sixth day token for the dragon, all I had to do was get back to the island where the dragon would meet me at sundown. The cheerfully devoted dolphin chattered a traveling chant, lifted me on its spine, and wave rode me back to my wee lush island to await the dragon and present my sixth day token."

The Tale Teller bows his head in profound silence awhile, "The dragon didn't come at sundown. I sat by my small fire in the solitary dark, dispirited, bewildered and bereft, now a Dragon Rider with purpose, but no dragon to ride to its fulfillment. I rage and wail and moan, and in my angry tears I meet my father again yelling telling that I'd never amount to a damn, and that as lily livered as I am, I am no child of his; and I am small and powerless and alone again with my inadequacies. "What is the function of a dragon rider without a dragon to ride? I wail bereft into the eternal still silent empty void of who I think I am, and as I sit abandoned alone watching puddling stars. They lean close and sing to me.

Shawn Gallaway – Shining Star

As stars sing and I re-member. I *forget* who I think I am. I plumb forget. I have not a memory thread left. Maybe who I think I am simply doesn't matter anymore. Maybe all my data points of self no longer connect into a scenario where I keep on being who I always was. Whatever the source, I had to start living like I want to be and express my true *I AM*. With stars listening close and playing a healing air, I'm thinking how I'd *like to be*, who I'd *admire* being, and *why* I'd admire being such a man. With no prelude at all, I *am* that man. I *do* admire him. On the Holy Instant of *getting* that functionally, I decide I will. If I am being given a chance to revision and reinvent who I think I am, I *am taking* it.

"At sunrise on the seventh day a spot crosses the face of the rising sun. With no data points to apply and nothing else to do, I wait to see what came of this odd sun spot. I see wings of the serpent emerge from the sun-shadow-spot, riding rising ray waves of light on its trajectory to me on my once again idyllic island. At the call of the dragon I respond, but not from my head. I leap on a nearby sunbeam, dance along it awhile, then quick step left to an adjacent ray and stride confidently from ray to ray until I meet the dragon in the heart of the sun on a new day of creation. We were One for the first time all over again. We speak of feats and deeds and dramas of the sundry paths and detours we see, choose, and walk each and every Holy Instant of time. The dragon asks "*Who do you think you are?*"

I am breathless as a newborn and remain so until my body is bereft of air. The body itself must inhale to live and so I do. Over and again. It gave me a kick start of oxygen to ride on, and I *choose* wisely and responsibly *now*.

I follow the Code of the Dragon Rider – which I somehow know by heart – to do with faultless faith in the One Source of All Life, everything that comes before me to do *this day,* even the acts and deeds that are *preposterously* beyond my ability. In authority of truth I know the answer and I reply with calm confidence. 'I AM a dragon rider. *Your* dragon rider. I came to change the world. I cannot do that without your help. Without you, I cannot return to the world to be *able* to change it. Will you carry me back to the Feed and Grain?

"Sure thing." The dragon agrees, "Seventh day breakfast first. I brought a special treat for you, you will be pleased. It's something you *cannot* live without." The dragon pulls from his mouth a splendid small crystal goblet without a stem that catches and arrays rays from the rising sun. Turning away, he pours liquid into the cup, turns back with a '*Ta-da! Your favorite treat,'* and gives me the crystal chalice.

"I smile at the deep red richness of the wine and in gratitude, raise the cup to my lips already pursed for the first sip, and I gag, I retch, I puke, I spew, I hack and cough until my nose spouts like Spindletop before it was capped, until there is nothing liquid left in me.

"With seeping red eyes, I take a gallant look at the piquant liquid and retch again until I cannot breathe and fall boneless to the sand. There I unleash and release all the tears of my life that I never cried before. I crawl to the surf wanting the odor washed away and there I collapse and heave more until I am gulping as much sea water as I'm spewing puke. Before I drown the watchful wyvern hooks a claw into the waist of my pants and drags me from the surf to sand still wet with my tears.

"When I can breathe again, I bawl and blubber over the EGO lies I believed and lived over my span of years. The agony of my sins of omission and commission and my willful fall from grace, my mistakes and their outcomes, all are ghosts of the undead rising to dance with me while the dragon watches.

"When I recover, and heal from boogying with my boogeyman bad guys, I lumber up, shake off the sand, and sit to talk with the dragon about the song of the stars and what I learned from it.

"After I confessed my sins, the serpent gave me the penance of practicing atONEment with my *sins*. He informed me that *sin* is an ancient archery term meaning to miss the mark, in this case, Oneness with the Source of Truth.

"*AtONEment?*" I sputter.

The serpent launches into a *rather good* lecture on the evil men do under the influence of accepting as the truth, the whole truth, and nothing but the truth that they *could* fall from grace! *Que tonto, mi amore! And more delusional still, that if you fell from grace, you would never recover from it. Really?*

Grace, He explains, *is an eternal gift eternally given and forever actuated by the asking. There is no qualification, not one, of deserving, winning, or earning it.*

We exist and have our being in grace, yet we are more truly accurately, innocents unaware, caught in the fast hands of an angry god.

"Did I say this all happened at sunrise on the seventh day?" Several in the circle nod. "The sun tarries awhile to watch what follows. I had to tell the dragon how every one of those mean petty nasty small thoughts came to serve me. "*Serve me?*" I shriek.

"Indeed, they do! How?" The beast settles serenely into an easy slouch, lays its head on a paw to wait and to watch until I solve his puzzle.

Well folks, dragons live forever, people don't. That is a vital thing to remember when working with a wyvern, particularly one who is probably a *Sensi* master warrior dragon or ascended master with no *concept* of space or time. I set myself to the dragon's task and a trivial eternity later I parse out all the *good* things about everything I once thought was bad about me, my life and the world as I knew it.

"The dragon then set me to the task of making all the things I named 'bad' come out of me and take a form so I could see and talk with them, and they *did* that!

"Real stern like I ask each of my bad actors to tell me exactly how have served me. The short story is that *every one* of them said they came to protect me from the things *I feared* might, could, would, should, or ever *had* hurt *me*. They came to *protect me* from what I believed was true about me that I denied and repressed. I ponder the mission for a brief eternity, then thank my inner actors for their wisdom and service. For that loyalty, I gave each of them their freedom as a parting gift.

"They protest that they do not want to leave for there is nowhere else for them to go, they were formed from *my mind*, my beliefs and my fears. They live in, always have done. I pretend to consider this and soon I feel their anxiety, for it is *their* fate of 'freedom' or 'protective service' I'm deciding.

"I rub my chin and I say '*if* I let you stay you must tell me *how* you will serve me in future'. They huddle awhile, and ask if I'm willing to try thinking of as like dials and gauges on the dash of an auto. They are *not* there to alarm you, but to give *alert* to what should be done to keep all things working silent and smooth."

"Well *done*," the dragon professor approves. Sitting erect now he asks "Where's my sixth day token?"

"I give the dragon the glowing orb, and this time the enamored beast does not complain about excessive adornment but sets about placing the pearl on various parts on his body, head and paws, and liking *all* of them.

With wisdom in my journey kit and no time for a navel gazing dragon, I hop on it like I always knew how to mount a dragon, and I ride that mythical worm like I always *was* a dragon rider. *This* darling dragon is, and becomes part of, *my own self.*"

In the profound silence that follows the dragon rider tale, the cocoa woman murmurs timidly, "What was in the crystal cup the dragon gave you to drink?"

Tale teller emits a bilious burp "blood.

"Human blood." They a share look of horror and without thought, the healing woman eats his pain, tasting the weight and hate of the daily dramas of his history, his story. She knows why he came to feed on the blood energy of others. Silent she asks to know why he came to see himself so needy of what lies outside of him that he blinded himself to the wealth that lies within.

"I am blinkered. My first semi-sane thought is: *I am a dragon rider! And you are dead on to my habit of quick offence and harsh defense. Retaliation in small doses.*

"I scowl tasting the gall of his bitter bile, *administered with a hard heart, fast fingers, and deniability.* He knows she heard. Nothing changed.

"Except *the pain is gone, almost as if she ate it.* You *did* eat it. She nods a wee wise smile. "Teach me," I whispers, "I *really* want to do that."

The woman starts back protesting "You didn't ask me to stop, or to know what happens to me when I eat your pain. It's all about you. You have no spare thought for any other being, man nor beast."

He eyes her, cocks a brow and replies, "If you taught me to eat pain, I would gladly eat your hard habit of thinking of yourself last and projecting your ever-last belief onto others. Then this conversation never happens because we have no pain left.

"We'd be holding only sweet and joyful memories that would weave into our mythic tales. That is my *only* hope when I'm back home fessing up to my Truth Ghosts," he grins, "while you stay here doing good, right and beautiful things. Yours is a better story."

Her smile is thoughtful and slow as she says "Maybe I *did* teach you to eat pain because I have none left. I am free as a bird and high as a kite. It's *all* good." She eyes him long and asks "what changed?"

Tale teller wells with emotion, sighs, and replies, "It was the star's song. I could not feel alone, nor even imagine being separate from anyone or anything. It felt so good and right, so true, and real, that I *chose* to believe that, and on my will, I changed. Listen…, and you will hear.…"

Shawn Gallaway – The Wind is Always

Into the silence that follows, Time says, "I'm supposed to give you something from the dragon," he places a fist sized pouch in her hand, from which she draws a crystal goblet with no stem. The newly confirmed woman releases the anger reserved for the Great Deceiver that housed in the small hard heart of the man who would be Time. "Thank you," he says softly. "You should know that the dragon requires, and I will, go back to recover the family and their possessions, and return the Rolls Royce."

Across the circle the dancing daughters huddle and whisper, both sets of eyes round on the tale teller, "let's go see what's there," they nod agreement, rise, and walk to bend before the man, who squirms under their inspection.

"I told you there was something there." "I told *you*," the other counters.

"*What's* there?" he asks covering his nose reflexively until a dancer slaps his hand away.

"It's a star. Wee, pale and indistinct until you remembered again with the saving grace of that sixth night when the star shone, twinkled and glowed like the first star, the leading star, the way shower star.

"Anyone knowing your star brand will clearly know when you are faking truth or fiddle with facts or figures. I suspect the star looks like a mole then. A cancerous one." She gives him a pointed petite pout.

"Or," the elder options, "you can obviate that whole cancer scare by deciding to just let go of the script for your mean man self, stop investing your bright mind and light energy in creating *more* separation. Choose instead to just be and become a better man who is *worthy* of a living a good life.

"That means amending for the rapacious greed that led you to us in this place and time." She grins, "Oh, remember to apologize to the dragon so he doesn't singe your tail feathers when next he sees you."

The eyes of the slapper sister narrow on his. "Think again about telling us the star song and the dire dragon drilling you with questions, and your responses to the wise wyvern. Just *think* about the feelings you were having and everything you were remembering and telling us. See, there it is again. Oh, how sweet, what a *divine* tattoo, and how telling too, for a clever tale teller."

"Oh," Jacob's head pops up, "I forgot to give you Michael's message, he left his mark on you. He said the mark was on the place where your bat body first came in contact with Michael's upright silver sword, and by this mark every man with eyes to see would know you and the truth of you."

Jacob scratches his chin, "It seems that the way people see and know that truth proof could produce better outcomes, depending on you and your choices right now. So, tell me, tale teller, will Michael's mark be an insignia of you and who you are, or an ugly abiding warning to be cautious in your company?"

The tale teller masks his nose and mouth below high arched brows, slides his hand slowly down his face and chin, remembers the man to whom the stars sang sad and soulful and sure and sure, he turns smiling eyes on Jacob and replies, "Well, sir, I do hope to meet that dragon again, as friend and master rider, not as piteous penitent; and I've a road ahead to travel that's littered with wrongs to make right, and rights to be won and celebrated.

"None of it can be done by the man I was. I'll be wanting to stay on Michael's Mark" he grins, "to best do, and to best undo, and all of that."

Into the hallowed silence that follows a voice calls: "I'll buy the master's slave," Smithy tips his head to where the woman stands, "and the tale teller trickster can take that money to the master too." He turns to Counselor "I reckon you can make the purchase legal?" Counselor nods, "and then, can you prepare her man-u-mission document, did I pronounce that right?"

"You did, I can, and I will do all that is needful to make her free as the good Lord meant her to be."

"Well, former *slaver*," Ben teases, "I can help with the dragon's requirement that you see your master and his family restored to their home and life." Silence follows.

"I've been talking with the local law in Mississippi and they tell me the plantation house and barns weren't burned, some horses came back, some slaves returned and keep care of the house, farm and animals. When you go back with the gold and jewels you took and stowed in the boot of the Rolls.

"*Of course,* I looked, it's my *job* to look!" Ben grins, "it occurs to me that you can play the returning hero role and *even* get your old job back.

"It is my *personal* wish, and I'll take it as a personal favor that you do all you can to convince the master to free the slaves to leave, or to stay and be paid for their work."

"I'll remember your kindness Sheriff." The tale teller tips back his head to laugh at the curious turns life takes while you imagine you're managing it.

"I'll call the master's horses along my way, you see I taught them to untie themselves from tie lines, to free themselves from stalls, and to come to my call. Never knew why I did that, but now I feel downright farsighted. I take it as my personal mission to win my family's freedom and see them safely back home again."

"On that note," Ben informs, "I'll give you an escort out of town and set you on your way to Mississippi; I've lined up mates along the way to keep watch over you and give you good speed."

"Thank you, sir, that's mighty fine help you give. In return, I will tell your mates along the way all the good news I find, and when I'm home I'll pass good news to the locals and ask them relay it to you."

"Deal." After they shake on the bargain, Ben asks, "What is the name that dragon gave you?"

"Time Turner, and I aim to live up to it."

"Good deal!" Jacob rubs his palms rapidly, "As you left on your seven-day dragon cruise Smithy's clock chimed two bells." He nods to the clock, "Smithy's clock still says it's two o'clock. While you were out gallivanting around, we learned at least a dozen new dance steps, discovered an artist, saw her work, commissioned some of her art glass, and Smithy agreed, though not out loud, that the artist could turn his metal forge into a glass forge.

"Despite all that *time-consuming* entertainment, Smithy's clock *still* says two o'clock, the sun still casts two o'clock shadows, and I for one, am six o'clock hungry. Would you *kindly* demonstrate for us what a Time Turner might do in an unlikely situation such as this?"

Time studies the unassuming face of Smithy's Big Ben wall clock, shakes his head and says "*that's* not the clock in need of righting." He turns away to long-leg across a nearly nearby galaxy to stop before a clock so towering tall it appears to curve back on its spine to admire an infinite blue sky puffed with cotton candy clouds and peppered with plump birds twittering and tweeting. The hands of the clock show two hours, same as Smithy's Big Ben.

Interesting, Time thinks. Stepping to the cabinet he pulls a key from a pocket, fits the key in the lock, turns it, hears the click, and watches as the drawer slides open with a whispery whoosh and out steps a crane. The kind with wings and feathers. *Disturbing!* "What floor please?" the crane asks. "All the way to the top," Time replies and does not know why.

Arriving at the heart of the mechanism he sees that it is broken in shatters and shards, and he does not know why. He asks, and the heart of Time responds: "I am Time," she wails, "I am infinite, everywhere present, even in the void where *nothing* is.

"Yet I am *required by man's* small concept of me to *only* move forward!" Time whines, "I'm the grandmother who lives too long in her estate while heirs and relatives impatiently await, or perfidiously plot, her sudden death. I am the temporal equivalent of *white noise!*" Time whines through her chimes. "I am used, scheduled, clocked and *measured! I will not* be proven!

"I am *Time!* I am *eternal, without* boundary, form or dimension; my essence *cannot* be held in thought nor confined in concept. Ideas, now, ideas are formed by a brain firing neurons that have no shape or mass and no functional use for time. Ideas turn my key, they transport me, inspire me, give me utility, character, and cause; I can work with that.

"But," she glares, "I will *not d*ie! Nor will I be *man size* small! I took a work stoppage. It's an idea that will catch on. Until then, *Time is functionally dead.*"

"Houston, we have a problem and it's bigger than eternities of neglected grandmothers. It won't be fixed by a crew of space techs, and while some ascended masters might help, there's nary one in sight.

"That's when I remember my name and I ask myself, what *would* a Time Turner *do* in a case like this? Well, I imagine such a man might sweeten the bitter tea Time's prepared for her solitary detention, so I start talking about all the things I admire about clocks and timepieces, the fine wheels and gears made of copper and other shiny metals, and how all hers need is a bit of cleaning and a nice oil rub. All the while, I'm doing what I'm telling her, so when she sighs a smile I ask *"doesn't that* feel better?

If you take a quick peek inside here you'll see how much better you look too, why in no time at all you'll be humming, whirring, and tolling like a brand-new clock.

"Listen to you, already purring like a contented kitten. When I'm done here I'll polish your fine case and its fittings until you shine like sunrise on water." When Time chimes her next interval, she sings, intones, resonates and rings like a divine diva.

Shawn Gallaway – It's My Time

Oh, look, now Smithy's clock tick tocks too at exactly two past two.

The Angel Garden Reunion

The meeting room of The Angel Garden is set up with two rows of tables ranked behind the podium at the point where the center aisle meets two columns of chairs with aisles on either side. It is an unusual set up for a Daughters of Isabella meeting and each Daughter entering the space notes the odd plan.

They shrug for this is not the first D of I meeting to be unusual because, by nature, women are daughters, mothers, and sisters. All Daughters know that Mother Energy is essentially different from Father Energy. Ergo, if both are here, both are needed, though no one knows why.

Yet every Daughter knows that RO called this irregular meeting. All daughters know that RO is President the D of I. They also know RO doesn't waste time. Daughters, you see, are never obedient. But they are compliant. In the case of this special meeting, they are simply curious, and curiosity always gets the cat.

Plus, it's an excellent time to gather and share gossip and speculate on unknown outcomes, like the purpose of the two rows of tables flanking the podium. Anything new and novel is worth conjecture. It's a guessing game for women who discuss the possible outcome of the different options available. Sometimes women even wager on them.

Some, they imagine, may change and be attentive, helpful, and devoted life mates instead of....

Everyone knows what's not said. They've seen bruises make up can't hide. They've seen underfed children, they've heard the bourbon bottles in the trash at houses were the wife is not seen.

None of that's happening this evening. The ladies put their handbags on a seat, reserving it for when the meeting is called to order, then turn to the wit and wisdom of their sister Daughters.

'What do you think the special meeting is about?' and 'What do you think those tables are for?'"

"I'm curious about the *purpose* of this meeting President RO called." A Daughter says to another. All nod agreement. "RO doesn't do anything without a reason. And her reason is always a good and helpful one.

"That *means* that the Daughters have a key role in determining the outcome of whatever purpose it is that this D of I meeting was called. Anyone ever play 'Clue'?" All Daughters nod with fond smiles.

"What clues do we have?" All Daughters shrug, palms up. "Oh look, RO is here at last, let's take our seats and learn what's going on."

RO steps to the podium and welcomes all to the meeting. "I called this special D of I meeting so I can tell all of you some things you *will not* believe." She waits for the Daughters to process the paradox of duality and then, one by one, to slip back into their unity as Daughters of the One.

"I know all of you are wondering about the tables behind me, and why they are here, so I will tell.... No." RO amends abruptly, "I will *show* you what you will not believe without seeing it, not even when you do see it. 'Believing without seeing' is a core D of I practice. There is a Judas in all of us.

"Ladies and gents, what I am about to show you is impossible. It cannot have happened." She gives her Wise Woman smile and adds: "Yet there is physical *proof* that the impossible *did* happen. My question is: Are you willing to accept *proof* of miracles?" The Daughters nod as one.

RO raises a hand, snaps a finger, and smiling men enter the back door carrying baskets brimming with fruits, berries, vegetables, tubers, and herbs. They put them on the tables and fade into the audience.

"Can I – can we taste of what's there?"

RO giggles and says, "Not while I'm talking, dear. Every one of you would be chewing and smacking your lips, and *not* listening to *me*! That is *not* why I am President of the D of I."

She looks at the Daughters, at the Knights, then Bam and Melt White, without whose help The Angel Garden project would not succeed. *It wouldn't even get off the ground.*

What a lovely tight devoted group of people you have brought together, Earth Mother. We must swear them to silence. You know how obedient daughters are. And their husbands, sons, uncles, and cousins.

All of us are necessarily involved. Lead us through this twisted twining way of secrecy so your objective is achieved, and remains secret in our hearts long after our work for you is done.

RO smiles, invites everyone to take a seat, and when all are seated and attentive, she begins with a question. "How many of you are wondering why I called a special meeting of the D of I?" All raise hands.

"Are any of you wondering why Knights are invited to a special meeting of the Daughters?" All nod.

"It is because we need you. Every one of you – to help with a special project."

"What's the special project?" Someone calls out. All people there nod their curiosity.

"First, let's discuss the confidentiality requirement for this meeting. What we talk about tonight, the votes we take, and what we will agree to do, will be held in the strictest confidence within this group. You will tell no one who is not here tonight about this meeting and the purpose of it.

"And, you will tell no one what happens afterward. Are there any questions?"

"I have one, and I think I speak for everyone when I ask you why the secrecy, what are we protecting?"

RO eyes him levelly, inhales fully, and replies calmly: "We are protecting a miracle."

"A miracle?" It is a single question gasped as one by Daughters and Knights. It's awhile before everyone remembers that RO won't talk again until all of them are listening.

A command and control figure in the group shushes everyone, tells them to sit down, to breathe deep, and just listen, "or the meeting could take all night."

Curiosity always gets the cat, and curious cats always get quiet to watch and listen, just like the perplexed people do. Peeps are curious cats too.

RO smiles as she looks around the room catching an eye and sharing a smile with everyone in the room. "A miracle", she whispers. She smiles when all are silent and listening close. "So, what miracle are we protecting then?" She asks each person there. No one has an answer.

"We are protecting the miracle of The Angel Garden, and we need your help. Every one of you."

"So, the Angel Garden is the miracle that we're signing up to protect, is that right?"

"Yes."

"For those of us who don't know, what is 'The Angel Garden'?" A husband asks curiously.

RO smiles, "I thought you'd never ask!"

"Well", the man grins, "I like to help out when I can. After you tell us about The Angel Garden, then you will tell us what we can do to protect the garden, is that right?"

"I love a skeptic! It makes a dialogue so much more vibrant and engaging. Any other skeptics here?" RO grins and looks to the doubter and says: "You are in good company, as you can see."

Without looking, RO reaches back, feels for a basket, reaches in and grabs a red bell pepper, holds it up and tosses it to the doubter. She looks around the room and asks: "Any *other* doubters?" All laugh and raise a hand. Bam and Melt pass a fruit or a vegetable to everyone.

It it's not quiet for a long while though no one is talking. The sounds of flavor savoring fresh fruits and vegetables fills the room, and oohs and aahs are the most discouraging words ever heard in the room.

"Any skeptics left?" RO demands with a satisfied smile for everyone is shaking their heads 'no'.

"You may wonder why Counselor and I called this joint meeting of Daughters and Knights." Most nod, some recall and remember but wait as the impossible tale unravels itself into the whole unit of one.

RO shrugs. "I told you we are here to protect a miracle. And that the miracle is The Angel Garden."

"Can we see it?"

"Not today, dear. But the *last item* on the agenda for our meeting is Bam and Melt telling true tall tales about The Angel Garden, and *maybe* best of all, they brought their instruments. We'll enjoy some picking' 'n grinning' and tall tale spinning' *when we have finished the meeting* agenda."

RO grins. "Otherwise I will call Counselor up here to keep us on our agenda. "*None* of you want my husband to have to come up here and be snarky with the lot of you."

Counselor stands, turns, and reports: "Where reason does not rule, faith is simply an *incredible* blessing that gives over and again. That's where we are folks. That's our choice point.

Shawn Gallaway – Choice Point

"Among humans, faith is at war with reason. Fallen ones like us, still fall from grace *because we do not ask*. The Master said: *You have not because you ask not. The girl asked.*

"Heck, as I hear tell, she *demanded* God save the garden, or they and their *neighbors* would starve. Her faith produced the abundance you see. You are her *neighbors*. She asked for you too. Every one of you."

Counselor grins amiably and adds: "I am asking every one of you for your help. I know you'll find this redundant, but you *will* swear as Knights that you will never speak of what you know, or what you will come to know." He pulls a forefinger and thumb across his lips and raises his hand in oath. All the Knights zip their lips and raise their hands in oath binding. The Daughters do the same.

Counselor turns to face RO with a smile of encouragement. He knows what comes next, and that what comes next is impossible. It is simply unreasonable to think it *could* happen.

He knows that if anyone can sell a bunch of skeptics on believing in the impossible it is his lady wife RO. Plus, she'll make it fun, and laughter always softens the hard places inside a man. "You're up, RO."

"Don't dither, Mother," a smiling daughter cautions RO. "Make us proud. Again. Like you always do."

RO laughs, looks at the Knights and Daughters, turns her palms up and asks: "What's a mother to *do*?

"We need loads of volunteers to help in all sorts of ways. We need truck drivers with tarps to pick up The Angel Garden produce and bring it to the D of I storeroom.

"How many of you have trucks with tarps and are comfortable driving on country roads?"

She counts hands, looks to Counselor and says, "Looks like there are enough to rotate drivers by week day so we don't set a pattern to make people curious." Counselor nods.

"Drivers, stay on country roads where you can, and don't stir up dust. Real farmer's *always* drive slow just to watch things appear, change, and disappear. They *see* the curvature of the earth. They *feel* the sunset melt them like ice in a cup, and they learn and know that when a man melts he free flows again.

"How many of you have pressure cookers? Oh, lots, that is excellent!

"How about canning jars with rings and flats?"

"Canning jars we have," a Daughter offers. "And we have canning rings. But most of us don't have flats. We used them last time we had anything to can."

"We need to buy flats then, Counselor. How do we pull that off without spilling the beans that we have something to can when nobody *else* does?"

"Hum, I take your point. Okay, who has any ideas to offer?

"Well," Bam White says, "Me and Melt both can be practically invisible, and we both haul 'junk' for folks all over five counties. I reckon we could trade for some boxes of flats here and there without anyone getting nosy enough to ask why. Most stores that carry canning supplies got nothing to do with 'em but dust 'em. They'll be glad to pay us in inventory they can't sell. We'll trade for fresh flats when we can."

"Oh," RO exclaims, "That is *so* perfect, Bam and Melt! The two of you are an indefinable blessing to our towns and our counties. Thank you." With a big warm smile, RO continues.

"We'll be canning produce from The Angel Garden in the D of I kitchen. Who *likes* keeping kitchens clean and washing pots pans, jars, etc.? Oh, lots, mostly guys, which is *so* perfect! Thank you, God!"

"Who's going to pack The Angel Garden produce for the drivers to pick up?" A curious customer asks.

RO grins and asks: "How many of you wondered the same thing?" She doesn't count hands. They're all up. "Well, I will tell you what you will not believe, and it's true.

"Archangels will pack the crates, baskets and boxes and put them on the loading dock. They'll help load your trucks too."

"Loading dock? Archangels!" A wide-eyed man nods quickly and says: "Okay, *that's* really all I need to know about that." He shakes his head mourning: "I *do* wish I had a truck with a tarp though."

"Counselor, is there anything you want to add?"

"There is. There's a table in the back with Volunteer Sign in Sheets. The sheet has a place for your name and phone number, fill that in.

"Check the boxes to select the work you'll do, the frequency, and times you're available to collect and preserve the produce from The Angel Garden.

"Canning days will be all hands-on deck at least within the confines of the D of I kitchen.

"Daughters, most of you will come with your Knight husbands. Talk it over so the two of you are on the same page when volunteering your best help times. Preserving food is more fun when it's a group effort.

"Any Daughter and Knight Couples who enjoy making jellies and jams? Oh, that is excellent! Ladies, can we be real? We'll talk by phone and get everyone scheduled so everyone gets to have fun pickling eggs."

"There are eggs?" Counselor asks. "I love pickled eggs. We're signing up for pickling eggs dear heart."

"Done." RO agrees. "We're dealing with a miracle, people. We must have faith that we will have what we need when we need it. We know it our hearts, and that's where change happens.

"Daughters, talk with your Knight Husband this evening and call me tomorrow with your schedule.

"Okay, ladies and gents, have you got anything else related to our joint meeting this evening?"

"Well then, we go to our entertainment for this evening, Bam and Melt White, come on up, you two."

Everyone hoots and hollers until Bam and Melt are up front waiting for silence. Bam and Melt grin and wave 'hello'.

"Thanks for helping out with The Angel Garden Project." He strums a few strokes on his ever-handy fiddle. "We couldn't do it without you.

"Plus, Melt and I got different stories to tell about The Angel Garden mostly because the girl wouldn't talk to me. She'd talk only with Melt.

"And," Melt clarifies, "Dad is the only one of us who talked with the dragon and so my dad is the one will tell the dragon tale."

Shawn Gallaway – The Source

"*Dragon?*" One bold man speaks for all, and his face shows the skepticism everyone else feels.

Except RO. And Hester, who's sitting in the back row keeping her head down.

RO grins at the doubter and says: "Let's hold questions until the end of our agenda, or we will not finish in time. And then I will be cross." She pouts. "And that will make Counselor cross; and there's just no future in that. Deal?"

"Deal." The attendees agree in one voice.

"Bam," RO says with a small frown, "I think you begin." RO looks at Counselor who nods agreement.

"Well, Ladies and Gents, I reckon I gotta begin with the first in a series of impossible events. My first impossible event was to ride on a dragon, and I did not go *willingly* on that wild ride." He waits till the audience stops whispering '*dragon?*' and turns to face him again, eyes round with wonder.

"And, riding that weird wired wyvern made me the man I am today." He grins with them and goes back to his tale. "The dragon you see is the Thunderer."

"I thought Zeus was the Thunderer." Someone protests with open puzzlement.

"Zeus is the Thunderer in mythology.

"Metaphysics teaches that thunder means the Perfect Mind, the Complete Mind. In metaphysics, thunder is a feminine power. Thunder is loved for bringing life." He smiles.

"Thunder is hated for bringing death." Bam frowns. "Thunder moves in all creatures. Thunder is the 'I AM' voice that speaks softly in silence as perception and knowing. Thunder is the *real* voice crying out in everyone, and they recognize that voice for its seed indwells all and everything.

"Thunder says: 'I AM awareness of the Father. I know the hidden thoughts, the eternal mystery. I know the primordial consciousness. Because 'the Father abides in me and me in him', as The Master put it.

"Dragon is the Thunderer. And there was some powerful need for dragon thunder in The Angel Garden.

"I situated myself on the dragon and rode that wonderful wyvern as we winged so fast we broke the sound barrier which got me and the dragon into The Angel Garden.

"It was *not* a soft landing. It wasn't even one you'd fairly call a *hard* landing. We crashed in a belly-flop. And that is my prelude for the Lilly pond in The Angel Garden. Look, you can see the V of the dragon's ribcage where it fell, and on the other side, a V where the tail pressed a channel there. The dragon likes lilies of all shapes, sizes and colors, and so it pulled out all Earth Mother's lily gifts and planted them in the pond."

"And the water came from...?"

"Angel tears." Bam waits.

"Wait a minute, you said "*Earth Mother's* Lilly gifts'? There is only one God!"

Bam nods agreement, and argues: "*However* the Divine *One* made all and everything in his image and likeness, and there *is* duality in everything in life.

"So, doesn't that *necessarily* mean there *must be* a female counterpart that is *not* separate from the One, but *is* separate from the masculine which is *also* not separate from the One?"

Bam offers a condolence, "And isn't that a *good* thing? I don't know what I would *do* without Lizzie, and Melt, and our girls. I personally *like* the dualities of life.

"I think I wouldn't find a reason to get up in the morning if I wasn't out looking for ways to help others knowing without proof that they'd help me when I needed help and they could help." Bam smiles and says: "I need your help. Every one of you."

He meets all eyes. "And I too need your vow of silence for what I am about to tell you, and for what I have already said to you. As RO said earlier, we're here to create a space for a miracle. The Angel Garden produce is the miracle. We are here to preserve that miracle.

Counselor rises, turns to the door and calls: "Knights, join us please." Two dozen Knights enter with baskets and burlap bags and as they place the items, the Knight names what's in the bag or basket.

"Where did this come from?" Someone demands as the chosen Knights finish their work and take seats.

"I already answered that question," RO says simply. "Do you remember?"

"The Angel Garden? So, there is such a thing! Where is it?"

"Well I *could* tell you," RO offers, "but you would first tell me *why* you want to know the location; and that is extraneous to the agenda for our meeting. You have a copy, don't you?" The man nods.

"We are here to talk about *produce* from The Angel Garden, and what we will do to keep and to preserve it. You are part of the solution, or, part of the problem. You choose. Make your choice now."

"I'll stay. And I'll remember the Knights Oath. And..., I want to peel an ear of that corn and eat it."

RO chuckles, "You are not alone. So, how are you at kitchen work, especially heavy lifting, the sort of things that need done during cooking, canning, and preserving?"

"I do all of that. How about the picking and packing?"

"Ah," Hester offers, "the Archangels do that and set the baskets outside the gate. That's covered."

"I am glad we're sworn to secrecy because nobody in his right mind would believe what you just said. It makes me feel like a kid again when I still believed in Christmas. When do we start?"

"You are not a patient man, are you? Well neither are we. We have an agenda. We're following it!

"Bam, pick up where you left off, please."

"Guys, angels don't have trucks. We need men with trucks and tarps to come to The Angel Garden to pick up the produce and bring it to the storeroom back of the D of I kitchen. When you load your truck, cover it with a tarp you tie down. Most of you are country boys, use country roads. Pretend you are rum runners if it adds zing to doing the same thing with something that's merely miraculous and *not* illegal.

"No caravans, please, caravans of trucks covered with tarps attract attention. Back up to the dock of the D of I kitchen to offload baskets and crates you bring in, and put them in the pantry off kitchen. Put peppers with peppers, corn with corn, gourds with gourds, and so on. Rows and aisles will be needed in the storeroom, and we don't know the quantity. Assume abundance.

"Next comes canning day," Bam says, "and it's back to you, RO."

"Daughters.... Don't you *love* being Daughters, *and* daughters?" She sees the nods all around.

"Women are Earth Keepers. That is our role. It's why we created the D of I space that serves as a school cafeteria. School's on break, and we need it for preparing and canning produce from The Angel Garden. We need pressure cookers. Who has one?" She raises her hand and sees that most mother Daughters do too.

"How many would *like* cooking and canning together in a kitchen as big as this?" All Daughters raise hands, and most of the Knights too.

The other Knights confessed that they were *masters* at cleaning kitchens, washing dishes, pots and pans, and they really *liked* cooking and canning.

"How many of you are volunteering to help until we've preserved all the fruits of The Angel Garden?" All Knights raise their hands. All Daughter Mothers do too.

RO smiles. "Excellent! Bam, you are up."

"I brought my banjo to accompany me in telling my impossible tale. Are you all up for some picking and grinning while I'm telling about riding a weird wild wyvern I did not want to ride?" Whistles give answer.

"You see, the wyvern told me that my job was to coordinate getting The Angel Garden produce from the garden to the D of I pantry. That's it. A delivery boy."

Bam grins, "That is my living. This time I do it for a good cause and it help a lot of folks stay alive and maybe even to thrive. We need help though."

"I keep wondering as I listen, so I'm going to ask. "Are we trying to hide this?"

"No!" Bam scowls. "What we are *truly* doing is planning to maintain a low profile so *our town* doesn't appear in the news attracting unwanted attention and speculation about what we're doing, why, and *how*. How many newspapermen do you think would write that The Angel Garden is a miracle?

Shawn Gallaway – Breathe A Little Magic

"Plus, the dragon said to do it this way, and the Archangels in The Angel Garden agreed. They pick and pack produce from The Angel Garden and put it on the dock for same day pick up.

"There's a loading dock there now," Bam says informationally. "The produce is grouped by type. All a driver has got to do is drive out, load the truck, tie down the tarp, and play slow rum runner on the way to the D of I pantry.

"If you see someone you don't know at The Angel Garden, it's an Archangel. Don't gawk. They'll help load trucks with berries first so they can be cleaned, cooked, and canned while they're fresh.

"They'll probably pick tomatoes and soft veggies the next day, and keep doing that until everything from The Angel Garden has been picked, packed, processed and canned by its best-by date.

"You might find it interesting to know the girl is the only person can freely go in The Angel Garden. Her mother must ask permission of the Archangels.

"And, if she asks, she receives, just like the Master said."

"Will we work on Sundays too?"

"Would a farm guy *expect* to work on Sundays after church too? Yes, of course he would!" Bam grins. "And your lady wife Daughter already knows that canning doesn't stop because it's Sunday – and, you'll already be at church anyway, you'll just stay after the service is complete and come to the kitchen.

"I said more than enough and its Melt's turn at telling tall tales true and well, and peeps a mine, you won't believe this tale either. And you'll know it's true anyway. Come on up here, Melt."

When Bam tries to step away, Melt pushes him to the stage to sit, and says: "Cover my back, Dad. As you know, it's hard to tell tall tales true and well when you don't believe 'em yourself."

Bam puts his hand on Melt's spine where it curves making room for the heart. Melt melts, and begins telling his tale.

Shawn Gallaway – I Am The Love

"You're probably wondering what Dad doesn't know that I know, because Dad knows *everything* there is to know about everything there is.

"Am I right?" He sees universal nods and smiles.

"I know the girl's tale, because she only told it to me. And hear this, people, she said if I ever tell her tale I *must* play music and I must tell her tale tall and true and *exceedingly* well. I gave her my word."

"So, there I was at Hester's because she'd called and said she needed my help. Help that only I could give. Help that only *I* could receive. That got me cat curious, so I went.

"Hester met me at the door and invited me into the kitchen where she poured water for us and squeezed a slice of lemon and of lime into the water.

"Tasty! We needed a tall cool drink before we could *accept* the tale Hester was about to tell. Believe – we did not. Then or now.

"In our trials, we often forget that Faith is the gap-filler between hope and fear. The girl has *amazing* faith! The truth is that her faith has nothing whatsoever to do with the logic and reason. Faith and fact are *not* at war in the girl." Melt smiles melting hearts, opening minds, and making room for miracles.

"So, there we were sitting on the cedar chest in front of a window overlooking the garden that I couldn't see, unless I did *not* look at it directly. What I *could see then* overloaded my mind, for in my mind I *knew* it was *impossible.*" Melt rubs his palms up and down over his face and tarries a moment in silence.

"'Your faith is weak. Your doubt is strong', she said to me.

"She looked me in the eyes with gloomy grief, and said: 'You can't go into The Angel Garden. Your doubt would kill everything in it. *Then* people would *starve*'.

She whispers 'I hoped you could help'." She turns to the window seeing things I *would* not see. I saw that. "I'm disappointed, that's all," she admits.

"'The cat-fighting angels are horrid!' She said, palms against the glass overlooking the garden. I didn't ask. I waited, knowing she'd tell. That she *had* to tell.

"There were too many impossible things happening in The Angel Garden, and some of them are as zealous for evil as the snake in Eden's Glen. Fighting evil is outside her skill set. She couldn't fight Archangels. Someone *else* had to do that.

"Turns out it was Hester who had to be Earth Mother to The Angel Garden. Dad didn't even know that at the time. Nor did Jacob. Not even Hester knew. Yet.

"The dragon knew though. Dragon is the Thunderer. Thunder changes things. Thunder means 'Perfect Mind', or 'Complete Mind'.

"For those of you who are wondering, yes, Zeus is the Thunderer. So is the dragon. Dragon is the sound of thunder.

"Thunder is a feminine power. If you ever see a dragon and don't know if it's a male or a female, default to female. Treat it like you would a *Lady*, a woman of high rank.

"That means treat it respectfully for if you don't, the dragon won't let you ride, and if you do finagle your way on board, it will be a *wild* and terrifying ride."

Melt waits for silence to fall, then says: "Thunder is loved for bringing life. Thunder is hated for bringing death. Thunder existed before creation, it moves in all creatures everywhere.

"Thunder is the real 'I AM' voice speaking softly. Thunder dwells in the silence as perception, knowing. Thunder cries out in everyone and all recognize the voice for the seed of Thunder indwells everyone and everything. I AM is the voice of the father who knows hidden things. Thunder is the eternal mystery.

"The dragon is the guardian within that opens new realms to you. Thunder protects creation and helps manage emotions. Thunder helps us to act *only* from balance and self-control.

"The dragon took Hester into The Angel Garden – after it thundered through her for what she will tell you was an infinity of time during which the sun did *not* change position."

Melt reminds: "Dragon *is* the Thunderer who changes man's mind into Perfect Mind, Complete Mind. Hester will tell you the next part of the tale for she's the only one who can. Hester, you're up" Melt says stepping away.

It's no longer easy for Hester to be timid or rigidly reserved since her Dragon talk and her Dragon ride; and, she has a key role to play in preserving the fruits of The Angel Garden. She steps to the podium with a poised grace that wasn't hers before.

"Thank you for being here, and for being willing to," she unexpectedly giggles, infecting everyone, "preserve The Angel Garden produce. I must start with my Dragon tale because the dragon reformed my mind about who I think I am.

"Before the dragon blowing my hair back and dropping me to my knees, I could not go into The Angel Garden. I would not *believe* what I could not see. I could not see mostly because my faith was too small. Not my faith in God. That I had.

"The faith I was lacking was my faith in *me* as a unique creation of the Divine across *all of time*. All my faith in *me* would fit into a thimble with space left. The dragon thundered that *wee self* out of me and opened a space in me for something new.

"In that Truth consciousness, I went into The Angel Garden on the back of my weird wyvern redeemer. I was stunned by what I saw. The Angel Garden was ruined!"

Tears brim in Hester's eyes but do not fall. "The Archangels sent to support and nourish The Angel Garden were fighting – as the girl put it – 'like a whole *basket* of cats from Kilkinney'.

It pissed me off." Hester giggles, "I ordered those two Archangels to come to me *now*, pointing to the dry dirt at my feet." They were angry. And, they had a common enemy now.

"Well, I am a mother! I'm not taking sass from a couple of fallen angels who aren't doing the jobs the Divine One sent them to do. And I'm not cleaning up after them either!" Everyone laughs aloud.

"I flew into The Angel Garden on the back of the Thunderer *knowing* what I came to do. I *thundered* into The Angel Garden to save it. The Archangels listened to me, but not without a lot of grouchy grumbling.

"So, I motherly asked the Archangels why they were naked as jay birds are on the day of their birth.

"Seriously folks, they were *clothed* in bruises, scabs, and powder dry dirt. And they had no shame."

Hester shrugs, "Mothers don't put up with no shame sass from wayward children..., even if they are Archangels.

Hester smiles now, "I did what any Earth Mother would do. I kicked butt and took names. I shamed the Archangels into being buddies and partners again.

"I did a disappointed mother version of 'ordering' them to clean up their act and just *do* the job the Divine One sent them to do to support and nourish The Angel Garden and then to restore it to what it was *before* their stunning fall from grace.

"And then, I knew a thing that I didn't know at all. I demanded: "Wasn't part of your mission here to cry Angel tears to water the garden?

"And then, motherly concerned, I asked them: "Where have you lost your wings?

"Where are your beautiful bright white angel clothes?

"Where are your white light halos?" They had no answer of course they were dim bulbs. They'd fully forgotten the reason *why* they were sent to The Angel Garden.

Hester grins, "You see, they both *thought* being assigned to The Angel Garden was a demotion from when Michael was the D.O.'s strong right arm, and Gabriel was Michael's strong right arm. More than that, Michael and Gabriel were best buds – before.

"However, the Archangel in The Angel Garden with Michael was named 'Gab-re-EL', and they *weren't* getting along well at all.

"All that dark energy and fighting filled the garden dome like Black Sunday. Or as the girl phrased it 'like a *whole basket* of cantankerous cats from Kilkinney'.

"Okay, I like this limerick so I'm saying it: 'There once were two cats from Kilkinney. They each thought there was one cat too many. So, they fought and they fit, and they scratched and they bit, until instead of *two* cats there weren't any'.

"Well those Archangels had to straighten up and fly right, and I did what any good mother would do in that situation.

"I shamed them. Brutally, caustically, sarcastically, the way *your* mother would have done had you gotten so out of line as to willfully destroy what God had made! *Really?*

"Not happening on *my watch*!

"Shame worked." Hester fans her hands. "Plus, I said no more 'casual Fridays' *any* day of the week. I expect you two to look angelic while you are here. And that *means* you do *not* have scratches, bruises, scars, cuts, or *dirt* on your bodies!" Everyone is laughing at Hester's delivery of her tale. She continues.

"You are not in The Angel Garden to bleed. You are here to weep tears of *joy* for have been assigned to The Angel Garden. It's a plum assignment, you *foolish, fickle* fallen angels!

"How *far* you have fallen from grace to even *imagine* that the Divine One would give *you* a demotion! *Que tonto! Que increable estupido!* He gave you a *plum* assignment. He even cherry picked it for you!

"And if you eat all the cherries I'm coming for you!"

Everyone laughs and claps. Hester grins. "The Archangels laughed too. They laughed so hard they cried tears of joy! Like they were supposed to do from the beginning.

"Now the Angel Garden is whole and healthy again, and the Angels are proud and happy. I think they are the ones who are creating new plants in The Angel Garden..., even *tropical* plants like papaya and pineapple. Who'd have thunk it?

Shawn Gallaway – The Artist

Hester waits until the applause and laughter stop, then, moist-eyed smiling, she says: "I want to personally thank every one of you for so generously dedicating your time and effort in the next few weeks to helping preserve the produce from The Angel Garden.

"Bam and Melt will be our distributors for the surplus canned produce." She pauses for the shock to settle and grins assurance.

"There *will be* surplus, even if we generously share with our families, friends and neighbors.

"See those two Archangels are not just picking and grinning in The Angel Garden. They're creating new fruits and vegetables, and opening inner spaces for them to grow and thrive.

"And, we all know the Whites always follow heart guidance, and people in need that we don't know but they do, will also share the wealth of produce from The Angel Garden."

She grins, "Let's call it a tithe. The Divine One does. And Earth Mother is always generous, true, and *unavoidably* at one with the One.

She claps her hands in girlish glee: "*Thank every one of you for being Thunderers!*"

Shawn Gallaway – The Sword and The Shield

Best Friends Forever

The young woman met Lena when she traveled with her parents to Mississippi to meet the woman Jay would marry later that week.

It was love at first sight between Lena and the young woman about the same age.

Not romantic love, oh no not that!

It was forever love. It was a love that had no beginning, and no ending.

Soul friends. They said it as one when Lena and the young woman were left alone to get to know each other while Jay and his father and mother went off in search of a wedding ring that Jay would slide on Lena' finger the next day and make them man and wife for life.

The young woman gazes into Lena's eyes with a small smile playing on her lips, leans close and whispers into Lena's ear: "I do believe that I like you *way* better than I like my big brother Jay."

"Why do you say that?" Lena asks with such open-faced candor that the girl woman knew she'd hear a half-truth before it was full out of her mind, let alone from her mouth.

The young woman stills herself, centering into the core of her, the heart of her, to hear in the silence the true answer to Lena's question. There are three answers, each one true and telling of Jay, and of her new best friend forever.

"There are three answers to that.

"First, because you look me in the eyes while I say whatever I say, and you will know if I lie, or tell a small truth, instead of the whole truth. You don't judge me for my omissions, even when you hear the hard, hurting things Jay says to me, and about me.

"Nor do you weigh and balance more than one iota of what I say to Jay. Nothing changes. Sometimes Jay is an angel, exactly like he looks, glowing gold in the sun.

"But sometimes Jay's energy is dark, predatory, menacing, quick to judge, and then to lash out with angry, punitive, punishing energy.

"He's got fast hands, I've got to hand that to Jay.

"With Jay, Lena, I'm never sure *which* Jay it is that's talking to me, and often, stalking me. It's creepy.

"My saving grace is that I can *hear* with the crystal clarity of a discordant note in a symphony when Jay's not telling the truth or any part of it, but is only reciting the words that he thinks I want to hear.

"It's not a lie, but it's not the truth either.

"'Leave 'em guessing when you go', is a phrase Jay's fond of saying.

"I love Jay, unconditionally. I don't know why I do, but I do.

"And third, because I get to be your sister-in-law when you marry Jay. And I know that we have been sisters before, in other lifetimes."

"Do you remember any other lifetimes?" Lena askes with candid curiosity.

The woman smiles, and with open-eyed honesty, replies. "No, not in my conscious mind where the co-creator lives and is totally devoted on the facts, figures, and data points of the physical world. But, then, the conscious mind hasn't the processing capacity to do anything beyond that.

"However, when I shift my conscious mind to a heart-centered awareness with 5,000 times greater processing capacity, all the facts, figures, and data points of the physical world are recalled with precise visual and auditory details, and can be analyzed, charted, weighed, and measured.

"Besides, the Great Mind of the body reveals itself in pictures, feelings, and words spoken in silence to the One who hears in silence."

Lena is silent a moment seeking some missing element between the two of them. She finds none. She considers all possible outcomes. She puts her hand on her friend's, and suggests: "Then let's ask the Great Mind to walk side-by-side with us as we follow the path that lays before us, for wherever it leads, we will walk the path that is ours to follow, knowing that the great good is already come."

"There is a way out. Without a great escape caper." They say as one, and know it's already done.

Shawn Gallaway – I Choose Love

Two Babies

The girl woman is in the bathroom putting on makeup when Lena opens the shower curtain she turns to smile her friend a welcome to the new day the D.O. has made. She sees the bruise, and is struck dumb.

Lena hasn't taken down her towel yet, and the bruise on her abdomen is angry black and bitter blue. Lena's eyes are puffy as though she's been crying.

In the time that she's known Lena, she has never cried. *There's not a shred of victim consciousness in her.*

Nor does Lena have the capacity in heart, or in mind, to be content with the victor consciousness.

There's only one option left for her. Verity consciousness. Awareness of Truth at its essence, at its core.

The young woman smiles inwardly as Lena grabs her towel and covers the soft spots in her body with it's warm, absorbent functionality. Yet the young woman did see the bruise on Lena's abdomen. Exactly the size of Jay's fisted hand.

Reality bites! She holds her tongue and speaks no words. She doesn't have to. She knows that Lena will hear her silent words. Her keen inner ear is as sharp and wide-open as her mind.

Jay aborted your baby of love, Lena.

I hate Jay for that.

I hate Jay for not *punching me in the gut to abort the baby his seed by proxy was inseminated into me.*

Is that good enough for you? The D.O. puzzles with divine indifference to any answer she might make.

I hate it when you do that!

Anything change for you because of your hatred against your brother? Or, your anger against Me because I tell you the truth tall and clear for I have nothing to hide from you. In live in.

No. Nothing changes, the puzzle troubled woman replies. *I think small of myself. I imagine that I can hide from what I don't want to see because I've mastered the art of hiding in plain sight. Jay saw me out when I was still in grade school. He always saw me. I think of myself as the victim because of that.*

Is victim enough for you, my beloved daughter?

No, it's not!

What's next?

Victor consciousness.

When have you played out the victor consciousness lately?

Like – daily – since I was raped! Not so much before then.

How's that working for you? How are you manifesting your truth as the victor? I'm not seeing that in you, dear heart. What am I missing?

It's not working. I'm having a pity party and nobody's invited but me. Being victor is above my pay grade!

What's next.

The girl woman is silent an infinite moment, knowing that the D.O. lives in, and because of that she knows as well as the D.O. what comes next.

Verity consciousness.

Tell me about that.

Truth consciousness is the Absolute. That which accords with God as divine principle; that which is, has been, and ever will be; that which eternally is. The truth of God.

The basic principle of Truth is that the mind of each human may be consciously, choicefully, and at core, unified with Diving Mind through the indwelling Christ presence.

By affirming at-one-ment with God-Mind, we ultimately know and abide in that perfect mind which was in Christ Jesus. Jesus lived in the great mind of the heart. And, so did Buddha, and Krishna, and the living breathing Llamas of Tibet.

The heart is love. Love is the active consciousness in man. It is the faculty through which man inhales, thereby receiving love from the Divine One. Inhale is followed by its paradox of exhale. Exhale releases oxygen depleted air from the lungs feeding it into the breathing ecosystem of Earth Mother.

And, my love, the heart is only the visible expression of an invisible center of consciousness that lives in, 24X7, seven days a week. Come visit sometime, the D.O. rebukes like a father whose kid never visits.

From the heart, divine substance is poured when – or because - man sends forth loving thoughts. Heart represents the subconscious mind. 'Out of the abundance of the heart his mouth speaketh' (Luke 6:45). The road of Truth is the straight and narrow path along which Spirit directs and which proves so smooth and safe that one refuses to allow oneself to be misled by habit into trusting only sense perception.

So, what is the sense perception that's become so habitual in you that your perception of life has assumed the power to overthrow Truth? Isn't your sense perception of you as the victim and you as the victor consciousness the exact same dark consciousness that opposes you – by playing the role of victor? Not good enough! Try again.

What's the next level of consciousness?

Verity consciousness, which is awareness of the truths of Being, that are without beginning and without end. Verity consciousness is the willingness to face the facts of existence.

Being, God, the Mind of the universe is composed of archetype ideas, such as: life, love, wisdom, substance, Truth, power, peace.

Love – The pure essence of Being that binds together the whole human family. Of all the attributes of God, love is undoubtedly the most beautiful. In Divine Mind, love is the power that joins and binds in divine matrimony the universe and everything in it; the great harmonizing principle known to man.

Be love, daughter a mine, even when you are fully engaged in every random element of life and living it. Especially then, be love. Love yourself generously so that you have more than enough love to give away.

Escape by Low Profile

Lena came to her friend one day after Jay had left to do his day's work, and him without a job. She said: "We need to get out of Jay's reach as quickly and quietly as possible. And we have to disappear."

"Disappear?" The girl woman puzzles. "What have you got in mind, girlfriend of mine?"

Lena pulls the car keys out of her handbag, jingles them, and replies with a smile: "I have the car. We're going apartment hunting."

"Okay, what do you have in mind?"

"Renting apartments in a small complex in an old neighborhood on a back street. A quiet place with trees and greenspaces close enough to walk to and through to explore the ways that nature connects and grounds busy humans and lets them find peace with what was, and what is, and for what will be.

"I've been asking God for that. We'll find it. Then we will go to ground and practice being invisible."

That worked for them for long enough to renew their rental agreements.

Then Jay found them, sniffing them out like a hunting hound tracking a scent, their profile was no longer low enough.

Pearl Handled Pistol

Jay tracked his sister down, and found Lena in the process. In the same small quiet complex. *Bonus points! Things are looking up.*

They weren't. Lena filed for divorce. She wouldn't take Jay back. She had a protective order against him.

That was not part of Jay's plan.

That meant that the only place he could crash was on the carpeted floor of his sister's living room in his extra-long sleeping bag with one of her pillows beneath his head.

Jay was not a happy camper. He did not sleep deeply and well. Sometimes the tremors of Black Molly withdrawal were so overpowering that Jay stopped breathing.

It terrified him to have been only seconds away from death. *I can't live like this,* he thinks, and instantly knows it is an admission badly phrased.

My sister is right, I have gone brain dead from Black Molly abuse. And the very truth is that I cannot, and will not, abide the pain of living through withdrawal.

There is another way out, another way to end it all. I have my pearl handled pistol. Like the one Jesse James used to shoot himself in the head so he'd not be taken alive and hanged as an outlaw.

My brain will be dead before pain signals reach it.

Jay chambers a single bullet, that's all he'll need. He cocks the trigger, puts the barrel to the roof of his mouth, counts ten inhales and exhales, and on the tenth exhale, he pulls the trigger. There is no pain.

Lena and the girl woman are safe again. Physically. Mental and emotional wounds take longer to heal.

Shawn Gallaway – Into the Dream

Sometimes healing takes more than one lifetime.

Putting woundedness into black words on white paper counter-pointed the pain for me.

It opened my inner eye to see dark and light at play in my life.

That shadow play resolved the emotional and mental trauma I experienced in writing this pair of hard tales.

May you find healing here.

May these words of light written on paper of light inspire your passion for healing your wounded inner child. That is my wish for you, dear reader.